A Broken Window

A Novel

Anne Leigh Parrish

To John, Bob, Lacey, Lauren, Sam, Frida, and Tsuga

". . . a poet's heart . . . is always breaking. It is through that broken window that we see the world."

—Alice Walker

A
Broken
Window

Chapter One

Happiness was a shock. So was knowing she belonged.

It was an old house, built in the 1930s. The bedroom window looked into a cherry tree whose blossoms fell like pink snow in April, Steven said. The bathrooms had original green-and-white tiles. The kitchen had been updated, meaning the previous owner had a gas line installed which Sam loved because she preferred it to electric. When she moved in, the burners were a sight. She scrubbed them clean, and the rest of the house too. Steven was a typical bachelor and didn't mind dirt and disorder. Basic maintenance wasn't on his radar either. The radiator in his study was broken and he graded papers with a blanket draped around his shoulders. He'd applied for a research grant that would take them to Boston for the spring term. There was an obscure poet he wanted to write a book about, Clara Levy, who brought out her first volume in 1950 with a newly established press, The Hedgerow, in Cambridge. Sam suggested England, or if not there, then California. She'd lived in LA for a few months, and though she was an upstate New York girl, born and bred, she was tired of winter, and this one had been particularly harsh. Steven said no. She asked why it had to be Boston. Okay, the press was there, but couldn't he get whatever he needed online?

Steven confessed his soft spot for Boston. He'd done both his undergraduate and graduate work at Harvard, so for him it would be like going home or returning to a place he was happy, since his actual home in Creve Coeur, a suburb of St. Louis, wasn't happy. Expanding on this, the blanket clutched and his breath visible in the chill of that room, he said it was wonderful how the word "home" could so easily be associated with happiness. His right eye had a difficult stye on the lower lid, a condition he was prone to. His beard, coming in thicker every day since he stopped shaving, was ginger. The hair on his head was brown. He was six feet four inches tall, which made plane travel uncomfortable, and a California King-sized bed necessary. Alcohol was consumed daily but in moderation, cigarettes were avoided altogether, and he never exceeded two cups of coffee a day. Sugar intake was strictly limited, as was salt. He had a passion for Reggae and the work of Juan Miro. The stained glass of Medieval cathedrals sometimes crept into conversation when his mood was quiet, and he reminisced about traveling in Europe when he was young. What made him wonderful, even extraordinary, was that he believed in her, asked little of her, and was delighted by her presence in his life. His zeal helped her overcome the feeling that they were a cliché, the professor who fell for his student—risky behavior in this #MeToo climate. She worried what his colleagues might think, and he said no remarks had been made. That seemed unlikely, since he described the English department as close-knit, except for the adjuncts, who kept to themselves. The hierarchy was entrenched, and their low status meant a lack of security and low pay. That fall, all her classes were taught by them, the best of whom was Professor Morris, seated behind her wobbly desk up front, guiding their discussion of "Paradise Lost."

When Professor Morris ended Sam's reverie by asking if anyone had any questions, Sam raised her hand.

"Isn't it possible that Milton saw Satan as a rebellious figure because it made a better poem, and not because he was trying to say the Puritans were right?" she asked.

"It's clearly politically motivated," the student who sat next to her said. His name was Clarence.

"But what mattered more? Politics or art?"

Professor Morris asked, "*Is* it a blatantly political piece? I say it isn't. Does politics inform it? I don't how it can't. None of us writes in a vacuum."

Clarence raised his hand as the bell rang. Professor Morris said they would continue the discussion next time and wished everyone a lovely weekend.

Sam put on her coat and backpack. Outside, the air was bracing, and the sky was chrome.

Politics and poetry shouldn't mix, she thought. She was certain that Milton was just making people think about human nature, not the specifics of the world they lived in.

She was halfway through her sophomore year. At first, she loved being in a serious atmosphere, but she was tired of how people pulled poems apart and approached them mechanically. Then there was the whole discussion of what you could or couldn't say, depending on your race and gender. Sam once suggested that woke thinking amounted to censorship and was treated badly by several students. She pushed back. The discussion then turned to the value of sensitivity readers. Sam said they weren't necessary, and that if you didn't know how to write without using stereotypes you should hang up your laptop. Eventually, she was given some ground because she was older than her classmates, who regarded her as an oddity, a thirty-something trying to find herself after other pursuits had failed. The professors didn't care about her age, only about how well she took criticism. She took it better than she once did, but still tended to get flustered.

One day, a fellow student, whom Sam described to Steven as a beanpole because he was tall and so skinny his collar bones protruded, asked what she was trying to convey with the phrase,

"The rich wet vein descending from heights we stood on once." She said the image just came to her, and she gave it words.

Beanpole didn't like that answer and said it was fine to write from one's gut, as it were, but there had to be an internal logic that let another person connect. Sam said she didn't know how anyone else would connect with her work, it was a gamble, a chance she always had to take. She said poems weren't recipes, were they? Here Professor Barns, whom Sam didn't like nearly as well as Professor Morris, jumped in and said in any kind of writing you had to put yourself in the reader's shoes, see your work through their eyes, and determine where they might get lost.

Sam then asked Beanpole if he got lost in her poem, that is, if he were confused. He said not really, he knew what she was driving at. The professor asked him to say what that was, and he suggested the vein Sam referred to was love itself, or the experience of love.

"See? You got it," Sam said, then laughed. Beanpole looked at her skeptically but accepted her invitation for coffee after class. She didn't want any hard feelings.

The content courses were harder. She'd taken Steven's Survey of Romantic Poets and struggled with rhyming lines. They felt artificial and Steven said this was the point, to elevate poetry above usual speech and purpose, even if the subjects were universal and thus accessible. He suggested that she think of it as an earlier fashion, like women's dresses from a different century. It's just what people did, what they liked, and what they were used to. Poetry was an ancient art, one that was usually spoken, and rhyming lines kept the listener engaged. Steven knew best, of course, and while Sam found the idea interesting, she wanted to write her poems the way she wanted. And to have them loved. People seemed to, and she wondered if she were shallow or sentimental, like a Hallmark greeting card. Steven assured her that she wasn't. She was an original. Also, a courageous artist.

She walked briskly against the cold. Snow was on the way; she could feel it. She always could.

She felt something else, too, as she walked over the gorge, a subtle suggestion in the way the icicles caught the low sunlight, or how the rushing water quieted as if dampened by the cold. Her head turned just in time to see Timothy's old Mercedes roll by. He must have seen her too. Did he know she'd be here now? Their breakup had been hard, but she didn't think he was stalking her. This was the main road between downtown and his house. He was just probably on his way home from somewhere.

As she continued along her route, the fraternities, including the one Timothy lived in years before, fell away and were replaced with houses. Many had pumpkins past their prime. In one yard, a deflated pilgrim lay rumpled on the grass. Sam didn't see why anyone would decorate for Thanksgiving. Perhaps a hay bale or some corn stalks, but a pilgrim was cheesy. Christmas was another story. You could pull out all the stops for that one.

At home, Steven was chopping vegetables for a chicken dish he was fond of. On the counter was a bottle of white wine and two glasses. She pecked him on the cheek, and he asked how class was. She said it was fine.

"Guess what?" he asked.

"What?"

"I had an email from Martin Alistair, you remember."

"The guy at Hedgerow."

"He's willing to let us come by his place and go through anything he has on the press's early days."

"That's awesome! You must be so pleased!"

Steven did a quick jig.

She hung up her coat and put her pack in the dining room on one of the chairs they never used. The table doubled as her home office. As she put out their plates and silverware, she wished again that they didn't have to leave. She was comfortable there, in his cozy home. Back in the kitchen, Steven had put the vegetables in the pan with the chicken and everything gave off a lovely, rich smell. He asked her to open the wine, and she did. She tasted it, stood before the window, and stared uneasily into the inky darkness beyond.

A little later, they sat down to eat. Steven slid a piece of chicken onto her plate. The candles flickered. He liked having them with dinner. The shutter slats were closed. They didn't go with the style of the house. Neither did the wallpaper in the powder room. The original owner's wife had once worked in publishing, and the book jackets of her firm's most popular titles had been haphazardly glued everywhere, even on either side of the mirror.

"I can't wait to show you Cambridge," Steven said.

"Will it be cold?"

"Until April, possibly May."

"That doesn't sound too great."

"Same weather as here. You should be used to it by now."

She asked him to tell her more about the press he wanted to write about. He'd told her a lot already, but she knew he liked talking about it and making it fresh.

"Edith Alistair was a trailblazer," he said. "She bought a bookstore on Harvard Square, then she set up the press. The first book she brought out was by a lesbian. In 1949. Can you imagine?"

"That took courage."

"I'm trying to track it down. The book, I mean. It was a tiny print run."

"What's it called?"

"*You, Forever.* By a Laura Brown."

He explained that the son, Martin, didn't know how to find a copy and Steven had been hunting everywhere online.

"Well, if you do find one, I bet it will be expensive," Sam said. Steven agreed. He'd tried to find information about the author, but had no luck there, either.

"It's still in business, right?" she asked.

"The press? Sure, but they haven't published poetry for years. They moved to fiction, then non-fiction, and now it mostly brings out academic works."

"They could publish you."

"The press publishes a book about itself."

"Why not?"

"Well, strictly speaking, there's no reason it couldn't, but I'd like a wider audience, and that means a university press. I'm hoping Dunston will take it."

"Would it publish one of its own?"

"We're always encouraged to query here, first. I had lunch with Maxwell last summer to sound him out. He was interested and liked the proposal I submitted. Of course, Baker just got turned down. He'll go begging to Chicago, I imagine. They're a bigger press, so it might work out for him."

Sam admired how Steven thought strategically about his career. She asked if he wanted coffee, and he said he did if she didn't mind making it. She cleared the table, set up the coffee maker, and turned it on. She gazed again through the window over the kitchen sink. The house she used to live in was a ten-minute walk away, and if the road didn't bend, it might be visible through the naked winter trees. Timothy was probably there right now, having another or sleeping it off.

She wished she didn't care, but she did. That's what happened when you loved someone.

Chapter Two

He came often in dreams, and the sense of him lingered after she opened her eyes and took in the bare branches of the cherry tree. They were together for three years, two good, and one not so good.

Melissa was the beginning of the end. There was nothing like the reappearance of an old girlfriend with a twelve-year-old son—a son they didn't know about, until then, to cause an earthquake.

Melissa wasn't a schemer. She didn't want anything from Timothy except for him to know their child. Sam thought being a father would be good for him and might overcome the weight of alcohol and self-pity, so she invited them over. Timothy didn't take his eyes off Melissa once. With him, she was polite but cool. Sam admired her calm and quiet dignity, and they became friends.

Late last summer, about two weeks before the fall semester started, Sam called Melissa to say she'd moved out of Timothy's house. Melissa already knew because Mark, her son, had told her. He stayed over at Timothy's every other weekend.

"I hope it wasn't because of me," Melissa said.

"It was because of him."

They agreed to meet for coffee on campus near where Melissa worked. She was waiting when Sam got there, wearing a pale pink sleeveless dress. Melissa always struck her as belonging to an earlier era. It was both odd and interesting. As soon as she sat down

Melissa said, "I think you did the right thing. Leaving him, I mean. Please don't take offense at that."

"None taken."

Melissa said Timothy was finding her absence hard, judging from what Mark said. He talked about leaving town, moving to California, and setting up a photography studio. In other words, la-la land.

"Things aren't easy for him," Sam said.

Had she trained herself to say that, after three years of covering for him? And how did that sound to Melissa, given that he had money, no responsibilities, and could do what he wanted while she was a single parent?

"No doubt. But I'm worried about letting Mark spend time with him when he's drinking," Melissa said.

"I can't imagine Timothy would do anything to endanger him."

"Not intentionally, no."

Sam wanted to beg Melissa not to keep Mark from seeing Timothy and knew that wasn't her place.

"Is he trying to get back together with you?" Sam asked. Melissa sipped her coffee and returned the cup to the saucer.

"He just keeps trying to extend our time together. Like, when I go pick up Mark, he asks if I want to stay for dinner. I always say no."

Sam nodded.

"The thing is, we were together hardly at all, way back when. I don't know why he thinks he knows me. He doesn't know me. Not at all."

"You're just another dream."

"Yeah."

They promised to stay in touch, though Sam could tell talking about Timothy made Melissa uneasy.

He had that effect on people, even members of his own family.

His older sister, Angie, and Sam's best friend wasn't surprised when Sam told her they'd broken up.

"He didn't deserve you," Angie said.

"I don't see it that way."

"I know. But you pulled your weight, and he didn't pull his, so it comes to the same thing."

Sam said nothing, yet felt Angie had no right to be critical. Her relationship with her boyfriend, Matt, wasn't exactly rosy. There was a woman Matt had been involved with who floated in and out of sight from time to time.

Timothy's twin sisters, Marta and Maggie, who lived in New York City, weren't surprised, either.

I love him, but he's a self-obsessed jerk, Marta texted. And Maggie wrote, He can never hold on to what matters.

Timothy's mother, Lavinia, invited her over to the house as soon as she heard the news. They were good friends, though at first, were suspicious of each other. They came to value traits in one another, chiefly hard work and a practical approach to solving problems. Sometimes, their opinions about Timothy aligned against him. He must have found that hard, Sam thought.

Alma, Lavinia's housekeeper, ferried in a fancy silver tray with Lavinia's best china tea service. Sam was mad about tea. They sat in the living room, though Sam would have preferred the humbler kitchen. Lavinia wasn't born to money and struggled through many lean years with her first husband, Potter, Timothy's father. When they divorced, she married her boss, Chip. Then Chip died after being struck by lightning on the golf course of the Dunston Country Club. Potter's second marriage broke up, and now he and

Lavinia were back together, remarried. Sam and Timothy attended the modest ceremony only a couple of months before.

Lavinia poured Sam a cup of Oolong. She wore a linen pantsuit in a pale blue that made Sam think of a tropical ocean. Her fingernails were painted pale pink. Sam admired her small build, though there were times when she seemed frail. How she managed to bear and raise five children was a wonder.

Sam sipped her tea. On the table in front of her were two dozen long-stemmed white roses in a crystal vase. The center of each blossom was a pale green, reminiscent of spring itself. She wanted to write a poem about this color and how surprising it always was.

"You did the right thing. Three years is a long time to listen to excuses," Lavinia said. She held her cup and didn't drink from it.

"Yes."

"You're sad."

"I'm just processing."

"And . . . I'm sorry, I've already forgotten his name."

"Steven."

"Right. How's it going with him?"

"Great."

Steven was committed to a common future. He'd been on the market for a while, as he put it. His last relationship was even longer than Sam's, over five years. His ex was a poet too, now in California, teaching at Berkeley. He wanted certainty, something he could count on, someone to always be there. He didn't talk about marriage, but Sam assumed he'd raise it before too long. As to children, she couldn't say.

She laid all this out to Lavinia.

"Can you see having a child with him?" she asked.

"He'd be a good father."

"You thought that about Timothy too."

Sam paused. She'd wanted a baby and Timothy didn't. That's why they broke up, or why she gave up on him, to be specific. At the time she assumed she would still want a baby and would act on it later, when things settled down. She was only thirty-two, and she still had time, but the whole idea of nurturing a new life, which once seemed beautiful, now seemed impossible.

Lavinia asked Sam if she heard anything from Foster, Timothy's younger brother.

"Not since I moved out, but I'd like to invite him over for dinner. I think he and Steven would get along. Steven loves animals. He wants to get a dog, in fact," Sam said.

Foster worked for a vet and was planning to become one himself. He and Timothy weren't close, but they looked out for each other. Sam was reluctant to call him because he might blame her for the breakup. She was afraid of his low opinion. Recognizing that made her feel like a fool.

Lavinia asked about school and Sam told her she was having second thoughts.

"Oh? Why?" Lavinia asked.

"I just want to write. Coursework tends to get in the way."

"The classes don't help you write better?"

"Not really."

"Did you think they would? I mean, is that why you enrolled?"

"I think I just wanted to see how I'd like it, and if I'd even be up to it."

"And you found out that you were."

Lavinia said she didn't finish college, and sometimes wondered if she'd missed out on an important chapter in her life. Of course, she had no idea what she'd study if she went back. Literature, perhaps. She always loved novels.

They sat with their tea. Lavinia said that despite all her life changes, Sam looked great, and she was glad to see her.

"Thank you for inviting me," Sam said.

"You'll always be a part of the family as far as I'm concerned," Lavinia said.

"I appreciate that."

Sam felt a rising wave of sadness and said she better go. She said she'd come again soon. That was months ago.

Steven didn't understand why Sam wanted to invite Foster to dinner all of a sudden but wasn't mean about it. She said it had been a while, they used to sort of be friends, and since she'd be gone over the spring, she wanted to touch base. Steven asked if Foster were another admirer and she said no, she could handle a romantic involvement with only one Dugan male at a time.

Foster didn't return Sam's text messages for three days, then wrote with an apology and said he was snowed under with school. Dinner sounded fine. He asked if he could bring anything. She said whatever he liked to drink, like sparkling water or Italian lemonade. Foster was scrupulous about avoiding alcohol. Then she asked how he felt about tofu.

It's spectacular, he texted.

They settled on the following Saturday after Foster finished his shift at the clinic. The vet he worked for was helping with his tuition and hoped Foster would join his practice when he finished school. Foster didn't think he could just take the man's money, so he kept working, but not for pay. Lavinia had made a sharp remark about that more than once. Foster ignored her.

Steven made a vegetable stew and asked Sam to taste it. When she said it was too spicy, he added coconut milk to smooth it out.

"You have a highly sensitive palate," he said and gave her a quick kiss. "And the soul of a poet," he added.

"And the heart of a lion?"

"A lioness."

She went to shovel the front walk for the second time that day. A steady snowfall had erased her morning's efforts. The walk was long, and she worked up a sweat. She removed her insulated jacket and kept working, her breath swirling away in silver plumes. Her neck was cold because she'd cut her hair just last week. All her life she'd worn it long, and found it took a surprising amount of courage to tell the stylist to go ahead. Steven said short hair made her an even more commanding figure than before, though she was formidable already because she was just under six feet tall. For much of her life, she was also heavy. She lost the excess weight during her first year with Timothy. It took a while to get used to being thin. Buying new clothes was strange, then great fun. Timothy never liked what she wore, new or old. He found her taste too plain, "hippyish," he once said. Steven didn't comment except to say she looked nice, even when she didn't. Since moving in with him, her fashion sense had improved and now light wool dresses, tailored slacks, and leather boots made up her winter wardrobe. Jewelry was something she'd developed a taste for, particularly silver and turquoise. A place down on the Commons boasted pieces from tribes in New Mexico and Arizona. Steven bought her a bracelet with turquoise when she moved in with him. She loved it but found it hard to wear when she was working, because she often wrote by hand.

The snow picked up and swirled madly. She didn't have far to go. The few cars that passed were quiet, their tires muffled. Then one with chains went by, and the sound was harsh.

She reached the end of the walk. Steven opened the front door and asked how she was coming along.

"All done!" she called across the distance.

"Great. Come inside, before you freeze!"

He closed the door, and she stood, sweating heavily. Now that she was no longer in motion, a chill settled. Yet she lingered to watch the snow in the purple light of late afternoon and recalled a poem she just read written by a woman who lived in the Pacific Northwest, Abigail Lois Pratt.

One world becomes another
When snow falls
Be like the snow
Silent, lovely, frequent
Unique, prized
Cold

Falling snow used to fill her with longing. Later, it became a nuisance. Now, she loved its beauty. A healthy progression, she thought.

Steven had set the table and opened the wine. Sam told him everything looked just beautiful and went to take a fast shower. Afterward, she put silver clips in her hair and looked like a girl from the Roaring Twenties, in her loosely fitting green dress. The freckles across the bridge of her nose suggested youth and innocence. As a child, when she studied them in the mirror, she searched for a secret pattern or invented one that changed according to her mood. Deep sorrow caused them to form a swan's neck. Good cheer made them suggest a giraffe. Timothy said she was just projecting her obsession with her height, and she supposed there was truth in that.

Foster had arrived when she returned downstairs. His cheeks were red from the cold. He said he'd been out walking his latest adoptee, Mirabelle. The new owners would rename her, and he hoped to talk them out of it because the dog, a pit bull mix, responded to it well. Sam gave him a quick hug and he said she looked great.

"You too!"

"I think I'm underdressed."

"Nonsense."

Foster wore wool slacks and a pullover sweater.

"I see you've met Steven," she said.

"Obviously," Steven said. He handed Foster a glass of the sparkling water he brought, with a wedge of lime in it.

They took their drinks into the living room where Steven had set out cheese and crackers. Foster regarded the cheese with suspicion, then ate some crackers. The fire, which had struggled to rise after Sam lit it, was now drawing well.

"I'm glad you could come. It's been too long," Sam said to Foster.

"It has."

"How's school?"

"I'm learning about parasites and communicable diseases."

"Sounds rigorous," Steven said.

"It is, but sometimes it's not as hard as I thought it would be. Other times, it seems impossible. I think it's a function of how much sleep I've had."

Foster asked Sam how her semester was going. She said fine, pretty much as usual. She wasn't enjoying the coursework as much as she once had. She preferred to spend her time writing and thought the degree wasn't worth getting, at the end of the day.

"You only need it if you want to teach, or go to graduate school, right?" Foster asked.

"Essentially," Steven said. "But Sam's not interested in a teaching career, I think we can all agree on that. She's free to dig in on her art."

Sam ate a cracker. An icy draft reached them from the poorly glazed windows.

"Almost sounds like you're deciding for her," Foster said.

"No, no, not at all. We've talked about this a lot," Sam said.

They hadn't. The one time she raised it, Steven seemed uncomfortable, and she said nothing further. He might worry about what his colleagues would say if she dropped out. She didn't want to make him look bad, but that wasn't enough of a reason to stay in school when everything told her to quit. She searched Steven's face for signs of what he was thinking, but his expression was pleasant and inscrutable.

Foster asked if she were looking forward to living in Boston. She said she was. He said he'd been a couple of times and really liked it.

Steven said dinner was almost ready.

As Sam and Foster went into the dining room, and Steven segued into the kitchen, Foster leaned in and said Timothy was having a tough time.

"I'm sorry to hear that," Sam said.

"He showed up at my place last weekend. I made him a sandwich, gave him coffee, listened to him ramble about this and that and finally asked him to leave because I had to study."

"You know he's not my problem anymore, right?"

"I just thought you should know."

They took their seats. Sam poured herself some wine, then called into the kitchen to ask if Steven needed any help. He said no and appeared a moment later carrying a large ceramic bowl he put on the sideboard. He filled a smaller bowl for Foster, one for Sam, and the last for himself. He asked Foster to help himself to a chunk of bread and he did, then passed it over to Sam.

The stew was good, but still too spicy. Foster didn't seem to mind. He said he appreciated the ingredients since he was trying to eat healthier, which Sam thought silly because he was skinny and always had been.

Steven asked Foster what kind of dog would make a good house pet. He thought the time had come to adopt one when they came back from Boston, of course. Assuming Sam was on board.

"Small or large breed?" Foster asked. He leaned back in his chair comfortably. Though his coloring was different, he looked a lot like Timothy, especially around the high cheekbones they'd inherited from Lavinia.

"I don't know. I like bigger dogs. I've heard small ones can be fussy," Steven said.

"Dogs are needy in general. Small dogs more so, I think. But they tend to live longer, if that's a factor. Parting is always so hard."

Foster told them about a family whose pug had reached the end. They all crowded into the room to be present for the final injection. The parents were teary-eyed, but the two children didn't give anything away.

"They probably didn't understand what was going on," Steven said.

"They knew they would never see their pet again."

"It's so sad. I don't think that's something children should go through," Sam said.

"They told us in advance they all wanted to be present. We couldn't overrule them," Foster said.

He talked about his childhood pet; a mutt named Thaddeus. He was found wandering around the neighborhood. No one knew who the owner was. He probably didn't have one. Foster's mother didn't want a dog, his father was all for it, but then his father had random enthusiasms, courtesy of his fondness for whiskey. Foster was only eight at the time and didn't keep up well with feeding and walking, so Angie jumped in and took charge. She said she hated Thaddeus, but Foster knew she loved him. She let him sleep on her bed, a habit Foster didn't recommend to anyone considering adopting.

"You have to act like you're the leader of the pack. A dog is happier when he knows his place," Foster said.

"I wouldn't like a dog on the bed," Sam said.

"Wouldn't be any worse than me," Steven said. They all laughed.

Steven asked Foster which was better, looking at a shelter, or going through a breeder. Foster said if you wanted a purebred, you should find a breeder, but if you were open to just a good all-around mutt, then a shelter was the way to go.

Steven nodded thoughtfully, yet Sam could sense his mind was elsewhere.

Foster said he'd brought an apple pie for dessert but left it in the car. He could get it now if they liked.

"That sounds great!" Steven said and stood up to clear the table.

They ate their pie in the living room. Foster asked Steven what he'd be working on in Boston, and Steven told him a bit about the press and the woman who founded it. Then he excused himself to do the dishes, and once they were alone, Foster told Sam Timothy needed to go into rehab. The family had discussed it.

"Will he go, do you think?" Sam asked.

"If you talk to him."

"Oh, God, Foster. Don't ask me to do that."

He said she didn't have to. That was entirely up to her. The family considered her one of them, and always would, whatever she decided. He just wanted her to understand how worried they all were. Timothy was on a downward spiral, and it was bound to end badly.

"Get Melissa to talk to him," Sam said. She wished Steven would return. Water ran in the kitchen sink, and dishes were going into the dishwasher. He was taking his time, giving them a chance to talk.

"I tried. She said it wasn't her place," Foster said.

"That's ridiculous. They have a child together."

"And you had three years together."

Sam asked what she could say that would make Timothy listen.

"Just tell him you don't hate him, that he didn't ruin your life," Foster said.

Sam was sure Timothy didn't think that. He never felt guilty about anything. But maybe he did now, and alcohol was making it worse.

Sam asked if they were considering an intervention.

Foster said they were, but frankly if Sam could get him to listen, a lot of time and trouble could be spared.

"Except for me," Sam said.

"I know."

Sam realized wanting to stay close to the Dugans meant she'd have to do it. She should do it anyway, because of how she and Timothy broke up. She'd handled that badly. When she said she was leaving him, she assumed he'd seen it coming, but it took him by surprise. He was so sunk himself he didn't know how unhappy she'd been.

"All right. I'll text him. No promises as to how he'll respond," Sam said.

"No promises required."

Steven returned and apologized for being so long in the kitchen. He sat down in the empty chair by the fireplace. Sam thanked him for doing the dishes.

Foster said it had been a great evening, but he had to get going. Tomorrow was a big study day.

Sam and Steven stood at the living room window and watched him drive off.

"Listen, I need to get in touch with Timothy. He's in rough shape, and everyone thinks I might be able to help him. I hope you don't mind," Sam said.

"No, I don't mind."

"Are you sure?"

"Of course!"

Steven said he had just a few essays left to grade, and they wouldn't take him long.

She followed him into his study where he'd rigged up a portable heater and an extension cord. Sam said she was calling a repair person on Monday. It was time to get it fixed.

"I suppose you're right. I don't know why I put it off," Steven said. He sat at his desk, a stack of papers at his elbow. He put on his reading glasses and picked up the first one. The student addressed the issue of Wordsworth's use of figurative language. Sam read, daffodils are how the author returns us to the world, while clouds are what remove us from it. Steven's pen hovered over these words, then he put a plus sign in the margin. Once again, poetry was pulled apart, and analyzed instead of experienced, but, of course, that was an oversimplification. People had to be able to find common ground when they talked about any art form, and this was how that happened.

She left Steven alone and went back to enjoy the fire for a little longer before going to bed. Her phone was on the mantlepiece, and she picked it up.

You need to stop drinking, she texted Timothy. Get help if you must.

Chapter Three

Over the next week, Sam sent Timothy three more text messages. He answered none. She called Foster and gave him an update. He thanked her for trying. He was getting ready for finals and didn't have time to talk. Sam called Lavinia and asked if she'd heard from Timothy, and she said she hadn't. She knew Foster had asked her to reach out to him, and she wanted to thank her for doing so. Then she said she had a gift for her, and she could drop it off whenever it was convenient. Sam thanked her and said she'd let her know soon.

Sam studied for finals too, though her heart wasn't in it. She'd put in her official withdrawal from school two days before. She had yet to tell Steven. He was looking forward to Boston and was trying to line up a tenant for their place while they were gone. A visiting English professor from Brown was the most likely candidate. He and his wife had been at Dunston since late summer and were living in a house they needed to be out of around New Year's. Steven knew him and thought he would take good care of their things, but of course, letting other people live in your house was always a gamble.

Steven assigned Sam the task of finding a place in Boston. Martin Alistair gave her the name of a realtor he knew, and she forwarded Sam a list of options. Most were three bedrooms. She and Steven each needed a workspace. It was important to have onsite parking too, preferably in a garage. A six-month lease was hard to find but she did, in a townhome in West Cambridge with a wood-burning fireplace.

Steven signed off on the townhome, paid the deposit, and scheduled a visit with the couple hoping to rent their house. Sam needed an excuse to be absent when they came, because she didn't want to answer polite questions about what she'd be taking in the spring semester when she was introduced.

Timothy supplied it when he texted and asked if she could drop by. He had a Christmas present for her. He hoped she didn't mind. She did mind, less about seeing him than about returning to the house where she'd felt hopeful, then desperate.

Steven was put out when she told him Timothy had asked to see her, especially on such short notice. She said it couldn't be helped and was sorry she wouldn't get a chance to meet their tenants.

"Prospective tenants. I haven't decided yet," Steven said. He didn't look up from the book he was reading.

"Okay."

"I asked for a couple of references. They're getting those to me today, I think."

"Good."

He glanced at her over the top of his bifocals.

"Did you ever trash a place you were renting?" he asked.

"What? No, of course not."

"I did."

"Seriously? When?"

He patted the space on the sofa next to him as a request that she join him. She was due at Timothy's in a few minutes, but she did as he asked.

He said during his sophomore year of college, he had a tough time. His parents were getting divorced, and once a week, like clockwork, each called to complain about the other. Steven's younger brother was still living at home, and he, too, had a case to plead, usually for Steven to ask the parents to lighten up and act like adults. As the elder son, he felt responsible. He heard them out but had nothing helpful to offer. They said they didn't want him to choose sides, but that's exactly what they wanted. His mother accused the father of cheating on her, which Steven was sure he did, and his father said his mother had lost touch with who he was. Both things were true, but his father's cheating was worse than his mother's losing touch. While he didn't side with his mother, because she was hard to live with, and made his father unhappy, he spent most of time talking to her. His father accused his mother of alienating Steven from him, which put him in the position of having either to defend his mother or say he was fine with his father's cheating. He didn't want to do either and hated being caught in the middle.

One night, after getting a bad mark on what he thought was a good paper on John Keats, he downed an entire six-pack of beer, hoping it would make him feel better. All it did was worsen his mood, and soon he was thinking about his parents and how angry they both made him. They were paying his rent, and in his drunken rage, he equated them with the space around him. He punched holes in the doors, which was easy to do because they were cheap hollow-core ones; he battered the walls and damaged the plaster.

Here Sam interrupted.

"I thought you went to Harvard on a full scholarship," she said.

"It only covered the tuition. They covered everything else."

"I see."

Well, long story short, he made a mess of things. His roommates were furious; the landlord was pretty upset too. His parents had to cough up plenty to repair the damage. And while they didn't stop the weekly phone calls, they did stop lobbying him. So, in a way, his childish rage proved useful.

"You could have just been honest with them and said the situation was hard on you too," Sam said. Steven's expression darkened. She'd said the wrong thing and had to think quickly.

"Are you worried that our tenants will do that? Trash the place, I mean. They're established and responsible, or so I assume," she said.

"Of course. But you can never be sure about people."

He told her he'd heard that the author Vladimir Nabokov had been a visiting professor there at Dunston University way back in the 60s and rented a nice house from someone taking a sabbatical abroad. The guy came home to an absolute mess. Things had been broken, the place hadn't been kept clean, and even the neighbors made repeated complaints, none of which had reached the owner while he was away. The point was that there was always a risk in renting out your home.

Sam waited to see if there were more and when he added nothing she said, "Well, I'm off. Let me know how it goes," and kissed his cheek.

As she drove the short distance to her old house, she realized Steven had deliberately delayed her. Had he hoped she'd get distracted and forget her appointment? Or just that she'd change her mind? She felt bad for him but was also annoyed at such a lame attempt.

There was a wreath on Timothy's door and Christmas lights strung over the front hedge. He must have heard her car because he opened the door as she came up the walk. He had a scraggly beard but otherwise appeared the same—tall, lanky, too handsome. Up close she could see the strain in his eyes.

"You cut your hair," he said.

"I did."

"Miss it?"

"Getting used to it."

They stood, staring at each other. She gestured to the hedge.

"I like the holiday cheer," she said.

"That was my mother's doing."

"Ah."

"She feels it her duty to drop in unannounced and force something on me."

"She's concerned. Everyone's concerned. You should appreciate that."

They went inside. Liquor bottles and empty beer cans were everywhere. The kitchen sink was stacked high with dirty dishes. Sam resisted the urge to swoop in and make everything right. She took a seat at the counter, though there was room at the table. The table was where she'd worked on her poetry. She couldn't sit there now.

He asked if he could get her anything. She said tea would be lovely. He looked lost. She said unless he moved everything around, he'd find it in the cabinet to the left of the stove. He pulled out a box of peppermint tea. It was her favorite kind. She had two boxes of it over at Steven's.

The kitchen smelled of garbage that needed to go out. The countertop was sticky, and she put her hands in her lap. She said again that she liked the decorations outside and asked if he were going to get a Christmas tree.

"I won't be here for Christmas," Timothy said.

"Really? Why not?"

"Harcourt and I are going to Las Vegas."

Harcourt was an old college friend who started a homebuilding business that went bust. Timothy invested in the company last summer and pulled out his money when he realized Harcourt didn't know what he was doing. They'd parted on bad terms. Obviously, they made up.

"What's he up to, these days?" Sam asked.

"Trying to put the business back together. He had to sweet talk his dad into funding him again."

"And he's going to Las Vegas?"

"We both need a break."

"Uh huh."

Timothy looked at her crossly. He said he didn't need her disapproval.

"Fine." Sam stood up and put on her coat.

"Hang on, I want to give you something."

"That's why I'm here. I thought you'd forgotten."

Timothy went into the bedroom and came back with a poorly wrapped gift. He gave it to her and said to open it. She did. It was a framed photograph of her, taken the summer they met. Her face wasn't visible, and the focal point was her hands, holding a book in her lap. She was sitting under a tree on campus, killing time until her next class. She didn't remember why Timothy was there that day. The frame was silver and clearly expensive.

"It's beautiful, Timothy," she said.

"Give it to what's-his-name."

"He has the original. This one's for me."

She said she was sorry she didn't have anything for him. He said it didn't matter; he was just glad to see her.

"Listen," she said.

"I know. I'm falling apart, I need to get a grip, etc."

"Well?"

He said he'd cut way back on the drinking, despite what she might think, given how bad the place looked. He was going to work hard on his photography and being loaded all the time made that impossible. When he got back from Vegas, he was going to go through his files, edit the better images, and set up a website. He also wanted to buy a high-end printer for those he might want to frame. He'd taken measurements. Everything would fit in the spare room—barely. He'd have to get rid of the small sleeper bed in there. Did she know anyone who wanted one?

"What about when Mark stays over?" Sam asked.

"His mother doesn't let him do that anymore. And frankly if she ever relents, and I hope she will, he can have the sofa. Won't kill him."

Sam said she should get going and thanked him again for the picture.

"Have a good trip," she said.

"Thanks."

He focused on her for a moment.

"Angie says you're moving to Boston," he said.

"Just for the spring semester. Steven's getting a grant."

Timothy nodded. The kettle screamed and he turned off the flame under it. He said she probably didn't want that cup of tea now.

"Not really. But thanks anyway," Sam said.

He walked her out. They stood awkwardly, wondering if a hug were called for. They remained apart and Sam got in her car.

She drove around the corner, then pulled up next to the curb. She texted Foster that she saw Timothy and he looked okay. She wasn't going to see him again, so she hoped that one visit would suffice. Then she wished him a merry Christmas.

The visit depressed her. She texted Angie to see if she could come over and when she got no reply, assumed she was working down at the bar Matt and her dad owned. Sam didn't like the place, or she'd have dropped in. Bars were pointless, no matter how cheery some people thought they were. Some people, in this case, being Timothy.

She went by the grocery store and picked up a couple of nice poinsettias for the house. They'd last well beyond the new year and the tenants could enjoy them. Light snow fell. She forced herself into the holiday spirit. She'd bought a beautiful sweater for Steven, hidden in her dresser, and would wrap it while he made dinner. Her first thought had been to knit him one, but she didn't know how she could work on it without him seeing. For herself, she had her eye on a silver necklace she saw in a catalog. She'd dropped a couple of hints, and if he didn't get it, she'd buy it for herself.

The houses all looked so pretty under snow. She'd miss Dunston so much!

She thought again how reluctant she was to leave. Steven didn't even ask how she felt about it. The grant application was made before they got involved and he simply assumed she was on board. She could tell him she wanted to stay behind and live in his house alone. She'd offer to pay rent, but he wouldn't be happy about that. He thought he rescued her from Timothy, but she was on her way out of that situation before he came along. He wanted to see himself as her savior. That was a problem. If he perceived her as being dependent on him, he'd never want her opinion on things that mattered.

Sam carried in the poinsettias and put them on the counter next to the dish drainer. She removed her coat and tossed it on the kitchen table. Voices drifted in from the living room and when she appeared there a moment later, Steven introduced her to Professor Lyall Tate and his wife, Professor Bannock.

"Please, call me Claire," Professor Bannock said.

"I've agreed to have them as my tenants," Steven said.

"Wonderful!" Sam said.

There were cocktails on the coffee table but only two glasses. Sam couldn't tell who was abstaining, then saw it was Claire when, after a moment, first Steven, then Lyall, each lifted a glass and took a small sip. Steven asked Sam if she wanted anything, and she said she'd get herself some wine. She offered some to Claire who said that sounded great. Sam went into the kitchen and Claire came too.

"This is a lovely house," Claire said. She was short and only came up to Sam's collarbone. Her long black hair was streaked with gray. The sweater she wore had silver buttons down the front. Her velvet slacks had the same kind running down the outside of the legs. Professors weren't usually such snappy dressers, though being a woman meant she had to try harder at everything.

"I'm glad you like it. Which do you prefer? White or red?" Sam asked.

"Oh, I don't know. Whatever you're having."

Sam went into the dining room where Steven kept wine on the sideboard. She chose a cabernet and brought it into the kitchen. She poured them each a glass and asked if Claire wanted to return to the living room or let the others continue their conversation uninterrupted.

"I think I've had my fill of who's up for tenure this year," Claire said. She explained that people in her department worried about it too, of course, it was just hard to listen to sometimes.

"What do you teach?" Sam asked.

"Economics."

"I took both Macro and Micro. Hard stuff."

"It can be."

Sam moved her coat from the table and hung it on the back of a chair. She invited Claire to sit.

"Thank you," said Claire, then when she was settled asked how Sam's classes were going.

"Fine. But I just officially withdrew."

"Because you're moving out of town for the semester?"

"I won't be going back, I don't think. I just want to work on my own stuff."

"And what stuff is that?"

"Oh, I'm sorry, I should have explained. Poetry. I'm a poet."

"That's wonderful! I don't understand why a writer needs a degree at all. I mean, isn't the idea to get published? And if your stuff's any good, that happens anyway, right?"

"Right."

"And you've published?"

"I have."

Claire asked how many poems she'd placed. Sam had to think for a minute.

"I don't know. Fifteen? Twenty?"

"Wow! That's great!"

"I guess it is."

"Tell me how you do it. Writing a poem, I mean."

Sam said she started with an idea, usually an image, then built a little world around it.

"I like that," Claire said.

"It's more complicated than that, but that's the essence."

"And how do you decide where to submit your work?"

Sam said there were lots of small literary journals around, both in print and online. She made it a point to read many of them to see what people wanted in their pages, then she chose a couple and submitted. She never thought she would get accepted. It came as a big surprise. Sometimes, she still couldn't believe it. She didn't talk about her publications with her classmates. One of her professors said last year she recognized Sam's name because she subscribed to a journal Sam recently appeared in. She, that is, Professor Gibbs, seemed impressed. That, too, felt weird.

"I think they call that 'imposter syndrome.' It's important not to fall prey to it. If you're good, you're good. And, you seem good," Claire said.

Her enthusiasm was welcome. Steven praised her too, of course, but he'd gotten distracted by teaching and working on the grant. They used to talk about her work regularly. She couldn't recall when they stopped.

"What do you teach? I mean, what level?" Sam asked.

"Everything. I'm an adjunct and take whatever they give me."

"Oh, so you'll never get tenure."

"Not unless they bring me on permanently. I've been at it for a couple of years, and so far, no interest."

"That sucks."

"It does. But I do a lot of outside consulting and earn more from that than I do from teaching."

"What do you consult on?"

"I help Native tribes invest in casinos and other businesses."

"Sounds lucrative."

"It is, for me and for them."

Steven called out to Sam, and they got up from the table and went into the living room.

"I'm afraid we need to get going," Lyall said.

Steven told him that since they'd be gone a couple of days before he and Claire moved in, he'd leave the key and some general instructions with the English department secretary.

Sam said she hoped they would enjoy living in the house as much as she and Steven did. Then she wished them a wonderful holiday season. As they got their coats on, Sam cleared the coffee table. Steven saw them out. When they'd gone, he found her in the kitchen and asked how her visit with Timothy had been.

"Mercifully brief," she said.

"What did he want?"

"To give me a Christmas gift. I left it in the car. I'll go get it."

She was gone for only a moment, but when she returned, Steven had taken himself off to his study. She stood in the kitchen, wondering if she'd done something wrong, or if he were more upset about her seeing Timothy than he let on. She went in and handed him the picture. He held it and gave it a long, hard look.

"That's you, isn't it?" he asked.

"How can you tell?"

"You have distinctive thumbs."

"Really?"

"Yeah. They bend slightly at the first joint."

"I never realized that." She looked at her hands as he went on looking at the photograph of them.

"He's good," Steven said.

"He is."

He gave her back the picture. He asked if she had any regrets. She said no, it was the right thing to do. Now she'd done her duty and wouldn't have to think about it again.

"I mean about breaking up with him," Steven said.

"You can't be serious."

"I guess I'm not."

"Good."

She kissed the top of his head and took the picture into the living room. She put it on the mantlepiece.

On Christmas Eve, Angie and Matt dropped by. They were due at Lavinia's later and needed shoring up, as Angie put it. Steven had met Angie a couple of times before, but not Matt, who was forty-two, the same age as Steven and stunningly handsome with black hair and blue eyes, which caused Steven to stiffen visibly as he shook hands. They brought wine and Matt offered to open it.

"Of course! Let the barkeep do it," Steven said.

Sam suspected Steven had a snobbish streak, and here it was. Matt didn't notice, or if he did, didn't react. He was swift with the corkscrew and poured out the glasses in the living room where Sam and Steven had spent a pleasant afternoon decorating the tree and hanging stockings over the fireplace. The room took on a false note after Steven's remark, but she was sure she was the only one who felt it. Angie settled into her chair and lifted her glass to the light. She complimented the wine's gorgeous color, then drank. When they were all seated, Sam asked Matt how things were at the bar.

"Busy, but not too bad tonight. Something about Christmas Eve keeps people away. Even the most dedicated drinker seems to prefer home and hearth," Matt said.

"That's quite poetic," Steven said.

"Thanks."

Angie wanted to know when they were leaving for Boston. Sam said the first week of January. Matt said Boston was cool.

"I thought you'd only been there once," Angie said to him.

"Yeah. But it's still cool."

"What impressed you, in particular?" Steven asked.

Matt leaned back on the sofa and sipped his wine.

"Paul Revere's house, I think. It was amazing. The whole place was slanted, and the ceilings were so low. Of course, people were shorter then. You know, smaller," he said.

The fire crackled.

"It's important, to have a sense of history," Sam said. Everyone agreed.

Angie asked when they were coming home. Steven said in June, they'd have to see how it was going.

"What do you mean?" Sam asked.

"We could hang out for the summer. If Claire and Lyall can stay on here," Steven said.

Sam explained these were the tenants who'd be living there.

"Risky business, having tenants," Matt said.

"They're professors, not students," Steven said.

"Still. They might have a wild party, you never know."

"Oh, be quiet," Angie told Matt.

Matt stared at her crossly, then said, "For your information, some of my professors were big partiers."

"Where did you go to school?" Steven asked.

"Right here, Dunston University. Majored in English."

"Really."

Matt said he went on a scholarship, which was great, but an English degree didn't give you a marketable skill.

"Not like owning a bar," Steven said.

"Exactly."

Steven said his brother owned a couple of small motels in the St. Louis area. He, too, had a Liberal Arts background and found it didn't yield much in the way of income. When their uncle died and left them a little money, he bought the first place. He had a knack for business, he discovered. People not only wanted a clean, comfortable place to stay but a nice, inspiring atmosphere. He decorated the wood-paneled walls with framed pages of poetry. It was interesting to see his tastes change over time. At first, he was all for Shakespeare and John Milton. Then, perhaps because of something a guest said, or his wife, he put up more recent work, even by women.

"Shocking," Sam asked.

Angie laughed.

"He loved Edna St. Vincent Millay, but I told him Emily Dickinson was always good. Also, that he should avoid Sylvia Plath and Anne Sexton. The guests didn't need nightmares," Steven said.

Sam asked if anyone were hungry. She could put together a plate of cheese and crackers in no time.

"Mom's serving dinner, but I could have a little something now," Angie said.

Sam went into the kitchen, hoping Angie would follow so they could talk. She wanted to follow up on the tension between her and Matt and see if it had to do with the former girlfriend Matt was still in touch with. Angie knew about her, and also that his involvement was restricted to occasional phone calls. More or less. At one point last summer, Timothy pressured Matt to leave her alone, citing how unfair it all was to Angie, and he did, for a while. Then Timothy got sick of the situation and didn't want to waste his time on it anymore. Sam was glad he'd stuck up for his sister, however briefly. Angie was her best friend. Her only friend, she thought, sometimes.

But Angie stayed behind with the others. Sam came back with a plate in each hand. She arranged everything on the table.

"You remember Mrs. Winterhurst at Lindell? She used to do that," Angie said to Sam.

"Do what?"

"Put up poetry quotations."

Sam had to think. She said she didn't remember her.

"That might have been before you started, actually," Angie said.

"You worked at Lindell?" Steven asked Angie.

"Ten years."

"That's a long time to clean rooms."

"I was a social worker."

"Really? You must have a master's degree. You need one for that position. At least, that's my understanding."

"You're well-acquainted with my former profession. And yes, I have a master's."

Angie and Matt nibbled the cheese and crackers. Steven served more wine. Matt noticed the picture on the mantlepiece and asked what it was. Sam told him.

"If I dropped in on my ex, I'd get a lecture a mile long," Matt said. Now, it was Angie's turn to glare.

"Foster wanted me to reach out to him. So, I did," Sam said.

"Yeah, I guess he's been drinking a lot," Matt said.

"Do you hear from him?" Sam asked.

"Sometimes. Not as much lately."

"I call him every couple of days. We all do. The family, I mean," Angie said.

"Poor Timothy," Sam said.

"Why do you say that?" Steven asked.

"Because he's having a hard time, why else?"

The icy tone of her voice made everyone still for a moment. Angie said he'd be okay, but that it was up to him to decide how to get there. Matt said he was still adjusting to being on his own, and sometimes that took more time than you expected it to.

"True," Steven said.

"He said he's drinking less," Sam said.

"He had plenty the other night down at the bar," Matt said.

"You should have stopped serving him then," Angie said.

"I was about to cut him off when he stopped on his own."

Another silence fell, broken by the cheerful snap and crackle of the fire.

Then Angie and Matt had to go. Sam promised to call before they left for Boston.

"We'll miss you," Matt said.

"I'll come back," Sam said.

She asked Angie to give her love to Lavinia and the rest of the family. Angie promised to do so.

Steven cleared away the plates and glasses while Sam walked Angie and Matt out. When she returned to the living room he said, "Is it just me, or were they not getting along so great? I mean, they looked liked they wanted to take it outside at one point there."

"It's a long story."

"No doubt. But tell me another time."

He said he had a gift for her which she could open now if she wanted.

"Oh, are you sure? Don't you usually open gifts on Christmas Day?" she asked.

"I don't have any set traditions."

"I guess we're making it up as we go. Our first Christmas! Isn't that something?"

He asked her to sit and when she had, he pulled a gift out from behind the sofa. She could tell at once it was a book.

She tore off the red-and-gold wrapping paper to find a beautiful small leather-bound volume, *You, Forever* by Laura Brown, published by The Hedgerow Press in 1949.

"I thought you said you couldn't find it!" Sam said.

"I have a friend who's an antique bookseller in Boston. He did some scrounging for me."

Sam opened it. There was a handwritten dedication in faded ink: To Fiona

"We'll have to find out who Fiona is," Sam said.

"I will if I can."

"I'll help."

"You'll be busy with school."

"Steven, listen, I withdrew. I'm not going back."

He sat beside her on the sofa. He asked if she were sure she'd made the right decision, and she said she was. Then he asked why she hadn't discussed it with him, first. She said there was nothing to discuss. And wasn't it her choice?

"Yes, of course. I just hope you won't be bored," he said.

"In Boston, working on my poems, how could I possibly be bored?"

He leaned in for a kiss but rather than find her lips, he pecked her lightly on the cheek and suggested they turn in. Tomorrow, they needed to start putting the house in order.

"What about your gift? Would you like it before we go up, or in the morning?" Sam asked.

"In the morning, I think."

Sam looked at the book, still in her hands.

"Thank you so much for this. I will treasure it," she said.

"As I treasure you."

Later, as she put the book on her nightstand and reached to turn off the little lamp next to it, she reviewed her discontent. Timothy, of course. The arrogant way Steven treated Matt, and how he assumed she would go along with everything. Then she examined her happiness. She was through with school. It had never felt right. Her poetry felt right. That filled her with gentle peace, so appropriate for Christmas Eve.

Chapter Four

Peace vanished two days later as she removed the decorations from the Christmas tree, a task that always made her sad. After Steven carried it out to the curb for the yard waste truck to collect, and she'd boxed everything up for storage in the basement, she turned her attention to the kitchen. Lyall and Claire would bring in their own things, and since the place in Boston came furnished and stocked, everything in the cupboards had to be carefully put away. Steven owned three sets of dishes—the one they used every day, and two others kept in the pantry. Sam didn't understand why those couldn't stay where they were, and he said they had sentimental value, and he didn't want to risk them getting ruined. The only way dishes could get ruined was if they broke, and the only way they could break is if Claire and Lyall used them. He asked her to please stop talking about it. His mood was foul and had been since he came downstairs that morning.

She put the roll of bubble wrap she was using on the counter and begged him to tell her what was bothering him.

He confessed the grant was in jeopardy. At the last minute, the committee overseeing the funding sent him an email saying the money might not come through. An expected donation failed to happen, and there wasn't enough for all the worthy applications.

"You'll still draw your regular salary, right?" Sam asked.

"Yes, of course."

"Then, either way, we're fine." Sam had her own money, invested for her years before by her father, from which she paid her share of their expenses.

"It's not that simple. A grant isn't just an income stream. It's recognition. It proves I'm working hard, and that other people know it."

"But you have tenure. I thought you didn't have to prove anything anymore."

"I always have something to prove."

She asked when the final decision would be made about the grant. He said in a couple of weeks.

"Well, we'll just have to wait and see. No point in thinking the worst."

"You're right."

He stood, looking down at her, his thoughts elsewhere. Then he focused. He asked her where she got the green scarf she wore, and she said it was her Christmas gift from Lavinia. She'd told him that. Didn't he remember? He said of course.

"Thanks again for my cardigan. It's great," he said.

"I'm glad you like it."

"Do you like what I got you?"

"It's lovely! I'm going to read it the first chance I get."

He asked if she had time to pack up the books in the bedroom. He explained that Lyall was a great reader and wanted to keep his favorite titles close, so he'd always have something interesting to end his day with.

"Sure, no problem," she said.

When she went upstairs and assessed the task, she thought it would make more sense to clear one shelf for him, not all five since he'd probably never read that much while they were gone and knew her idea would be dismissed. She took Steven's books down one at a time. They were old paperbacks he'd had forever judging from the worn covers and yellowed pages. When she lifted *Fahrenheit 451* a piece of stationery slipped free and dropped onto the carpet. It was a letter dated the year before from someone named Molly. Sam was taken with the idea of someone using a pen and paper to write a letter. Who did that, anymore?

Steve—

You say you've thought this all out and looked at the situation from all sides. Which I suppose you have, except from mine. I didn't sleep with Professor Klein. He told you so, I told you so, but you decided otherwise. You're not God, you know. You are capable of being wrong. I think you decided I couldn't be trusted because you became interested in someone else, and rather than look that squarely in the eye, you had to find fault with me. Maybe there is no fault. The time had come, and we were through. I accept that. What I will not accept is you blaming me for something I didn't do. That's cheap and unworthy of you.

There was more Sam didn't read. The only woman from the past Steven spoke of was the professor out in Berkeley. This was someone else, someone recent, who overlapped Sam's arrival in his life. She wished he'd talked about her. She had been honest about Timothy, probably a little too honest, given that sometimes he came close to wincing, listening to her. While she felt it best to be open, Steven clearly felt otherwise.

As she continued her work, Sam wondered if Steven had asked her to clear the shelves so she'd find the letter. But that assumed he remembered it was there. Another question was why he kept it, and didn't throw it away after reading it.

Don't go down that road, it's always a dead end.

Three years of trying to figure out what Timothy thought about anything turned out to be a waste of time. If she wanted to know more, she'd have to ask Steven directly but only later, when the grant came through and things were easy again.

They rang in the new year with a glass of champagne and pizza. All around them, the house was barren, and Steven said, looking at it, that he almost had second thoughts, especially because the grant was still pending. Sam said he was being silly. He already told the university he wouldn't be teaching in the spring, and if they didn't go to Boston, what would they do? It was too late to change their minds now.

He agreed with a sullen nod. Sam shifted gears, determined to lighten his mood.

"What was your favorite trip to Europe?" she asked.

He ate part of a slice of pepperoni pizza.

"The summer after I graduated from high school. My folks got me a Eurail Pass and off I went, landing in one youth hostel after another," he said.

"Sounds like fun."

He told her about seeing the Mona Lisa at the Louvre. It was so small, he said, such muted, dreary colors. He never understood that about da Vinci. For a man so full of curiosity, that overwhelming passion to know, why did he portray the world as murky?

"To suggest that shadows, or darkness, is what knowledge must overcome," Sam said.

Steven picked something out of his teeth.

"Where did you get that?" he asked.

"I just thought of it."

He looked at her skeptically. Her face warmed.

"That's an interesting idea," he said.

Next, she asked him how he came to be so interested in Juan Miro. He said he already explained that but was happy to again, since she'd forgotten. He was at a conference in New York City and wandered into the Museum of Modern Art. He just loved that impression of childlike simplicity, an almost primitive take on shape and color even though the work was highly sophisticated. Miro's colors were vivid and wonderful.

"You probably think that sounds stupid," he said.

"Not at all. You like what you like. No need to delve too deeply into why. Even though I asked."

"Are you mad at me?"

"Of course not!"

"I haven't been nice lately."

"You're under stress."

He nodded. He said he was going to deal with cleaning up, then they could watch television if she wanted.

The next day, they packed their things, and on the following morning stuffed it all into Steven's Jeep and headed off. Sam fought back tears as they pulled away from the house. Sensing her mood, Steven didn't try to engage her in conversation.

They stopped for lunch at a diner outside of Schenectady. The lighting glared, and the hamburgers were delicious. Steven said she looked sad. She said she just wasn't a good traveler.

More silent, stressful hours followed, then the open country filled and became congested. Traffic was terrible. Sam had directions programmed into her phone and read them aloud clearly, yet Steven had trouble following them. The city struck her as small, with few skyscrapers, and she said so to Steven. He reminded her that the geography was bounded tightly by hills and water. Boston couldn't sprawl the way LA could, for example, or Denver, though he hadn't been to either. She told him he was almost certainly correct. She pointed out some buildings with ornate brickwork and asked him if they were Victorian. He didn't answer and she didn't press. She continued to watch everything closely. Some structures were clearly much older, Colonial or Revolutionary War era, with tall narrow windows. It would be fun to explore them if she could persuade Steven to. Or she could go on her own. She never minded discovering things alone. It was healthy, she thought, and meant she could be comfortable with her own company.

Finally, they reached the townhome and were greeted by Bethany, the property manager, who said she'd just about given up on them. She shook hands and said she understood that Steven was a professor, to which he nodded.

"I was at Boston College for a while, but I had to drop out. My parents said they weren't paying for me to party all day long," Bethany said. Her accent was thick. Sam didn't hear a single 'r.'

Steven leaned hard against a door in the kitchen that led to a deck. It opened with a loud squeak and Bethany said she'd get that looked at.

She explained about the parking space. It wasn't marked, but it was the one on the right. The man in the adjacent townhome was uptight about that. His spot was on the left, near the stairs. She said the dishwasher was new, but the washer and dryer weren't. If they had any trouble with them, they should call, and she'd see about getting them replaced. She did want them to know, though, that the owner didn't like spending money, so it might be an uphill battle.

She gestured to the spare bedrooms to the right of the entry door, then said the living room furniture was new and she hoped they liked leather. She led them into the master bedroom. The four-poster bed seemed a bit much, but if the mattress were firm, Sam didn't care. Steven leaned his head briefly into the bathroom, then followed Bethany back out. Sam sat on the bed, bounced a little, then lay on her back and gazed at the ceiling where a patch of fresh paint suggested a water stain underneath. She hoped when the snow melted on the roof they wouldn't get dripped on. She got off the bed and looked in the closet. There was plenty of room, though in the online photos it looked more spacious than it was. A clever camera angle could do wonders.

She wandered back out to find Steven alone in the kitchen, opening the drawers and cupboards.

"Oh, did she leave? I didn't hear her go," Sam said.

"There's a rice cooker."

"Yeah? Cool."

Sam said she wanted to get her stuff put away in the closet. Did he want to take a look and choose which side he wanted?

"It doesn't matter. Let's check out the spare bedrooms."

The first had a double bed and a desk under a window. The second was a dedicated office, complete with a desk and a printer. The walls were painted a deep blue, and the artwork was a series of abstract prints which made Sam suggest the room had been decorated with Steven in mind. He said he'd take the other one, and she could have this one.

"Oh, no, you need this. It's got more room," she said.

"I don't need a lot of room."

"I don't either."

"We can flip a coin if you want."

"Okay."

Steven had trouble with the quarter, so Sam took over. He asked where she learned to do that. She said she had no idea. She called heads and won.

He read her expression and asked what the problem was.

"We're here on your grant, or soon-to-be grant if you prefer. And so, you should have the better space to work in," she said.

"You'll never make anything of yourself as a poet if you don't start thinking of your work as important as mine—or as anyone's."

She was grateful he said so, but still felt uncomfortable. Later that day, when the unpacking was behind them and she set up her laptop and poetry journal in the blue room, she was happy to be there. Steven was right, as usual. Then she recalled Molly's statement that he wasn't, but, of course, that was a different situation entirely.

Who was Professor Klein? She looked up a list of Dunston University faculty online and didn't find that name. Someone might have been visiting, or Molly met him at a conference somewhere. Conferences could be loose and liberating. She knew that first-hand. Last summer, when she and Steven went off to one at Middlebury College, she saw her doomed relationship with Timothy in a new light. Knowing it was at an end was painful but also freeing. Molly—whoever she was—and Sam imagined her as small and dainty (she knew this was just her inner giant talking) would have let her rules soften and even drop away.

Since neither of them felt like cooking, they looked up a Mexican place nearby and ordered in. Bethany had thoughtfully left them a bottle of wine, courtesy of the management company, which they drank. Sam found it too sweet; Steven said it was just right.

The following day they met with Martin Alistair at his apartment in Back Bay, on the top floor of a stately building overlooking the Charles River. Martin was silver-haired and wore pressed wool slacks, a button-down shirt, and a gray cardigan. He ushered them into the living room. Sam went to the floor-to-ceiling windows and looked down at the gray ribbon of water. Light snow fell, and she studied how the flakes vanished when they hit the surface. Martin offered them sherry, and when they both declined, said he also had a pot of tea ready to serve. They accepted that and he disappeared and reappeared soon afterward with a tray.

They sat down with their cups. Steven put his on the table by his chair, Sam held hers. Martin asked Steven how he came to be interested in The Hedgerow Press, and Steven explained that while he was researching one of its poets, Robert Nedleman, who died about ten years ago, he found the name Clara Levy in the foreword of his third book.

Martin nodded.

"I'm just digging in. I have her volume, *Holocaust*, and it's such compelling work, I had to wonder about the woman courageous enough to publish it," Steven said.

"My mother was nothing, if not courageous. Many other things too, of course, not all of them good, but motherhood is a fraught condition. She didn't want me. That is, she didn't plan on my appearance in her life, but I suspect in those days that happened quite a bit. Or so I'm told."

There followed an awkward pause. Martin apologized for speaking of personal things. Steven said it was no problem at all. But could he tell them a bit about the press? In whatever order made sense. Sam put her empty teacup on the coffee table and leaned back against the sofa. A log shifted in the fireplace. Martin had lit the fire when they arrived and now it was robust and cheerful.

"Well, the story of the press is really the story of my mother," Martin said. He hadn't touched his tea.

"What was her name?" Sam asked.

"I told you. Edith Alistair," Steven said.

Sam absorbed Steven's rebuke. Martin looked at her with a kind, patient light in his eyes.

"She began life as Edith Parry in Urbana, Illinois. She met her future husband, Walter Sloan in high school. They married and came to Harvard. He was a law student; she earned a master's in American Poetry. They divorced in 1949. At the time, she was living with Henry McCormick, an English peer who moved here to study Shakespeare, if you can believe that. This was once his home. It came to my father when Henry died. My father was his butler."

Martin put his cup on the table next to Sam's and continued.

He said his mother was engaged to marry Henry, but he had a breakdown and had to go into a sanitorium. He had a history of mental illness, which she didn't know about when she accepted his proposal. It was decided he should release her from the engagement. She continued to live in the apartment with his butler, Malcolm Alistair. They had an affair, and he asked her to marry him when they learned she was pregnant. He was twenty-six years older than she, which couldn't have been easy for either of them.

"I should think not," Steven said.

Martin said in the early years, the press struggled. The poetry books didn't sell well, and his mother had to keep the whole thing afloat with her own money.

"It was a labor of love," he said.

"I think much of writing and publishing is just that. I mean, if one wanted to make money, there are easier ways to go about it," Sam said.

"There are indeed. My ex was in real estate. He did well."

Steven asked how many titles the press brought out, and over what time span.

Martin said around twenty-five and most of them between 1950 and 1962. Then, things changed. His grandmother became ill, and the family moved to Illinois to be near her.

"There I was, twelve years old, struggling with my sexual identity, plopped down in a small academic town. My father also felt like a fish out of water. An Englishman, who'd spent years in service, got out of it for a time, then found himself back where he started," Martin said.

"What do you mean?" Steven asked.

"He took care of my grandmother. Her close friend had died the year before and she was distressed, naturally. She was also becoming increasingly confused. Sometimes she thought my father was her late husband."

"And what was your mother doing?" Sam asked.

"Reading, mostly. Managing the press long-distance. I don't think she took on any new books during that period."

After his grandmother died a couple of years later, they came back to Cambridge. His mother had a different view of her publishing mission. Women authors all sounded so angry, and she had no patience for the tone many of them took in their work.

"She felt poets should be contributing to the greater good, and she didn't see rage as a way to do that," Martin said.

"But some titles came out, right?" Steven asked.

"Yes, indeed. All by male authors."

Sam was surprised. Based on Steven's brief account, Edith Alistair seemed dedicated to women's rights. Clearly, she was, for a time, then got distracted or disheartened. What happened to make her lose interest?

Steven asked Martin how long his mother was in charge of the press.

"Until 1994. Then she established The Hedgerow Trust to provide permanent funding and hired a man in New York City as managing editor. He had a small staff. He retired, and his assistant took over. Lisa Tettle. She's here in Cambridge and runs everything from home."

"But where are the archives? The unsold books?" Steven asked.

"In a warehouse. Lisa would know. But the papers are here. Jason Dobbs, the first managing editor, sent them over years ago."

"I hope we can go through them," Steven said.

"Of course. But I don't want them to leave the apartment. You'll have to work here, if that's all right."

Martin offered to show them where the papers were kept. Their route took them through the library, which had magnificent built-in bookshelves on every wall. He explained the collection reflected the eclectic reading interests of his parents, and that some books had belonged to Henry McCormick, but he wasn't sure which. Then he led them out and down the hall to the room containing the papers. Winter light poured through the windows like silver over the deep green carpet. The wallpaper featured a repeating pattern of climbing roses. There was a richly upholstered sofa with a side table and a crystal floor lamp. Boxes were stacked next to a writing desk covered with old envelopes, folders, bills, and receipts. Martin explained he'd tried to put everything in order and just gave up.

"My heart's not in it. It's so hard for me to see her handwriting, and read her diary entries," he said. He indicated a stack of leather-bound volumes on the floor. The one on top lay open.

"May I?" Sam asked, and Martin said yes, of course, she should feel free to help herself to anything. Sam lifted the diary and flipped through it. Most of what filled the pages were lists of things that had to be taken care of like trips to the grocery store or pediatrician. One item was a reminder to get the curtains hemmed. There were also recipes, book titles, and the name of a new restaurant. Nothing here suggested anything more than simple domestic concerns, except on the next page where Edith had written and underlined the name Philip.

Steven sat in the chair by the desk and looked through some envelopes, all of which contained personal letters. He asked Martin where the business correspondence for the press was, and Martin said he wasn't sure. He was afraid Steven was going to have to look through everything until he found what he needed.

"Has all this been sitting here since your mother died?" Sam asked.

"Heavens, no. It was in storage. I hired some college students to bring a few boxes up from the basement," Martin said.

"And what was this room used for before?" Sam asked.

Martin said it had been her private study. It hadn't been touched for years. He never had felt right about selling the apartment, and he just left things where they were. Once a year, a crew came in and cleared out the cobwebs. His ex thought he was foolishly sentimental, but it turned out to be providential because when his marriage ended, and they were deciding who would live where, he had this place to fall back on. He'd only been there a few months and was still adjusting to reoccupying his childhood home.

He went to the window and removed dead leaves from a wilted plant perched on the sill. He said he put it in here when he moved back in and kept forgetting to water it. It was a philodendron, a kind his mother always loved. That was no doubt why he chose it. Sam said he could put it in a different room, one where he spent more time, so he'd see it often and be reminded to care for it. Martin nodded and went back to plucking the leaves, which he put in the pocket of his cardigan.

Then he suggested Steven might like to have some time alone with the material. He and Sam would leave him to it.

"I won't be long. I just want to get a sense of what I'm up against," Steven said.

Sam would have preferred to stay too and continue with the diaries. As she followed Martin back to the living room she asked if he were certain they wouldn't be able to take anything home with them. He paused, hands deep in the pockets of his trousers.

"Oh, I suppose there's no problem. I mean, Professor Wells wants to write his book, and he needs this material. I'm sure he'll take good care of it. Besides, I don't know how much longer I'm going to be here," he said and added he wanted to get away, maybe to England and visit the estate where his father had lived as a boy. It had belonged to Henry McCormick's parents. Henry died young, and about ten years later, his parents died within a few months of each other when Martin was a teenager. The place was held in trust by the British government for a long time, and his father had tried to put the money together to purchase it but thought it would be a waste of time. Then his grandmother fell ill, and that whole saga distracted anyone from proceeding. Not long after, someone else bought it, and well, that was that.

"I'm curious about this Henry. You say your father was his butler?" Sam asked.

"Yes."

They were seated where they'd been before, Sam at the end of the sofa and Martin in a wingback chair. He asked if he could refresh her tea for her, and she said she was just fine.

"He was an aristocrat. An earl. Lots of money, the right school, the right wife, only she left him and went back to England," Martin said.

"He came here to study Shakespeare. I have to think he'd could have done that just as easily back in England."

"No doubt. He may have wanted a change of scene. In any case, he didn't complete his degree, so he might not have been that serious about his academic ambitions in the first place, which is why buying the bookstore appealed to him as a project. My mother was involved too, though she didn't have the funds to be an equal partner. She managed the place. Then his wife went home, and my mother bought it outright with money she inherited when her father died."

"How did your mother meet them?"

"Henry and her husband were friends."

Sam wondered how much longer Steven was going to be. Martin asked what she did.

"I'm a poet. That is, I'm trying hard to become one," she said.

"Do you also teach?"

"I don't."

"Well, that leaves you lots of time for your work."

"Yes."

She asked what he did.

"I'm a lawyer or was. I retired a couple of years ago. Now I do pro-bono work here and there, mostly landlord-tenant squabbles, but sometimes a criminal case."

"That sounds interesting."

Martin sighed and looked around the room.

"It can be," he said.

Steven appeared and asked where the bathroom was. Martin told him. A moment later, he returned. Sam said Martin had agreed to let them take the material with them. Steven thought that was wonderful because he had his eye on one box that he'd like to bring home.

"Let me know how it goes, and you're welcome here anytime. Actually, why don't I give you a key? Call ahead, and if you get no answer, just come on over," Martin said.

"Are you sure?" Steven asked.

"Absolutely. Hold on, just a minute, I'll go find the spare. I think it's in the kitchen."

Sam stood up when Martin did. She wished she could stay longer. The apartment made her feel peaceful. It was such a luxury, to be surrounded by all that quiet space.

Steven went to get the box he wanted. Martin returned with the key and gave it to Sam. She put it on her keyring. Martin walked her to the door. As they waited for Steven, he said he was more grateful than she could possibly know.

"For what?" Sam asked as she slipped on her down coat.

"Taking an interest in my mother, in her life, I mean."

"Well, she sounds like an interesting woman."

Steven returned with the box. He handed it to Sam while he got his coat on. They said goodbye to Martin and made their way down the hall and into the elevator.

In the car, Sam told Steven she thought Martin was sad.

"He didn't seem that way," Steven said.

"I spent more time with him than you did."

"Okay, then he's sad."

"What's wrong with you?"

"I'm not used to driving in this traffic."

"Go right at the next intersection. We're almost there."

When they reached their building, they found their assigned spot occupied, so Steven parked where the other resident was supposed to. He said he didn't want any grief and hoped the guy didn't want to get into it with him. Sam said she thought everything would be fine.

Steven carried the box inside and put it in the office he'd claimed. Sam went into the kitchen and made carrot soup. She'd only cooked a couple of meals since they moved in but enjoyed it, even though she had less counter space to work with than at home.

Later, as they sat down to eat, Steven apologized. He said he was just tense and would get into the swing of things soon. And the stuff over at Martin's was going to be a tremendous help.

"For sure. I'm glad he's okay with you having it here," Sam said.

After dinner, in the safety of her new office, and perhaps because Martin had spoken of his own past, she began a poem inspired by her grandmother, called "Her Face Curls."

It's okay not to be wanted
As long as she keeps her hands to herself

Her grandmother's abuse was both possessive and intimate. Sam had never thought of it that way before.

She put down her pencil. Confronting the past was necessary but it was like standing in a dark, cold room, waiting for her eyes to adjust and the heat to rise.

Right now, waiting was too hard.

She would try again in the morning when her thoughts were less bitter.

Chapter Five

Bitterness stayed, deepened by ragged dreams. The kitchen window shattered, and shards fell into the sink. Once fully awake, the details returned. Like everything in that wretched house where she lived with her mother and grandparents, the window was old and tended to stick. It was cold out and Sam closed it. She was strong then, at twelve, and the window slid down the track so quickly the glass fell apart. Everyone came in from the other room. Before Sam could say what happened her grandmother went after her. Her eyes were empty. Sam worked herself free, picked up the cast iron frying pan she'd washed and left to dry on the stove, and told her grandmother if she ever touched her again, she'd kill her. They all stood waiting. Then, her mother and grandmother went back to watching television; her grandfather nailed plywood over the opening and called a repair person to install a new pane. Sam threw the frying pan into the yard, went up to her drafty bedroom, and wedged a chair against the door. But no one disturbed her. No one spoke of her threat. Her grandmother insulted her often after that but kept her hands to herself.

Steven was already up. He'd spread papers over the kitchen counter where he sat on one of the stools, a cup of coffee at his elbow. Sam poured herself a cup too and took it into her office. She checked her email and found Angie had written to ask how she was settling in. She said she was bored out of her mind with Sam away, even the bar was boring, but then it had never really been all that fascinating. Sam wrote that everything was great, Boston was going to be a ton of fun, and she'd write more when she had time.

Time was slow. The poem wouldn't budge, so she wandered out and asked Steven how it was going. He said he was organizing Edith's business correspondence.

"This one is from a lawyer she consulted after a cop showed up at the bookstore," he said, indicating a yellowed, typewritten paper.

"A cop?"

"He threatened to arrest her on an obscenity charge over that book I gave you."

"You're kidding!"

"Remember, this was 1949. Lesbian literature wasn't a thing. At least, not in the mainstream."

Sam nodded.

She sat on an empty stool and dug through the envelopes. She pulled out one addressed to Mrs. Edith Sloan, care of a Mrs. Margaret Sloan in New York City. It was dated July 1948.

Dearest

The weather is close and muggy, and I suspect it is the same for you there. I don't like thinking of you so far away. I hope the job goes well for you. My summer work for Professor Clark is not interesting. I know the money is in estate law, but I'm not drawn to it. My mother says Kathleen came down from Chicago. Everyone asks after you.

All best,

Walter

Edith's first husband.

"They lived apart?" Sam asked and showed him the letter.

"Obviously."

"The war was over, though."

"People move out for all kinds of reasons."

Sam didn't find that likely. Divorce was frowned upon then, separating would have been too. But Edith was a woman out of time, given what she did with the press.

Sam suggested they walk over to Harvard Square and find where the bookstore had once been. Steven looked at her quizzically.

"You know, primary research," she said. She was restless. She needed cold air on her face.

"I want to read through her letters to prospective authors, see if she were encouraging or blunt. Get a sense of her style as a publisher, I mean."

Sam nodded. Did he mind if she went alone? She could pick up something for dinner on the way back. They'd seen that cute little grocery the first day there, remember?

"Take the car, if you want, but parking will be tough," he said.

"It's not that far. And I'd rather walk, anyway."

She dressed in light layers because she would work up a sweat. She always did. Her backpack was empty and ready for the market. With her phone fully charged, she slipped on a warm yet lightweight coat she bought just before leaving Dunston, then put her poetry journal in her backpack, and set out.

Her route took her along Concord Avenue. Despite the cold, there were a lot of other people walking, most alone, some couples, and a group of teenagers herded along by a weary adult. The traffic was heavy. LA had crazy traffic too, but the ocean was always there, like a soft whisper. Here, the sense of history was all around in the stone buildings and street names, Fayeweather, Brattle, and Lexington. Thinking about the past, and the people living then was fascinating on the one hand, but made her uneasy, almost sad, on the other. The sadness was deepened by recalling all the books Timothy read about ancient civilizations. She'd find them open and face down on the coffee table, and she'd use anything as a bookmark—a clean paper napkin, a twist tie from a loaf of bread, even a pencil—then closed the book to spare its spine.

Her skin was damp by the time she reached Harvard Square. The Turned Page had been where a boutique now stood. Steven found pictures of the interior in the box he brought home that showed two rooms separated by an archway. Sam went inside and there was the archway and both rooms, full of clothing racks. The smell of incense was heavy and cloying. She removed her coat and carried it over one arm. There were chandeliers with opaque glass. As far as she could recall from the grainy black-and-white photographs, these had been here in Edith's time too. The store had about a half-dozen shoppers going through the racks and looking into the glass cases at the back where necklaces and rings were displayed. A middle-aged woman asked Sam if she needed any help, and Sam said the place used to be a bookstore, way back when.

"Really?" the woman asked. She had red hair with white roots and green oval glasses.

"It was called The Turned Page."

"Cute name."

Sam took herself over to the glass jewelry case and focused on a turquoise ring with an oval stone in a simple silver setting. It matched the turquoise in her bracelet. The woman approached and Sam asked her if she could see it. The woman opened the case and explained the stone came from the Sleeping Beauty Mine in Arizona, where the highest quality turquoise was found. The ring slid easily over Sam's middle finger. She removed it and looked at the small tag tied to the band.

"Two hundred dollars?" Sam asked. The woman looked at the tag and confirmed the price.

"I can let you have it for one-eighty," the woman said.

"Why?"

"It's been in the case a long time. I think it's ready to find a home."

"What a lovely thought. I'll take it and thank you for the discount."

As she rang up the sale, the woman asked if Sam were a student. She said she used to be but just dropped out to write poetry full-time. The woman nodded and didn't ask for more information.

Sam left her gloves off so she could enjoy the new ring, but her hands got cold, and she went into a coffee shop a block down, called Devlin's. It was full of people, most of whom were using laptops or staring at cell phones. She ordered a decaf latté with non-fat milk, waited for the harried barista to make it, then found a table in the back where two people had just stood up and left their cups and plates behind.

She imagined The Turned Page as it would have been, with books on the shelves and dust motes in the air. Edith made her life there, spun her dreams, and worried if she could succeed as a publisher. She must have had other obsessions, other stars in her eyes. Sam needed to know what they were. The diaries must contain something more personal than what she read the other day, and after debating briefly with herself, she called Martin Alistair and told him she wanted to borrow them. He paused, then said he wasn't comfortable with them leaving the apartment. Her letters, well, that was another matter. Did she see what he meant? Sam said she did and promised to be extra careful with them. He hesitated and said he supposed he was fretting for no reason, something he had a bad habit of doing, and he was glad to let her spirit them away whenever she wanted. What good were they doing just sitting around anyway? In any case, he was leaving at the end of next week for an extended vacation. He'd had enough of the cold.

"Where are you going?" Sam asked.

"I haven't decided yet. Somewhere in the Caribbean, or the Bahamas."

He said nothing else, and Sam wondered if he'd hung up on her.

"Look, this is going to sound strange, but would you consider moving in here while I'm gone? You'd be doing me a favor. I've finally decided to sell the apartment this summer and it would be nice to have someone onsite until then," he said.

"But what about when you come back from your vacation? Won't you want to live here then?"

"No. It was hard to move back in the first place, and I think I'm ready to go. I have my eye on a condominium a couple of streets over. Of course, I could look for a tenant, but I doubt I'd be able to offer a reasonable lease at this point. And I got the feeling you connected with the place."

"Oh, I just love it, but I don't think Steven would want to uproot himself again so soon after settling in. I can talk to him about it, though."

He asked if she were free for lunch.

"Today?" she asked.

"Yes. Come around noon. You can go over the diaries and see which ones you want to borrow."

He suggested she take the train and told her which line and stop. She told him she was in Harvard Square, not the townhome. He gave her the information for that location.

"Let me check on a couple of things, and I'll text you right back," she said.

"Sounds great."

She called Steven. He didn't pick up until the fourth ring. She said she was invited to lunch at Martin Alistair's place. Did he mind if she went alone? Unless of course, he was ready to break off work and join them over there. He said he was on a roll and wanted to keep going. He'd found a slew of letters between Edith and Robert Nedleman, the poet who first mentioned Clara Levy, that bordered on romantic. Sam paused a minute to consider that Edith had been married, divorced, engaged, then married again and was still carried on a flirtation.

"Interesting," Sam said.

"What time will you be home?"

"I don't know. Why?"

"I'm wondering about dinner."

She reminded him that she'd offered to shop. What did he feel like eating?

"I can't think about that right now," he said.

"No worries, I'll figure it out."

"You're amazing, you know that?"

"Absolutely."

"Okay, then. See you later."

They hung up. She texted Martin she'd be there at noon.

She gazed idly around the coffee shop. A white-haired man studied a crossword puzzle as he pressed a pen to his lower lip in concentration. A young woman whose pushed-up sweater sleeves revealed colorful vining tattoos bent over a thick textbook. Sam pulled her poetry journal and a pencil out of her backpack and returned to "Her Face Curls."

She dropped back to getting ready for picture day at school. She fussed over her hair ribbon. Which was perfect—blue or green?

Her red hair should have made the complimentary green an easy enough choice, but she'd agonized over it. That intensity of feeling, returning now, gave rise to a simple stanza:

> Take from the chest the dress you wore
> When she pushed you
> Into the river,
> Down the stairs,
> Under the bus

Even when her hands stayed down, her grandmother was full of rage, especially when she was drinking.

> Her face curls,
> Planning her next attack

They called it "the cat," the way her cheeks pulled up into a leer when she was angry or upset.

"Someone let the cat in," her grandfather would say if Sam didn't wash the dishes properly or was slow getting the ironing done.

As always, reliving the past left her anxious. She sipped her coffee. It was cold. She wanted a refill but the time on her phone said she had to get going.

Martin's instructions overlooked a rerouting that caused the train to deposit her at the stop fifteen minutes late. He wasn't annoyed at her tardiness, so she didn't bother explaining the reason for it. He wore a different cardigan, dark green this time. He took her coat and ushered her directly into the dining room with a long oval table that could seat ten people. On the sideboard was a hot plate with a ceramic pot. Martin said he hoped she liked potato and leek soup. There was also a green salad and French bread. He asked if she wanted wine.

"Oh, I don't usually drink at this time of day, but then again, why not?" she said. He smiled at her. She realized he was lonely and grateful for her company. She wondered how long he'd been divorced.

He asked how she enjoyed Harvard Square. She explained about the boutique and the ring she bought. He asked to see it. She extended her hand.

"Have you been in? To the boutique, I mean?" she asked as he poured her a glass of red wine.

"A few years ago, with Aaron. My ex. I wanted to see how the place had changed, and how it hadn't. I must say, it left me feeling rather strange to be back there. I sometimes played in my mother's office while she worked. I wasn't allowed to make much noise, and when I did once, she got angry. Then she apologized. She didn't apologize, as a rule, and I never forgot it."

Sam said she'd been drawn into the past too, just that morning, working on a poem she thought had promise, but which was painful to write.

"Because of what it's based on?" Martin asked. He tucked his linen napkin into the collar of his button-down shirt.

"Yes."

"And that is? If you don't mind my asking.

"My grandmother."

Sam said she was a piece of work. She was dead now, of course, which was a huge relief, though it sounded like a terrible thing to say.

"Not at all. A person's absence from one's life can be freeing. I discovered that when my father died," Martin said. He slurped his soup. Sam found it endearing, there in that huge, elegant apartment, full of old-world charm.

"You didn't get along?" Sam asked.

"An understatement. I disappointed him in every way a boy can disappoint his father. I was gay, bookish, good in school, and not the least interested in sports. My father had no formal education, so I thought he would have appreciated my scholastic nature. And he wasn't athletic, either, but sports were important at the private schools they paid for. I was such a flop at rugby he stopped coming to the matches."

Sam said she thought that was a common story for people of Martin's generation. Gender roles were so strictly defined then, that it must have been hard realizing he didn't fit the mold. How had his mother dealt with his being gay?

"Oh, I don't think she took much notice. She tended to regard me with confusion when she regarded me at all. My father did most of the child-rearing. Very uncommon for a man to do back then. I always wondered why his assuming a role that went against the grain didn't make him more enlightened where I was concerned."

"He was worried about the discrimination you might face as a gay man."

"Perhaps."

Sam said his father's attitude was odd, given his mother was a pioneer in terms of publishing lesbian literature.

"She only published one book by a lesbian," Martin said.

"Really? I thought she was known for that."

"I think what she was known for was being a woman in a male-dominated industry."

The soup was good but bland. The salad was excellent, and the bread was superb. The wine warmed Sam's cheeks and she relaxed.

She said sometimes it seemed like women had come a long way, and sometimes it felt like they were still stuck.

"The patriarchy is the problem. That, and religion," Martin said.

Sam waited for him to say more, but he stood up and cleared the plates. She helped carry everything into the kitchen.

"Wow, this place is huge," she said, looking around.

"And a waste of space at that. I don't like cooking for one."

Sam put the dishes in the sink and wondered for a moment if she should offer to wash them, but Martin suggested they go see the diaries.

He'd arranged them neatly on the desk where Steven sat the other day. He explained his mother didn't start keeping track of her private thoughts until after she married his father, and he always wondered what it was about being his wife—or having him as her husband—that made her need to write about herself. As Sam would see, she didn't write every day, but there should be enough there to get a sense of the woman she was. There were six diaries, and he said she would begin another before filling the one before it.

"I think she got bored and wanted the feel of a new volume in her hand," he said.

They stood quietly for a moment. She asked if she might sit with them for a little while before she went home.

"Oh, please! I've already said my home is your home!"

"I'll just go grab my pack. I might want to take some notes."

"Allow me. I'll be right back."

After Martin returned with her pack, left the room, and closed the door quietly behind him, Sam dove in.

The pages were stiff, almost brittle from having sat so long. The top and bottom of each had yellowed. The volume she started with had a blue cover and a thin blue ribbon to mark the writer's place. The ink was either blue or black, clearly from a fountain pen since there were the occasional splotches.

May 2, 1951

Marty slept poorly, Joann reported. She was up every hour with him. I seem to have absorbed her exhaustion, though I slept over nine hours. Malcolm is his usual buoyant self. He asked for roast beef tonight. I have lunch with R. I might not get home in time, and Sadie is useless in the kitchen though Malcom loves her Cockney accent and refuses to show her the door.

A nanny and a cook, Sam thought. Yet Edith was exhausted. Just being a mother was a strain, even though other hands did the work.

April 14, 1952

I told Malcolm Marty is starting to look like my father. Malcolm said Marty looks like Marty. I don't believe in ghosts, so I can't believe in being haunted, but there it is. His words are still a jumble but one of these days they'll surely cut.

Afraid of her own child? Of his future rebukes and accusations?

She closed the volume. A moment later, she was at the window staring out at the river. Edith might have stood here often, gazing too, going down a list of chores, or seizing a brighter spot on the horizon she could navigate toward. When Sam returned to the volume, she found it disappointing. Edith maintained an even tone throughout. Sam didn't know what she'd hoped for. By the sound of it, Edith wasn't the kind of woman who boiled over, broke down, tore out her hair, or railed against the injustice of the female condition. There must be something here, though, and Sam wanted to find it.

She read entry after entry and the neutral tone continued. In the summer of 1954, Edith recorded receiving news of Henry's death in England. He was cleaning a gun, and it went off.

The standard euphemism for suicide. Poor Henry, unoriginal to the last.

How cold! Being practical was one thing: unloving, another.

That was it, wasn't it? The question of love, and whether Edith expressed it, or kept it to herself.

Sam had to use the powder room and afterward wandered into the living room to find Martin on the sofa, going through some papers. He looked up as she entered and crossed the room.

"They plead guilty, then are outraged when the judge tells them they have to serve five years before being considered for parole," he said. He removed his glasses and pinched the top of his nose. He asked how it was going.

"Pretty well. This might sound weird so forgive me, but was your mother aloof? As in, not open about her feelings?" Sam asked. Martin gestured to her to take the chair opposite the sofa. The room was warm, and Sam removed her pullover sweater. The static crackled as she folded it neatly in her lap.

Martin said yes, she was, but that was how women were raised back then. You were only supposed to show emotion to your husband and children.

"And did she?" Sam asked.

"Well, as I mentioned, she could get cross with me. As to affection, she didn't express much. That said, she was a constant, if limited, presence in my life. She would sit with me in the evening when she came in from the bookstore and asked how my day had been. Sometimes she read me a story. But, when I got sick, it was my father who was on hand, never her. It seemed completely normal until my friends at school talked about being down with the flu and their mothers feeding them soup, that sort of thing."

"Your father didn't work?"

"He had activities. He took classes and went to lectures. Always trying to improve himself, but no, no regular job, no nine-to-five routine. We were quite the odd family, in that respect."

"What did your mother do when she wasn't working?"

"I don't think she was ever not working, until we went out to Illinois to help with my grandmother, that is. At that point, she just read all the time and consulted with the nurses who came in."

"So, no hobbies to speak of?"

"Not really. She cooked well, but she didn't like it much."

Sam asked if she followed politics or the art world. Did she go to the movies?

"Sometimes. The movies, I mean. I don't remember her ever talking about politics or art, though my father liked to take himself down to New York now and then and prowl around the galleries. He never bought anything, though he kept threatening to."

And what about friends? Were there any?

Martin put the papers he was holding on the table in front of him. Friends, he said, well, there was a group of women for a while, when he was still quite young. His father called them "the hens." They were made up of the first poet she published, Laura Brown, and her circle. They were all lesbians, though one of them eventually married. His mother hinted the woman in question got pregnant during a moment of bad judgment and decided to go through with it to see what all the fuss was about. Living a normal life, he meant.

"She told you this?" Sam asked.

"God, no. But I picked up threads of conversation here and there. You know. Little pitchers have big ears."

He paused, clearly reminiscing. Then he said he had to meet a client, a man who was suing his landlord for not fixing the furnace.

"That's a problem, in this weather," Sam said. She thought of the broken radiator in Steven's study at home, and how the bitter cold hung in that room.

Steven!

What time was it? The clock on the mantlepiece said it was three forty.

"Excuse me for a moment, I need to make a call," Sam said.

She returned to Edith's room and pulled out her phone. Steven didn't pick up. There were no messages from him, either. She gathered up her pack and when she came into the front hall, Martin was there to help her into her coat. She thanked him for lunch and the diaries, even though she wasn't taking one away with her at the moment. She didn't know when she'd come back to continue reviewing them and asked when he was leaving. He said within the next four to five days and said if they didn't see each other before then, they would when he returned.

The train was crowded, and it took a long time for people to file on and off at each stop. She felt both squeezed and suffocated. She could never adjust to city life, but here she was for now, and she had to get used to it.

Breathe!

She leaned back and relaxed her shoulders.

So, Edith had no maternal instinct and saw Martin as a burden. Last June, Sam told Timothy she wanted a baby. She had for some time. Then the urge faded away, which seemed strange. What changed? Where had that yearning gone?

As Sam opened the door to the townhouse, she realized she'd forgotten to shop. She was closing the door again when Steven appeared and asked what she was doing.

"Hi! I lost track of time and didn't get to the store. I was just heading over there, now," she said.

He told her to come in and have a glass of wine. Dinner was underway. A couple of hours ago he realized he needed a break from Edith's letters and went shopping.

"Why didn't you let me know?" she asked and hung up her coat. He reminded her it wasn't her job to shop and cook.

"I know, but I said I'd take care of it, and I should have. Then I forgot. I'm sorry."

He said he found a missed call from her and was sorry he didn't try her back. He asked how her lunch went. She explained she went over Edith's diaries for a couple of hours and forgot about the time.

"You're really getting into her now, aren't you?" Steven asked. He washed lettuce, spread the leaves on the counter, and patted them with a paper towel.

"My work is kinda stuck, so I guess I'm easily distracted. Anyway, her entries are fascinating from a time capsule standpoint, but they stay on the surface."

"Diaries aren't always confessional."

"What's the point of keeping one, then?"

"Didn't you ever keep a diary?"

"Not in my house. My mother or grandmother would have found it, gone through every page, and tormented me over all of it."

Steven nodded but didn't follow up. She'd never given him the full story of her childhood, just the broad strokes.

When she met her father, after finally learning of his existence from her mother, she wondered at first if he thought she'd made her childhood sound worse than it was to gain sympathy, but he took her remarks at face value. She realized that in his work as a therapist, he'd have heard just about everything. He was grim about what she'd suffered, and said he wished things could have been different.

"Did you? Keep a diary?" Sam asked him as he set the table.

"A journal sometimes. When I was younger."

That night, after Steven was asleep, Sam lay awake listening to cars coming and going, and now and then a long-sustained honk; also, the neighbor moving around on the other side of the wall. What had him up at that hour? She wondered about going over and introducing herself one of these days, just to be friendly. Steven had said they shouldn't bother, they wouldn't be there long enough to settle in. Still, it might be nice to get to know someone other than Martin Alistair. Sam wished he weren't going away, though of course if he stayed, there'd be no chance to move in there. She had to tell Steven about the offer. She would tomorrow, if his mood were good. Telling him anything when his mood was bad was a waste of time.

Chapter Six

Sam was the first one up. She made coffee, poured herself a cup, and sat with her volume of Abigail Lois Pratt, *And Then Some.*

> The color of the season isn't white or
> Gray
> Just this gentle hue
> Carried within us
> Like a piece of sky
> Waiting for spring

That was from "Snow Country." Sam wished she could write like that! She worked on not feeling jealous when she read good poetry so she could learn and do better. She told herself she'd measure up one day. Claire was right. She did have imposter syndrome. She had a feeling Edith would tell her the same thing. In the dry lines of her diary entries, a steeliness emerged. Sam hadn't seen that yesterday, but this morning, when she woke up thinking about what she read, she felt it there.

Steven appeared, looking well-rested and in good spirits. The good cheer evaporated when he opened his laptop on the kitchen counter and read his new emails.

Lyall wrote to say they had trouble with the dishwasher and wanted to know who to call. Also, was it possible Steven got the garbage collection day wrong because the can hadn't been emptied unless they left it in the wrong location?

The grant committee still hadn't approved Steven's application but wrote that a decision should be made within ten days.

A student complained about receiving a B on his final paper and urged Steven to reconsider because he was applying to law school in the fall, and he needed his GPA to shine.

After Steven shared all this, he paused, as if waiting for some encouragement. Sam told him not to worry about the grant. She said she should go take a look at her emails, not that she was expecting anything, but she liked to check in at least once a day. Steven nodded, not listening. He typed something, stopped, resuming typing. Sam stood and kissed the top of his head. His hair needed washing.

In her office, she found a note from Angie saying the you-know-what had finally hit the fan with Matt and that she'd asked him to move out.

"Oh, no," Sam told the screen. Her phone was still in the bedroom, so she went to get it. Steven was staring at his screen, not typing. She sped past him quietly, got her phone, and zipped back into her office. She closed the door.

Angie answered on the first ring. The issue, in a nutshell, was that Matt was a lying snake. He was involved with that ex-girlfriend and had been all along, despite his repeated assurances to the contrary. He just didn't seem to understand it wasn't cool to be talking to her on the phone all the time, not to mention lending her money. He was probably at her place right now, asking if he could move in.

"I can't believe it," Sam said.

"Believe it."

"Are you feeling horrible?"

"Yes. But I'll survive. The wisdom of my actions will carry me through."

Angie's voice was throaty, suggesting that she'd been crying. Sam said she was sorry things ended up this way.

"It was only a matter of time. I tried not to see what was right in front of me and well, couldn't avoid it, in the end."

"And he denies everything?"

"Of course."

Angie said she was taking time off work. Her dad could run things at the bar. She told Matt she didn't want him down there. He objected at first, and she said if he showed up, her dad wouldn't like it.

"Potter wouldn't get violent, would he?" Sam asked.

"No. But Matt doesn't know that."

Angie said she had another call coming in and to hang on just a second. While she was gone Sam looked over her poetry journal, seeing what she could refine and improve. "Her Face Curls" was still stuck. Angie came back on the line. She said the other call was from her mother, who said she should get out of town for a while and clear her head.

"That's a great idea," Sam said.

"I need to go somewhere warm, but that takes planning."

"True."

"Hang on, another call."

Sam wrote:

Make for the door while her back is turned,
Wake sweat soaked from another nightmare

"Sorry, that was Timothy," Angie said.

"Yeah? What's he want?"

"To tell me Matt's over there. Figures. Anyhow, sorry that took so long."

"No worries. I scratched out a couple more lines of a poem."

"Amazing multi-tasker, you!"

They paused for a moment.

"Come here," Sam said.

"Boston?"

"Why not?"

"You have room for me?"

"No. But I have a line on a great place. I'll text you the details. Let me know if you want to do it."

"Okay, great. Thanks."

They hung up.

Steven took Angie's news with sympathy and thought her coming up was a fine idea. When Sam said she would ask Martin if Angie could stay over at his place, he said not to.

"Why not?" she asked.

"Because we need to get in there."

"So? The apartment is huge. She'll take up one corner of it. And anyway, he's leaving town for a while."

"I still don't think you should ask him."

"Oh, come on."

"It won't look good, that's all."

Sam told him about his offer to let the two of them move in. Steven asked why she hadn't mentioned that before.

"Because I knew you wouldn't want to," she said.

His brief nod said he saw her point. Then he tapped on his keyboard, signaling the conversation was at an end.

Martin said it would work out perfectly. He was leaving for the Bahamas in another three days and Angie could stay as long as she liked. Sam already had a key to the front door, but she'd need one to the building, which was locked every evening at ten. It might be a good idea to make a spare set for her friend to use. He'd take care of that if she wanted, and he'd also write down the access code to the garage. His car would remain where it was, but the spot next to that was also his and they were welcome to park there. As for keeping the place clean, he hoped she didn't mind seeing to that herself, unless she wanted the name of a good cleaning outfit who'd come in weekly, or twice weekly if she wanted. On him, of course.

"Oh, I'll take care of it, no worries. But it's a very generous offer. I swear you're about the best thing that's ever happened to me," Sam said. His long pause said he had no idea how to interpret her remark. She said she'd be over later today or tomorrow and hoped they'd cross paths.

But as the day wore on, she was busy with laundry and writing back to Lyall about the problems they'd raised. She didn't know why they couldn't look up the same information she did. Dishwasher repair people were listed on the internet like everyone else. As to the garbage collection company, it was the only one that served that part of Dunston. She copied their number and put it in her email. Then she had another call with Angie where they debated the best way for her to travel. Did she want to drive, and thus have her car available? Angie didn't like the idea of driving in Boston's weird tangle of narrow streets. She was thinking of taking the train. All those miles of looking out the window might get Matt off her mind. Now, they just had to figure out which day she would arrive.

Sam told her Martin's timing, and Angie said she'd let her know later.

Steven returned from looking at a gym he might want to join. At home, he had the athletic center on campus which he didn't use as much as he might, though his weight was fine. Exercise was just such a good stress reliever, he said, and he wanted to nail down the habit there in Boston. Sam could have her own membership if she wanted. A gym never made sense to her when you could walk and get the blood moving but she didn't say that. Instead, she promised to think about it.

The business correspondence Steven went over didn't yield much. A lot of it was technical and bore on paper stock, lettering, finding a new warehouse to store print runs in, and what to do with volumes that didn't sell. There were other matters discussed, of course, like the designs for dust jackets. In the beginning, Hedgerow used someone Edith Alistair knew personally, then she found a professional, a woman with a studio out in the country somewhere. The covers would be interesting to see, Sam said. Could they get ahold of them? Steven had already reached out to Lisa Tettle asking if they could look at the press's backlist. She wrote back and said Thursdays were good for her. The warehouse was in Sommerville. They could meet there.

Sam made a pot of tea while Steven told her about Edith's letters to her authors, not all of which were cordial. He pulled one from the stack and read from it:

"'If you do not agree with this arrangement, I warmly invite you to go straight to Hell.'"

"You're kidding," Sam said.

"Nope."

"Her diary entries are so dry compared to that."

Steven looked interested in her observation, then continued with what he'd been talking about.

There was one author, Joseph Preston, who seemed to have gotten under her skin. A whiner, Steven said. You know, never happy with anything. He didn't like her suggested changes to his manuscript. His book, *Long Way Around,* was heavy on journey images and Edith felt he should be more consistent in his choice of words.

Steven pulled out another letter.

"Here she writes 'I strongly advise you to say the road winds, not flows.' I wonder if the author were intentionally mixing up his metaphors as a way to unsettle the reader, keep him off guard."

"Or her."

"What? Yeah, or her. But you see what I mean?"

Sam suggested they track down the book in question and see what the final product looked like. What about the manuscripts themselves? Weren't they around somewhere?

"Good question. I think she would have returned them to the authors," Steven said.

That evening, heavy snow fell. Angie called and said she'd be up on Saturday. She'd stay a week, no more. Matt had been calling her, trying to make amends, and she refused to speak with him. Sam said she understood how hard that was and was sure it would get easier as time went by. Angie said she was looking forward to seeing her.

As they hung up, Sam wondered if she did the right thing by inviting her to come. The talk would be all about Matt and his endless failings. Of course, Sam would be supportive and hear her out. But it might prove tiresome before too long.

"You know what's wrong with me? I'm just too nice to people," she said to Steven. They were on the sofa in the living room watching a movie on television. Sort of watching, since Steven had a stack of letters on the coffee table he was occasionally skimming and making notes about on his laptop.

"Why do you say that?" he asked.

"I shouldn't have invited Angie up here."

"Oh, it will be fine, you'll see."

"I thought you didn't want her to come."

"I just wasn't sure it was a good idea to ask Martin to let her stay there, but you say he's fine with it, so there's no problem. Right?"

Sam said she planned to spend a fair amount of time over there with Angie and she hoped he wouldn't mind. He said no, not at all.

He might like having the place to himself, she thought. The townhome was about half the size of the house in Dunston. And there he also had had his office on campus to escape to if he needed to be alone and concentrate. When he invited her to move in late last summer, she worried that she'd be crowding him. There were two extra bedrooms, but they were full of boxes he hadn't sorted, mostly books and old clothes. Steven was a classic packrat. Purging made him anxious. She offered to help or to take charge of it herself, and he always said he'd get around to it one of these days. Claire and Lyall didn't mind not having the use of those rooms, they said. They would have plenty of space without them.

The next morning, Sam texted Martin to say she'd be by to get the spare keys and that he could give her the garage access code then. He texted back that anytime was fine. One the way, she bought him a second copy of Pratt volume she'd been reading at a bookstore near her train stop. Boston was full of bookstores, she was discovering, each a bit different in flavor and emphasis. This made her wonder where The Turned Page had fit in back in the day—what its competitors were like, whether the store under Edith did well by comparison. What she was like as a businesswoman, in other words.

Martin looked worn. There were dark circles under his eyes. He asked why she brought him a gift and she said it was the least she could do. He accepted the book graciously. He said he knew of the author and looked forward to reading her. He offered coffee, then said he'd had bad news about his ex. He was in the hospital with pancreatitis.

They sat in the kitchen this time. The coffee had a chocolate overlay, and the cup was delicate bone china.

"I'm sorry. Will he be all right?" she asked.

"It's not serious. But I'm the one he called, and that strongly suggests that he hasn't moved on."

"And that bothers you?"

"It worries me."

"Were you together long?"

"Almost twenty-five years."

"That's quite a while."

She talked about her breakup with Timothy, though she stressed they were together only for a couple of years.

"Yet, when the heart is wounded, time is irrelevant," Martin said.

They didn't speak for a moment. Sam found herself feeling sorry for him and had no good way to express that. She asked if he were ever involved with The Hedgerow, or if his career had kept him too busy.

He said he'd sometimes served as their lawyer. A few years ago, he defended it in a lawsuit.

"Someone sued the press? For what?" Sam asked.

"An author claimed the book we brought out copied her title."

"Which was?"

"*Miserable Women.* It's a book of essays."

"So, how was the suit decided?"

"The judge found for us. The title wasn't esoteric and basically in the public domain."

Sam asked if there were common themes among the books published by the press after it gave up on poetry. He said the fiction titles, which tended to be by women authors—a reversal of the spate of men his mother published in the sixties and early seventies—focused, logically enough, on women's issues. The non-fiction ones did too. There was a short series on suffragettes. Two researchers from Harvard had submitted a series of papers they turned into three—no, four books.

"I'd have thought they'd publish them at Harvard, not at a small local press," Sam said.

"It was hard for women to get work published then that wasn't strictly academic. Anything that emphasized social history, I should say."

Sam said Steven was scheduling a time to meet with Lisa Tettle and look over her stash of past titles. Martin was glad to hear that.

"I'm curious about the trust your mother set up. Who manages it?" she asked.

"The firm I used to work for. It's all pretty routine. Quick reviews of author contracts, annual tax filings, that kind of thing."

She said she assumed the operating costs of the press weren't great, so the trust must have gained value over time. It invested its money, didn't it?

"It does. Careful, not terribly interesting investments, but all socially acceptable. No African diamond mines, for instance."

She wanted to know everything—how much it was worth, who decided how to spend its money, if it had ever wanted to expand, set up a scholarship, for instance.

Martin wasn't put off by her questions. He said the trust was worth over ten million dollars. That sounded astronomical, of course, but he wanted her to keep in mind how much of his mother's money had gone into it and how many years had passed since then. One always hears about the miracle of compound interest, and here it was. The investment decisions were made in consultation with a financial planning company. One day, given how little the press published, he might use his authority to dissolve the trust and find another use for the money.

"That would be the end of Hedgerow," Sam said.

"It would. But nothing is definite. I'm just thinking about it."

He looked at his watch and she apologized for taking up so much of his time.

She took the spare keys and tapped the access code into the notepad section of her phone. Martin said if she needed anything, to just call. He'd made up one of the bedrooms for her friend. He could stock the refrigerator if she wanted him to and Sam said he shouldn't bother.

"It's no bother, really," he said.

"Have a wonderful time in the Bahamas. And thank you again for everything." They shook hands.

As she waited for the train, her phone rang. It was Lyall, calling from Dunston. He said they found someone to fix the dishwasher, and he'd straightened out the garbage pick-up too. Sam said to be sure to forward the receipt for the repair, and she hoped they were enjoying the house so far. Lyall said it was a lovely home but the radiator in the study still wasn't working right. Now, the room was too warm. He said he'd be happy to call the guy himself if Sam could shoot him over the number. She said she would when she got home—she was on her way there now.

"Claire says hello," Lyall said.

"Oh, well tell her I say hello, too!"

"How's Steven liking his old stomping ground?"

"Fine. He's working hard."

"I heard about the grant delay."

"Oh?"

"I know someone on the committee. I might be able to put in a good word, you know, put a thumb on the scale, as it were."

"You better talk to Steven about that."

"Okay."

Sam said she'd email him later. They hung up.

Steven was in his home office when she got back. He asked how her visit had gone. She said she learned a lot about the press—how much money it had, for instance, and that, one day, Martin might dissolve the trust and that would be that.

"Well, I hope he waits until I finish my research," Steven said. He seemed happy. She said it must be going well.

"I found some more stuff on Clara Levy in the letters Edith and Jason Dobbs exchanged. There were unpublished poems found in Levy's papers. She told the nursing home she was living in to make sure Edith got them. Anyway, Edith thought they could be collected in a new volume, but Dobbs didn't think it was a good idea. He felt the work wasn't strong enough. He was never keen on *Holocaust*, Levy's first volume. Her only volume, I should say."

"There was only one book from Levy?"

"Yeah."

"Oh."

"What?"

"Well, can you write a whole book about that? I mean, is she a deep enough subject?"

Steven explained—again—that she was *part* of the project, not the *whole* project. Honestly, he laid all this out to her before. If he didn't know better, he'd think she wasn't listening. She assured him she was, she had just forgotten. Her mind was a jumble, what with Angie on her way. He took her hand and asked how her work was and if she had anything she wanted him to read. Not yet, she said, but soon.

Two days later they went to meet Lisa Tettle at the Sommerville warehouse. More snow fell the night before and the roads were a mess. Steven said back in his day hard snow meant plows in the morning but so far, they hadn't seen one. Budget cuts, he suspected. The stupid Republicans had no idea what a common good was. Sam said she thought the State of Massachusetts was controlled by Democrats in both chambers, and Steven didn't answer. He gripped the steering wheel. The car was an all-wheel drive with good tires. She had offered to drive, and he told her not to be silly, he could manage just fine. Sam watched the city pass by. It was old and dirty. Even their high-end neighborhood was crowded and unwelcoming.

The address they had turned out to be a vacant lot between a diner and a gas station. Steven wondered if Tettle had deliberately misled them. Sam said that was unlikely. She told him to pull over, consult his phone, and check the message she sent him with the address. He did. He showed her the phone.

"4534 Adams Way, not 4734," she said.

"Oh, right. I don't know why I got that wrong."

"You're just nervous. It's okay."

The traffic whizzed past, and he turned to look at her. The winter light was unflattering, and Sam thought he had changed, lost something he had before. Confidence? Because the grant hadn't yet come through?

The warehouse was small, with two garage bays. The corrugated metal on the sides was rusty. The roof looked new. A large sign, which said Forbes Storage, fastened to a wooden post driven into the ground, was also new. Lisa Tettle was outside, waiting for them. She wore a short, insulated jacket and red mittens. She shook Sam's hand and said it was a pleasure to meet her. Steven held out his hand and Lisa looked at it as if she had no idea what to do next.

"I'm sorry, Professor Wells, is it? I don't know where my mind is these days. Come, let's go inside. I'm afraid it's not much warmer in there, but that's where everything is."

They passed through a small office with a desk, chair, and two filing cabinets. Lisa explained that the office manager was only onsite once a week, if that. Otherwise, she did everything from home.

"What's 'everything?'" asked Sam.

"Bookkeeping, mostly. She bills the presses that store their backlists here and so on. She also has to schedule deliveries. That is, when books are getting received."

"Do they ever leave? The books, I mean?"

"Rarely."

Lisa unlocked another door, and they stood for a moment in darkness which sudden, harsh brightness from the overhead fluorescent fixtures dispelled.

The place was stacked with boxes that weren't in alphabetical order. Lisa went from column to column, sometimes bending down, or standing on tiptoe to read the labels, many of which were handwritten. Sam and Steven studied the labels too. Some names were charming, Fair Winds Poetry, Larkspur Press, and The

Raven's Perch. Small presses, like The Hedgerow, struggling to stay afloat. Authors laboring to make sense of their dreams and nightmares hoping someone would give them room to breathe. One day, Sam's work might sit here, but that wouldn't be the best outcome, would it? Far better to be on a library shelf, or in someone's home, on a nightstand, or coffee table and a cheerful voice saying, "Let me tell you about this amazing young poet I've just discovered."

"Okay, here we are. It *would* be the last set," Lisa said. She stood before a stack of three boxes. Steven lifted the top one and put it on the floor. It was unsealed. He and Sam took out books and read the spines. They were all non-fiction titles. Sam asked if these were the most recently published volumes. Lisa said she thought so. In any case, the last title came out in 2017.

"What? Seven years ago? What's the press been doing since then?" Steven asked.

"Not much, to be honest."

"You mean, no one submits anything?" Sam asked.

"Well, we get off-the-wall things. A political manifesto, cookbooks, self-help titles, that kind of thing. Martin wanted the press to stay focused on scholarly work, nothing with a commercial flavor, and certainly not anything overtly controversial. The manifesto I mentioned was a screed against the evils of feminism."

"Good lord," Sam said.

"Exactly."

Steven had moved on to the second box, where he found titles published in the 80s and 90s. The third box yielded what he wanted—novels that came out in the 70s, poetry titles from the 60s, all by men, as Martin had said, and below those, seven books from the 1950s. He said he was certain, based on the letters he reviewed so far, that Edith had published over a dozen titles in those years. Where were they?

"Maybe they all sold," Lisa said.

"What about the original manuscripts?" Sam asked.

"From the authors? I have no idea."

Steven said he wanted to borrow the entire box, and Lisa looked uncertain. He reminded her he had Martin's permission and said he must have sent an email to that effect. She said, yes, she received it and, of course, he was welcome to take whatever he wanted. He carried the box into the front office. Lisa went to turn off the lights in the warehouse and lock the door.

"Listen, I've got an appointment, so if you're all set, I'll show you out," she said.

As they walked across the gravel parking lot together, Sam asked what else she did besides manage the press.

"Well, it doesn't take much time. I just keep an eye on the things and turn down authors who send us stuff we'd never publish."

"Does the press have a website?"

"It used to. Frankly, I think it should hire a designer and get a new one up and running. Then people could see what we publish or used to publish. And to answer your question about what else I do; I've got three kids under eight and my husband goes to law school at night."

"Wow. That's a lot to juggle," Sam said.

"Yes, ma'am."

Steven unlocked his car and put the box in the back seat.

"Thank you for making time for us," he said.

"Let me know when you're all done with those," Lisa said.

"Of course."

On the drive home, Sam said it seemed like the press was long past its heyday. How could Steven make it sound interesting? It used to be interesting, but it lost sight of its mission. No one seemed to have the time or energy to get it back on its feet.

"Publishing is a hard business, and you have to be fully committed. Not with three kids and a law-student husband," Steven said.

"It's not her fault the press isn't doing anything. I don't think it's her job to figure out what its new mission is. That's up to Martin, and he's not interested, as far as I can tell."

"I just wonder what she does to earn her salary."

"I'm sure she's not paid much."

"Even so."

Sam asked why he was being so hard on her. She seemed like a competent person, one who managed competing demands. She must have been a student at one point, someone with a background in literature. How else would she have gotten the job managing the press, otherwise?

Steven said nothing. He was back to gripping the steering wheel.

They reached the townhome and pulled into their assigned spot, which the neighbor had finally vacated. Steven turned off the engine. Sam opened her door, and he asked her to wait a moment. He had something to say which he hoped she wouldn't take the wrong way. He said her doubting his research project was getting to him. He depended on her opinion, and it was hard sometimes to keep going in the face of so much negative energy.

Sam looked through the windshield at the garage's concrete wall. In the corner hung an abandoned spider web displaying the talent and patient resolve of a now dead creature. She admired that touch of beauty in an otherwise utilitarian place. But then, the web was utilitarian too.

"If you mean you don't want me asking questions, just say so," she said.

"I don't mean anything of the kind. You just seem so negative."

She turned and looked at him. Timothy never confronted her when he was upset but sank deep into himself. Steven's discontent was in the open, like a lake of fire she could douse or sail through.

"What do you want from me?" she asked.

Now he stared through the windshield at the concrete wall. Did he see the web too?

He said he just wanted her support. Was that so much to ask?

"If you didn't have my support, I wouldn't be here. I'd have been happy to stay in Dunston and visit you on the weekends, but you insisted I come. And assumed I'd agree. You didn't even ask me how I felt about renting the house to Lyall and Claire. I wasn't present in your thinking, so please don't tell me how I've let you down."

Steven's hands left the steering wheel and rested in his lap.

"Wow," he said.

She got out of the car and went inside. She threw her coat at the coat rack and missed. In the kitchen, she filled the kettle with water and lit the burner.

Steven opened the front door, then he was in the kitchen. He removed his jacket.

"You left your coat on the floor," he said.

"Sorry."

"I picked it up."

"Thank you."

He held out his hand and after a moment, she took it. He apologized. She apologized too. He said he didn't realize she was unhappy in Boston. She said she hadn't realized it either.

"Well, it may help to have Angie around, even if she's miserable about what's-his-name," Steven said. He was opening the cabinets, taking stock of what they had. They were supposed to go to the store after meeting with Lisa. They both forgot.

She asked if he'd brought the box of books in from the car. He said he had. A few minutes later, she poured out her tea and carried her cup into the living room. The box was on the sofa. She sat and took out the book on top, *Tales of A Mermaid in Distress*, published in 1955. The pages were thick and sturdy. A cloth bookmark was tucked into the cover. The dedication page read To Jerome. Steven came in from the kitchen and asked her which book she was looking at. She lifted it to show him.

"Author?" he asked.

"Genevieve Spalding."

Steven said he'd brown some garlic in olive oil and toss it over pasta. Sam nodded and kept going through the book.

"Listen to this: 'The Finns have fine fins, being a sea-going folk / To find one is fine, to miss them earns a fine.'"

"Pretty infantile stuff, if you ask me," Steven said between chops of his knife on the cutting board.

Sam went to another poem, "Ask the Sea." She didn't read aloud.

Lock hope in a blue box
Ask the sea to take it
What good to you now, this ragged
Thing you once were guided by?

Was hope ragged? It could be when it wore out.

The smell of Steven's cooking drifted pleasantly. She went to see if he needed help.

"I'm sorry about earlier," he said and kissed her cheek.

"It's all right. I know you're stressed about the grant."

He said he forgot to mention it, but he got an email from Lyall saying he talked to someone on the committee and put in a good word for him.

"Oh, that's great!"

"He said he told you about that when he called."

"He just said he heard about the delay and wondered if he should talk to them. I said he should check with you first."

He looked glum.

"I don't like people going behind my back," he said.

"I didn't."

"I mean Lyall."

"So, he didn't check with you?"

"No."

They drank wine, ate dinner, did the dishes together, and went to bed. Sam was relieved when he rolled onto his side, away from her, and fell asleep.

Chapter Seven

The Amtrak station was only a couple of miles away, but heavy traffic made it slow going. Steven said there was some big sporting event, so Sam gave herself extra time, which didn't help. Then, Angie's train was early. Sam got a text saying she was waiting at the curb and to look for her red coat. The line of cars crawling past the passenger pick-up was slow too, and Sam wished she told Angie to find her own way to Martin's apartment. Finally, she saw Angie standing with a guy at the curb, and as she drew the car in close, she realized it was Timothy.

He had on a stylish insulated jacket with a loosely tied blue scarf, a backpack, and a camera slung over his shoulder. Sam double-parked and got out of the car. Angie rushed over to her and said, "I know, I know, I should have told you. Sorry."

Timothy approached. "Last minute change of plans," he said.

Sam had hoped to take Angie back to her place for dinner but having Timothy along made that impossible. She opened the back door of the Jeep, Angie put her suitcase inside and hopped into the passenger seat in front. Sam and Timothy stood staring at each other. A car behind them honked. Sam got behind the wheel and Timothy hustled into the back. She pulled away from the curb and said, "Okay, what the hell is going?"

Timothy said he came at Angie's request and didn't think he had to clear it with Sam first.

"How am I supposed to explain this to Steven?" Sam asked.

"Just say he came to keep my spirits up. It's not like they have to hang out together," Angie said.

"Christ, Angie."

"Chill out. I'm sure he'll be fine. Now, tell me about this fantastic apartment."

Sam said it was spectacular. Large, nicely furnished though the pieces were old. It had floor-to-ceiling windows.

"How did you come by it, again?" Timothy asked and Sam gave him a quick description of The Hedgerow Press and Martin Alistair.

"Man, the guy's trusting to let the likes of you have free run of the place," he said. Sam knew he was joking. He always said she was as reliable as rain and winter, two things he adored.

She looked at him in the rearview mirror. He caught her eye.

"Don't worry, I won't smash up the place," he said.

"I'm not worried."

"I don't drink much these days. Or hadn't you heard?"

"No one's feeding her information," Angie said.

"Not even my esteemed brother?" he asked.

Sam said Foster only asked her to reach out at Christmas because everyone was so worried. And from what she could see, the worry had resulted in better things. What she didn't say was that it had only been a few weeks since then. She didn't want to sound skeptical of his progress.

The traffic was worse than on the drive out. Timothy said he was glad to be back in good old Beantown. It had been years since he visited. Sam knew the story—his stepfather wanted him out of the fraternity and back home because his grades were tanking, and instead, he left town for a week, bummed around Boston, and had a blast. Reality caught up with him when his money ran out, and he ended up right where his stepfather wanted him in the first place—under his watchful eye.

The light changed, and no one moved. They were gridlocked. Sam lowered her window. Angie reminded her that it was freezing outside. After a moment, Sam raised the window. She was glad no one had anything else to say for the moment.

Finally, cars inched forward, and they arrived at Martin's building. She'd memorized the access code to the garage and when she punched in the numbers the gate lifted. The garage was brightly lit, and the spot Martin said Sam should take had the name Alistair painted clearly on the wall, as did the space next to it, where his blue Jaguar sat.

"Fancy," Timothy said as he got out. They passed a Mercedes and a Bentley as they made their way to the door that opened into the lobby. Timothy remarked on the marble everywhere, the crystal light sconces in the elevator, and the plush carpeting in the hall that led them to Martin's door. Sam wished he'd stop.

Angie said she was both exhausted and famished, and Timothy reminded her that she'd eaten a sandwich on the train. She asked what the dinner plans were. Sam said she was going to invite her to eat with her and Steven, but that wasn't a good idea, under the circumstances.

"So, now I'm a circumstance?" Timothy asked.

Sam couldn't get her key to work and struggled with it.

"Here, let me," Timothy said and pulled the keyring from her hand. The door opened easily. He gave the keyring back to Sam and stepped inside. Sam said the switch was just to the right of the entrance and a moment later everything was bright and welcoming. Angie wheeled her suitcase against the wall and looked around.

"You weren't kidding. This place is a palace," she said.

Timothy admired the tile floor and said it was totally old-school. Sam led them into the living room and opened the drapes. They stood at the window and looked at the river. Both Angie and Timothy said the view was spectacular, and Sam said the library next door had the same one. Plus, both rooms had a fireplace, and they could have a fire if they wanted. A service delivered wood right to the apartment. Wasn't that something? Angie said she loved a fire in the evening.

The apartment was warm, and they removed their coats and tossed them on the sofa. Then they inspected the bedrooms. The first one they came to had a king-size bed with a canopy. On the bare mattress, clean bedding lay neatly folded. The adjoining bath had a huge tub, and, seeing it, Angie declared the room hers. There was an adjoining bedroom separated by a door that could be locked from either side and another bedroom across the hall, which Timothy claimed. He said he wanted to take a shower, so Angie and Sam drifted into the kitchen to see if there were anything in the fridge and found a roasted chicken, containers of pasta salad, wedges of cheese, and a blueberry pie. On the counter were several bottles of wine. A note was taped to a bottle of Bordeaux that said, This is one of my favorites!

Angie opened one drawer after another until she found the corkscrew. She went to work on the Bordeaux and soon had the cork out. She brought everything to the table where Sam was already sitting. Angie joined her.

"Okay, why is he here?" Sam asked.

"Like he said, I asked him to come. I know I shouldn't be such a wimp, but I'm having a hard time. At first, I was so mad at Matt, now I'm just sad."

"I'm sorry."

Angie's eyes glistened. Sam encouraged her to try the wine.

Angie said Matt tried to love her, but at the end of the day, he couldn't. Now, this wasn't to say he loved Sharon, his ex-girlfriend, more. In fact (and Angie wiped a tear as she said this), he didn't love her at all. But he was drawn to her and found something in her he didn't find in Angie. Of course, that hurt. It was hard on the old ego.

"Absolutely," Sam said.

Angie said three people in a relationship never worked. Sharon was always there, getting in the way. Of course, she hoped she'd disappear. She hoped for that every single day.

"Sounds like you see things clearly," Sam said.

"I always did, even when I tried not to."

"So, what was the tipping point?"

"I don't know. The start of a new year. I think I resolved not to be such a fool."

Sometimes foolishness—or self-selected blindness—had its uses, Sam thought. Like when you're trying to put up with something you know you have to endure. But she was thinking about herself, not Angie, wasn't she?

"Well, I'm glad you're here," Sam said.

"Me, too."

The wine was delicious and helped Sam to relax. She wondered if she should bring a bottle back for Steven to try. At the thought of him, she was flooded with anxiety. She'd promised to let him know when she collected Angie from the train station. She trotted back to the living room for her phone, buried in an inner pocket of her coat, and discovered Timothy on the sofa, flipping through a magazine he'd taken from the coffee table. The stubble on his chin was gone. His wet hair was neatly combed. She couldn't remember if he used a comb when they lived together, and it struck her as a stupid thing to wonder.

"I just need my phone," she said.

"Yeah, better tell him I threw a wrench into things."

"It's fine."

"Then why are you doing the jellyfish?"

This was their term for when she was visibly nervous, if she had to give a talk in class, for instance, or when she went to meet her stepsiblings for the first time.

"Why do you think?" she asked.

He patted the space next to him on the sofa. She remained standing.

"Okay, fine. But listen, I know this is awkward, but Angie's hurting and she asked. What was I supposed to do? Tell her I'm afraid of seeing my ex?"

"No, of course not. I already said it's fine. I just don't know what to tell Steven."

"Tell him the truth. He's a big boy. I'm sure he can handle it."

When she took out her phone, she found a voice message from Steven saying his friend, the guy who ran the antique bookstore, called and asked him to dinner. He knew it was short notice, and he hoped she didn't mind the change of plans. Why didn't she and Angie go out somewhere, and they could all meet up later? She texted back okay.

She didn't feel relieved. If anything, she was even more agitated than before. She flopped down onto the sofa.

"Trouble in paradise?" Timothy asked.

She said she didn't like Boston. She was all settled in at Steven's when he springs the news of this grant on her. She didn't see why he couldn't conduct his research remotely. Everyone did that now, didn't they? He could have arranged to have any materials he needed shipped to him at home.

Timothy sat with his arms folded across his stomach.

"Did it ever occur to you that he might have wanted to get you out of Dunston for a while?" he asked.

"Why?"

"You're looking at it."

"Be serious."

"The guy's all hung up, wondering if your feelings for him are what you say they are. Not that you're lying. You don't lie. I lie. This, we know. But not you."

"So, what's he afraid of?"

"Losing you."

Sam said Steven had no reason to be insecure about her. She was one hundred percent committed.

"So, tell him I'm here, just in the spirit of being honest," he said.

"I think that would upset him."

"And you don't want to upset him."

"No, I don't."

Timothy looked cynical, and Sam reminded him how many times she'd protected him from all sorts of things.

"If you mean you were willing to act as a buffer between me and my family, for example, yes, that's true."

"Well, I'm glad you see that now."

"And I'm glad you're glad."

She couldn't help laughing. He laughed too. Angie appeared with her glass of wine. She asked what they were doing sitting there by themselves. Sam explained that dinner plans had changed, and the three of them should go out somewhere.

"With all that great food in the fridge?" Angie asked.

Timothy said he wanted to see if a pizza place he discovered years ago near Harvard Square was still around. He'd go alone, he didn't mind.

"We'll go too," Sam said.

"No way. I'm staying here," Angie said.

Sam asked if she were sure she didn't mind being on her own. Angie said she was going to help herself to something to eat, then take a nice, long bath.

Sam didn't know if they should drive or take the train. Timothy said the train was easier. They said little as they walked from the building to the station. Then Timothy said it felt colder than at home, which didn't make sense unless it was because the wind was funneled by the buildings. Sam pointed out that there was no wind, just a penetrating chill.

"It's only January. Three more months of winter," Timothy said.

"But you love winter."

"You don't."

"I should be used to it. I don't know why I'm not."

They waited on the crowded platform. Timothy said some people felt the cold more than others. His mother was that way. She kept talking about moving to Florida, though he knew she never would. Sam asked how she and Potter were getting along these days and Timothy said fine. Potter seemed to be staying on the straight and narrow, drinking-wise.

"Are they going to buy Matt out of the bar, do you think? Assuming the split with Angie is permanent," Sam asked.

"I'm sure they're talking about it."

"Are you guys still friends?"

"Yeah, of course. I put him up for a couple of nights. He was pretty wigged out, but he chilled after a while."

"Did he say anything about that woman?"

"He mostly talked about Angie."

The train came and they got on. There was a free seat and Sam took it. Timothy stood, gripping the leather strap fastened to the overhead bar running the length of the car. Sam kept checking her phone to see if there were anything more from Steven. There wasn't.

The train deposited them around the corner from the Square, which was full of students. The place where the pizza parlor had been was now a Thai restaurant. Sam said Thai was fine, she was hungry now and didn't care. The hostess said their wait would be at least thirty minutes, so they hustled into the bar and grabbed the only free stools. Timothy ordered a light beer, Sam had wine. She watched him sip his drink.

"I have cut back, you know," he said.

"I know. Was it hard?"

"It was."

"What made you decide to? Not everyone getting on your case, surely."

"I guess I got tired of feeling like crap all the time. Hangovers are hell."

The restaurant was noisy. Servers walked briskly. The bartender came and went up and down the bar, checking in with everyone.

Sam asked how the trip to Vegas went. Timothy said Harcourt blew a lot of money playing blackjack but came out okay in the end. His construction business was back on its feet. Sam asked if Timothy would work with him again.

"Only if I can have more control over the day-to-day operation," he said.

He said he hadn't been too bright before, just jumping in the way he had. He was so anxious to get out of the GAP. Retail wasn't for anyone with a brain.

"You were in management though," Sam said.

"It wasn't too engaging."

Finally, they were shown to a table near the back. The server dropped off their menus and left. Timothy scanned his and said Pad Thai was a far cry from a deep-dish pepperoni pie, but that's how it went.

"For sure," Sam said. She asked how often he saw his son these days. Timothy said they'd gone cross-country skiing and had a good time.

"And Melissa?" she asked.

"And Melissa, what?"

"Do you see her?"

"Not socially. She's got a boyfriend, you know."

"Right."

The server returned, took their order, and left.

"I'm not in love with her. I probably never was. That's a recent revelation, by the way. Proof positive that the old learning curve is still accessible," Timothy said.

"She represented something to you, some idea."

"She represented the past and all the things I screwed up."

Sam thought about what he said. She checked her phone. Steven had texted, sounds great! See u @ home!

She asked Timothy what he wanted to do in Boston while he was there. He said just a couple of things, nothing huge. Mostly, he just wanted to hang out with Angie, read, and think about the future.

He asked what classes she was taking online. She said she dropped out.

"Really? Why?" he asked.

"I just want to write."

Timothy put his hand on his bottle of beer and didn't drink from it.

"It was so important to you to get that degree. First one in your family to go to college," he said.

"I know. But I don't like the atmosphere and the way people talk about literature."

"Goes with the territory."

Timothy nudged his beer bottle with his forefinger.

"How does what's-his-name feel about it?" he asked.

"I don't know. We didn't talk about it."

Timothy looked skeptical but said nothing. His attitude put her on edge. She was never any good at explaining herself.

Sam told Timothy about Edith, Martin's mother and founder of the press. She was learning about her from reading her diaries. She loved their direct view into the past. Time disappeared. It was as if what Edith thought was happening in the moment, as Sam read her words. She didn't say anything vital, or earth shattering. It was just the idea of her sitting at her desk, sixty or even seventy years ago, with the world so different from how it is now, no computers, internet, cell phone, well of course the list went on and on, didn't it?

Timothy said yes, absolutely.

"Steven's looking at the business side of the press, of course, but I think the personal side is important too," Sam said.

The food came and they ate quickly.

Sam's phone rang. It was Angie asking how to turn the heat down. Sam didn't know where the thermostat was and Angie said fine, she'd go hunt for it. She wanted to know when they'd be back. Sam said they were just finishing up. Did she want them to bring her anything? They could put in a to-go order. Angie said she was stuffed.

Timothy offered to pay for a cab, so they didn't have to freeze waiting for the train. Sam accepted. As they rode through the lively streets, watching people walk in lightly falling snow, Timothy took her hand. She didn't withdraw it. Neither spoke.

In the elevator of Martin's building, Timothy said, "You shouldn't take that the wrong way. My holding your hand, I mean."

"I know. I'm not."

"I'm sorry Angie didn't tell you I was coming."

"It wouldn't have mattered."

"Sam."

"What?"

He kissed her and she let him. Then she said that was the last time that was ever going to happen.

They reached their floor and stepped out.

Angie met them at the door.

"I found it!" she said. She was tipsy. Her bathrobe was tied loosely, and her flannel pajamas peeked through.

Sam realized she meant the thermostat. She said the apartment felt cooler. They took off their coats, and Timothy asked if she had time to show him those diaries she mentioned earlier. They went into the office, which was just as she left it, except the dying plant was gone. Timothy lifted a volume from the desk and flipped through it.

"Well, she's got nice, neat handwriting. That was a thing, in those days," he said.

"Penmanship. Isn't that what it was called?"

"I think so."

She took the volume she'd been reading and told Timothy she had to get going. She thanked him for dinner. He said he planned to be out and about most of the day tomorrow, so he wouldn't see her.

Angie was in the living room staring into the fire she had just lit.

"This place is great. Look at that dentil molding," she said and pointed up.

"Yeah, lots of great period details."

She told Angie to call her in the morning when she got up. Angie promised.

Later, as Sam pulled into their parking spot at the townhome, pieces of the evening flashed through her mind, the brightest of which was the kiss in the elevator.

Don't even go there.

She locked the car and walked in with Edith's diary tucked under her arm.

Steven was in the kitchen drinking a glass of water.

"There you are! I was about to send out the dogs looking for you," he said.

She explained about Timothy showing up and having to deal with that. Steven set his glass on the counter.

"Why on earth would she bring him up here? Unless she hopes you two will get back together," Steven said. He stood close enough for her to smell liquor on his breath. She asked how his evening was, and he said it was good. Jordan took them to a high-end bistro with a great, new bartender. At least, Jordan seemed to think he was new. New or old, the guy knew how to mix his drinks.

"And you enjoyed several," Sam said.

"I did! Old fashioneds, if you can believe that. Very fifties."

"By the way, why didn't Jordan invite me too?"

"He did, and I said you were picking up your friend and couldn't make it."

His eye fell on the diary, and he asked her what it was. She told him.

"Not that again," he said.

"Why not?"

"Oh, I don't know. Don't listen to me. I'm still jumpy about the grant."

Sam said she had a good feeling that he'd hear soon. He said it didn't matter when he heard if the news were bad.

"It won't be bad," she said.

He touched her shoulder and said he was sorry he said what he had about Timothy. She should feel free to invite him and Angie. He'd make something special.

"You don't have to do that," she said.

"I owe it to you."

"Why?"

"For dragging you up here."

"You didn't drag me. Come on, let's hit the hay."

The bed's headboard had small LED lights installed so one person could read without disturbing the other, and Sam made use of hers while Steven snored. As before, Edith's commentary tended to be objective and unemotional.

Then, in April 1954, her tone changed.

Malcolm and I argued. Apparently, he feels I shouldn't ask anything of him in bed, other than what he is prepared to provide. I admit to having enjoyed my wine a bit too much this evening, but I spoke plainly when I said Philip would have denied me nothing, though of course, I have no proof, based on our limited encounters.

Sam flipped ahead. The more personal passages were always long, and the script was less even, due, no doubt, to the time of day she wrote and the amount alcohol in her blood.

Fiona told me I settled for less than I'm worth. How can she say that, given what Malcolm took on? My defense fell on her deaf (and drunken) ears. How tempted I was to tell her she knew nothing of these things. She'll never marry, never be a mother. Her marginal status in life shields her from the realities most women face.

Was this the same Fiona *You, Forever* had been dedicated to? It would be too much of a coincidence, otherwise.

On the 31st of August Edith wrote:

Philip, I believe I was in love with you. I always pushed this thought from my mind because I didn't see how it could be possible. But here you are, in that same mind, six years later. I am tempted to ask Aunt Margaret about you. I think I will. She already knows what happened, in that way one knows things without being told.

When Sam woke in the morning, she was alone. Edith's diary was closed and resting on her nightstand. She didn't remember putting it there and assumed Steven had when he got up. She pulled on her bathrobe. She lifted the blinds on the bedroom window and was met by a brilliant blue sky. Steven was at the kitchen counter, typing away on his laptop. He was dressed in blue jeans, a button-down shirt, and the cardigan she gave him for Christmas.

"Guess what?" he asked.

"What?"

"I got the grant!"

"Oh, wow. That's fantastic!"

She went to him and gave him a long, hard hug.

He told her to call up Angie and ask them over to celebrate. He'd call Jordan. He thought Angie and Jordan might just hit it off. Sam said Angie and Timothy had already made plans for that evening. Timothy had a friend out in the suburbs somewhere, and they were heading over there to spend the day.

Steven nodded, which meant he stopped listening. He went back to typing.

Sam went into her office, ashamed of the lie she told, but she couldn't deal with Timothy and Steven in the same space.

She pulled out her journal and began a new poem.

> Maybe love is all that holds us together,
> Keeping us from breaking away
> & forsaking the earth

Steven came into her office carrying her cell phone. He said it was Angie, and he just invited her to dinner.

"Why did you answer it?" Sam asked.

"Because it was ringing, and you were in here."

He handed her the phone and left.

"Hi," Sam said.

"What's this about our going to see a friend of Timothy's?"

Sam explained. Angie got it. She said she told Steven Sam must have misunderstood their plans.

"Why didn't you back me up?" Sam asked.

"Because it's early, I'm hungover, and didn't sleep well. Besides, it will be fine. We're bringing dessert."

"God."

"What's the matter?"

"Nothing."

"Come on, you can tell me."

"No, I can't.

"Has my dear brother gotten under your skin? Or has he been there all along?"

Sam said she didn't know. It was just that he seemed so different, so centered in himself. She was glad to see it, of course, but it made her think her leaving him had done him a world of good. She didn't mean her ego was suffering. It's not like she expected him to grieve over her forever. It just came as a surprise how well he seemed to be doing.

"Who says he's doing well? How do you know he's not just putting on an act?" Angie asked.

"Is he?"

"No, I don't think so."

"Well, there you go."

Angie said to chill, everything would be fine, Timothy might not even join them. Sam asked what else he'd do.

"Who knows? Wander around. Find a bar somewhere," Angie said.

"Not the best place for him to hang out."

"Stop worrying about him. If he gets smashed, he'll find his way back. Eventually."

Sam said she'd call her after lunch, and they'd see how things stood. Angie asked what things.

"Oh, I don't know."

"Look, if this is such a problem, tell Steven I'm sick or having a bad period or something. Tell him I ran off to join the circus if you want."

Sam laughed.

She asked how Angie would keep herself busy until dinner. Angie said she'd go where the good shopping was. And where was that, exactly?

"The Faneuil Market, I think," Sam said.

"Open on Sunday?"

"Should be. They got rid of blue laws ages ago."

"Have you been?"

"Not yet. Steven said we'd go some time."

Angie said she would talk to her later. Sam told her to buy something amazing.

After they hung up, she put the phone down on the desk. Disappointment descended. Had she wanted to go shopping, too? No, not really. Was she anxious about having Timothy over for dinner? Extremely, so when his text message came in at that moment saying he couldn't make it, she was relieved. Also, sorry.

Steven stuck his head in.

"She'll be here for dinner. Timothy can't come," Sam said.

"Oh, that's too bad."

Sam looked at him skeptically.

"Okay, so I'm not heartbroken, but it was the right thing to say," he said.

"It was. What are we making?"

"Pasta with something."

"Sounds great."

He said he'd get to the store. What were her plans?

She wasn't sure, probably return the diary she was reading from and pick up another volume.

"You're obsessed with those," he said.

"Not obsessed, just deeply interested."

"She was a steely businesswoman, that's for sure, but she had a big soft spot for Clara Levy."

Sam asked what he'd found out so far.

He said Edith wrote an introduction to the second edition of *Holocaust*, outlining Levy's life as she shared it when they first met. Levy went to Radcliffe and then worked as a secretary. She never married. She lived with one man after another, practicing was Edith called "serial, unmarried, monogamy." Then she took up with a painter in New York City. They split when his work failed to thrive, and her poems were consistently published.

"And here's the interesting thing—even though many of her poems were published in journals, she brought out the first edition of *Holocaust* herself. Isn't that fascinating?" Steven asked.

"It is. But a lot of writers self-published."

"Lord Byron, T.S. Eliot, and James Joyce among them."

"Wow. I didn't know Eliot had."

Steven looked at her lovingly. He said he was so glad she came to Boston with him, and hoped she would like it better soon.

"Thanks. Me, too."

She thought to mention his answering her phone and felt it would ruin the moment. If he did it again, she'd say something.

"Now go. I've got to work some more before I leave," she said.

Timothy holding her hand. Timothy, kissing her in the elevator. Timothy, with a calm, clear light in his eyes.

Maybe a heart is stronger than bone
Because it leaps miles in one beat
& destroys you from the inside out

Chapter Eight

Sam opened Martin's door and smelled fried bacon. She went to the kitchen to find dirty dishes on the table and two frying pans on the stove, both with congealed grease. Unwashed wine glasses were in the sink. On the counter was an open package of sliced bread and a knife smeared with butter. She took off her coat and draped it on the back of one of the kitchen chairs, and went into the living room where more dirty glasses sat on the coffee table. There were magazines on the floor and an empty bag of popcorn. In Edith's former office, things were as she last saw them. The library was the same, too. She wouldn't venture into the bedrooms.

As she walked along the hall, a door opened behind her, and when she turned around, she saw Timothy approach wearing a T-shirt, boxer shorts, and a pair of heavy socks.

"Whoa," he said. "Sorry. I didn't know you were here. Angie's out."

"This place is a mess."

"I know, I know, I was just heading into the kitchen to get to work. I made Angie breakfast."

"Oh, never mind, I'll do it."

"Nope. Our mess, our problem."

He walked past her and disappeared through the swinging door into the kitchen.

She pulled out her phone to send Angie a crabby text message, then decided not to. Timothy would clean up. If he didn't do a good job, Angie would have to deal with it.

In Edith's office, Sam put the borrowed diary on the desk and took another. She opened it and several small black-and-white photographs fell to the floor. She bent down to pick them up.

In one picture, a young couple stood in a small living room, side-by-side. The man wore a tweed jacket and held a pipe. The woman wore a long, belted skirt. Her hair was short, and her expression was intense, bordering on manic. Even before she turned the picture over and read Walt & Edie, Cambridge, 1948 she knew who they were.

"Well, hello," Sam said to Edith's image. She studied her face to see if Martin looked like her. He didn't. He must take after his father, Malcolm, the former butler.

The other photos showed another man with Edith and a large stone house behind them. The man was in a double-breasted pinstripe suit. His expression was inscrutable, while Edith smiled broadly.

The back said, showing Edith the family home.

There was one of an older woman wearing a fox fur and a veiled hat. Between the fingers of her gloved hand was a long cigarette holder. She was identified only as Aunt Margaret.

Why had Edith grouped these together? What did they signify? People she was fond of, people she missed?

The diary gave nothing intimate. It touched on domestic matters, a cranky author, an increasing worry about the state of her mother's health, and comments about a woman named Betty.

She says Mama broke the window trying to open it. Just put her hand right through. The doctor kept asking questions while he sewed up her hand—did she mean to hurt herself; did she try lifting it first, was the latch locked—poor Betty, having to shield her from this man's ruthless logic.

This entry was dated in the winter of 1959. Didn't Martin say they went out to Illinois to be with his grandmother? But that was later, Sam thought, in 1961 or 1962, so things must have been going badly for a while.

Sam thought about her own mother, Flora, down in Florida with her husband, Chuck. What if she got wobbly when she was older? Would Chuck be enough of a caretaker? Sam didn't hate Flora anymore, but she wasn't overwhelmed with affection, either. If she'd never asked Sam to look up her father to get money out of him, Sam wouldn't have learned the truth, that rather than being the product of rape, as Flora claimed, she was the result of genuine love. It should have reassured her about her value in the world, but by then, in her late twenties, she'd carved out a life for herself where whatever value she had came from her willingness to work hard, her physical strength, and her love of poetry. Into this independence came someone who wanted to be her father. That required processing, and he was happy to let her take things at her own pace. She was surprised to learn that he lived in her neighborhood and was married with three grown children she later met, though, of course, these things just meant he'd made his own life. Sam wondered if his choosing to become a therapist had anything to do with being rejected by Flora all those years before. Naturally, Flora begged forgiveness for her lie. She said it was to keep her parents at bay. She gambled they'd be understanding if they thought she was forced, but they were just as cruel as if they knew she consented. Sam understood and couldn't forgive, but neither did she condemn. She simply turned away.

Her phone buzzed, indicating a new email. She opened it. It was from Professor Morris who said she was sorry to hear that Sam had withdrawn from school and hoped it wasn't for personal reasons, like a family emergency. She also hoped Sam wasn't put off by her contacting her. It's just that she seemed so suited to studying poetry. In any case, she hoped she'd decide one day to continue. Sam was touched. She'd write her back when she had a chance to frame a response.

August 5, 1962

I see him everywhere in this town, on every sidewalk, at every soda fountain. I could be told he haunts the mathematics building on campus and not be one bit surprised.

August 6, 1962

Malcolm found us a nice little house. We'll be on top of each other, and I guess that's okay. We're enrolling Martin in school tomorrow. I feel for him, poor mite. Doesn't like it here. I don't, either. Mama comes and goes, is in and out. She knows me, then doesn't know me. Who's there, behind the eyes I know and love?

Snow fell, and gazing out the window of Edith's study, Sam was overcome with melancholy. She closed the diary and left the room. The drapes in the library were closed and she pulled them open. Timothy asked her what she was doing. He was now dressed in jeans and a flannel shirt.

"Why were you sitting here in the dark?" she asked.

"Just wondering what to do today."

"I assume you cleaned up the kitchen."

"I did."

"Thank you."

"Don't thank me. We agreed to keep the place in shape, which means I will since Angie can't be bothered."

"She'd have gotten around to it, eventually."

"Probably."

The fireplace hadn't been used, and Sam lit the kindling Martin had thoughtfully arranged below two stout logs with a long match kept in a container on the mantlepiece. She hoped he was enjoying The Bahamas. It felt strange to realize she missed him. The flames took hold, and she sat on the far end of the sofa. Timothy's camera was on the coffee table, and Sam asked if he had taken pictures earlier. He said he had.

She held out her hand, and he lifted the camera, turned the power on, and gave it to her. He asked if she knew how to scroll through the memory. She said she did.

There were pictures of the apartment's architectural details, like the glass doorknobs and the tile floor in the entryway. The river also featured, and the winter trees lining the shore.

"I'm glad you're at it again," she said.

"I was never not at it. Just sort of hit a dry spell there."

She watched the flames. She willed them to lift her mood.

Timothy said he was going to go out and shoot some more stuff before lunch. He was supposed to meet Angie when she was shopped out. He hoped whatever rant she'd treat him to about Matt wouldn't last longer than a few minutes.

Sam looked at him crossly.

"Oh, I don't say those things to her face, but I figure it's okay to be honest with you," he said.

"Try to remember how hard this must be for her," Sam said.

"I do, I do. I wouldn't have come up with her otherwise."

After a moment, she asked why he was staring at her like that.

"I was thinking about you dropping out. It seems so unexpected," he said.

"I was thinking about it last fall."

"You weren't even halfway through."

"I know. But, like I said, they want you to think a certain way. You're supposed to be fluent in terms someone came up with yesterday. It's like everyone joined a cult or something. I got sick of it."

He said he heard some departments had gotten full of themselves, wanting people to be woke—which they used to call politically correct. Of course, he'd majored in business, and if he had to bet money, no pun intended, no one cared about being woke over there. It was all graphs, dollars, and cents.

"But, if they don't care, or just act like they don't, they get branded as racists, or misogynists, or whatever. It comes back on them, in the end," she said.

He said any positive step they took was just for show, and it was the same in the real world. Okay, maybe there was some discussion of how to keep your board balanced, that sort of thing because the shareholders wanted to know that they're staying current with social concerns. But, at the end of the day, it was all about how much power you have. When you have a lot, you don't have to elevate stupid language just to please people.

"And an English department doesn't have much power."

"Exactly. I mean, who hires an English major for anything? And the professors are all hanging on by the skin of their teeth. God help them if they don't get tenure."

Timothy said the big donations went to computer science and engineering, at least if the alumni magazine he read was accurate. The humanities were losing ground every year, though studies show that studying history, for instance, or reading fiction—particularly literary fiction—is better for your brain than learning accounting, which makes sense. His stepdad, good old Chip, was a whiz with numbers and anything to do with money, but he couldn't think his way out of a paper bag. That might sound harsh, but there it was. Still, he was a good guy, and sometimes Timothy missed him.

"Your stepfather? I thought you hated him," Sam said.

"Only back when I was an angry, resentful, full-of-myself young man."

"What caused this change of heart?"

"I don't know. I grew up a little?"

Sam said the woman whose diaries she was reading, Edith Alistair, got a master's in American Poetry from Harvard in the late 1940s. Back then, that kind of degree might have been worth more than it was today, though of course getting a teaching job would have been hard because she was a woman.

"I believe it. Old Boys Network, and that sort of thing," Timothy said.

Sam leaned her head against the sofa. She said nothing was ever given the right emphasis. Things people should care about, they didn't. And vice versa.

"Well, to care about something, you first have to understand it. I assume you refer to poetry," Timothy said.

"All the arts."

"Luckily for me, photography is more direct—more accessible. But then, some of Man Ray's stuff is pretty bizarre."

Sam didn't know who that was and made a note to find out later.

She said she needed to be on her way to help Steven get dinner ready. Sometimes he got nervous when he entertained.

"I wanted to talk to you about that," Timothy said.

"You already said you can't make it."

"I know. But Angie said you told what's-his-name some story about our having a previous engagement."

"So?"

He said it wasn't a good sign that she felt she had to lie to him. They were early in their relationship, and this could set a bad precedent.

"You're concerned for my welfare," she said.

"Why is that impossible?"

"It's not. It's just a little late."

She didn't have to look at him to know his jaw had squared. Angie did the same thing. Lavinia, too, when vexed, which she often was.

"Before you run off, I think there's something you should know," he said.

"I'm not running off."

"Let me talk."

He said he was always concerned for her welfare, but didn't show it well. He was self-destructive—he didn't have to tell her that when it was always she who told him. And being that way made it hard to do the right thing by other people. He knew she understood that. He could tell from her face that she did.

"My face?" she asked.

"The way you're listening and trying not to."

"Timothy, look. I appreciate your concern, but it's none of your business."

"You'll always be my business."

"That sounds possessive."

He shrugged. She stood up. When she returned to Edith's study, there was a message on her phone from Steven. He wanted her to bring another box of papers back with her. He wasn't sure which it was, and she'd have to do some digging around. Specifically, she was to look for any letters between Dobbs and

Edith about an author named Penny Forbes, most likely from the mid-60s. She was the first of the so-called angry women Edith turned down. Then he said not to be late, Jordan was due at five-thirty. And could she please remind Angie of the time, too?

At her feet were six boxes. She sat down and turned one upside down. The contents fluttered onto the carpet. She put them in order by date, then she sorted them alphabetically by the recipient's first name. There was nothing to or from Penny Forbes, and scanning the dates, all in the 1950s, Sam understood why. Edith's change of heart came later.

In the next box, she found documents from the time frame Steven requested. She didn't organize these. Steven could do that himself. She sent him a text to say she was on her way. He texted right back to ask if she found what he wanted. She didn't answer. She put the papers she'd organized back into their box and carried it down the hall.

She didn't know if Timothy had gone out. The apartment was quiet as she got on her coat. She thought of taking a quick look at the kitchen and decided not to. Her phone rang. It was Angie. Sam put the box on a chair in the foyer and answered.

"Hello?"

"Hey. I'm still shopping. I've been at it for hours and all I found was one lousy sweater. Okay, it's a pretty nice sweater, but still."

"Great!"

"What's wrong?"

"Nothing. I'm just leaving the apartment. Dinner's at five-thirty. I'm supposed to remind you."

"Where's Timothy?"

"I don't know."

"He's not answering his phone."

"Don't worry about it. I'm sure he's fine."

"I'm sure he is, too, but he said he'd meet me for a late coffee."

Angie paused. Then she said Matt had called her a couple of times and she didn't answer.

"Do you think you should talk to him?" Sam asked.

"No."

Sam asked if Angie wanted to come directly to the townhome instead of going back to the apartment first. She could text her the address. Angie said the train schedule was a nightmare to decipher, but she'd do her best. Oh, should she bring anything?

"Dessert?" Sam asked.

"See if that blueberry pie is still in the fridge. I didn't have any. The temptation was huge, but I resisted."

Sam said she would. Angie promised to be at her place on time. When they hung up, Sam went to the kitchen. Timothy did a good job cleaning up. The pie was still in the refrigerator, with a piece missing. The label on the carton said it hadn't reached its sell-by date. She put it in the box of papers and carried it down to her car.

At home, Steven was tidying the living room.

"Where have you been?" he asked.

"What do you mean?"

"Never mind." He took the box of papers from her and started toward his office when she explained about the pie. He put the box on his desk and returned with the plastic carton. He pointed out that there was a piece missing.

"We can still serve it."

"You can't offer guests pie for dessert with one piece missing."

"They won't see that. We'll bring it out one slice at a time."

"That's ridiculous."

"What's wrong with you?"

He said he'd lost track of time and gestured to the papers spread over the coffee table and kitchen counter. Sam didn't understand why he wasn't working in his office and wondered if he found it too small a space, though now wasn't the time to ask, because his list of grievances was growing by the second. He hadn't gotten started in the kitchen, he thought they were out of toilet paper, and the powder room needed cleaning. Sam said she'd handle it. As to cooking, what kind of pasta was he making? He said just a hearty spaghetti sauce with browned meat. She asked if he had all his ingredients. He said he needed to buy a couple of bottles of wine, but otherwise he was set. She told him to get his sauce started, she'd double-check the toilet paper situation to make sure they were stocked, then he could go to the wine shop on the corner and get what he needed.

He stared down at her, his face tight and miserable.

"We can cancel if this is a bad idea," she said.

"No. I told Jordan we're celebrating the grant."

"We can pick a different day."

"I said, no."

"Fine."

She turned away and went into the guest bathroom where she put cleaning products under the sink when they first moved in. Steven must know she'd spent time with Timothy. Why else was he being such a jerk? But he couldn't know. This was due to something else, and it wasn't worth speculating as to what.

Scrubbing the toilet and sink led her back to her career as a motel maid, first, in LA, where the constant warmth was welcome, then later, back in Dunston, where she took home a volume of Dickinson a guest left behind. From then on, poetry was with her. Even working at the Lindell retirement home, cleaning in the residential wing, a book would be in the pocket of her smock for her to pull out and read on breaks and over lunch. She met Angie there and, through her, Timothy. All these things came her way because she was good at cleaning, having learned early at her grandmother's harsh, bony knee.

Make for the door while her back is turned . . .

Sam went to her office, yanked off her rubber gloves, and added those words to the poem, "Her Face Curls."

By the time she was ten, she was a master in the art of silent escape. She'd slip out and roam the woods behind her house. There was a favorite log she'd sit on and daydream about being somewhere else where people spoke in gentle voices.

She wrote:

Wake sweat-soaked from another nightmare,
Remind yourself as your heart now slows,
She's gone

She closed her journal, and finished the guest bathroom without wearing her gloves, which was fine, because she was down to wiping surfaces dry with paper towel. Steven was in the kitchen stirring something in a large pot. She gathered up his papers, put them in stacks depending on where she found them, and brought them into his office. His laptop was open, and his email list was on the screen. There were several he hadn't opened yet. She deposited the stacks neatly next to the laptop and left.

She vacuumed the living room and put away the vacuum cleaner. Steven's sauce smelled wonderful, and she told him so. He kissed her on the cheek and said he was off to buy the wine. She asked him to pick up a loaf of bread they could heat and serve. After an hour he hadn't returned. Sam resisted calling or texting him, then discovered it didn't matter when she found his phone on the kitchen counter where he'd been working. She hoped that he was taking a long refreshing walk and would come home with the clear light in his eyes she always found so comforting.

When he returned, his eyes were the same. She didn't ask what kept him. She took the wine and bread and thanked him for getting them.

"I took a brisk walk. I need a quick shower," he said.

"Okay."

Sam made a green salad and then covered the bowl with plastic wrap. If Steven didn't make a dressing when the guests arrived, she'd do it.

A little later, Steven appeared in the kitchen. He'd put on different clothes. He wore pressed khaki pants and an attractive pullover sweater. His beard was gone, and Sam said she didn't realize he was going to shave it off.

"I wasn't," he said.

"Spur of the moment?"

"Open one of those bottles, pour us each a glass, and come into the living room. I need to talk to you."

Sam did as he asked.

He brought in the candles from the dining room, placed them on the coffee table, and lit them. She handed him his glass and, after a moment, joined him on the sofa.

"Something's happened," he said.

"Did they take back the grant?"

"What? No! You can't take back a grant once it's been given."

"Okay."

He stared at the flickering flame of the candle nearest him, then sipped his wine. He said a complaint had been lodged against him by a former student, someone he taught the year before, a woman. She'd asked him to change her final grade. Her story was that he said he would if she slept with him. She didn't speak up before now because she was processing her trauma.

"What trauma? Did you threaten her?" Sam asked.

"No. Of course not."

"*Did* you ask her to sleep with you?"

"Yes."

"And did she?"

He nodded.

"I don't suppose her name is Molly," Sam said.

"How do you know about her?"

Sam explained about the letter found in the book she packed away. Steven asked why she hadn't said anything about it.

"I didn't think it was my business," she said.

"No, it wasn't Molly."

Steven said this other woman, the one causing trouble, was a decent student, but lazy. He caught her plagiarizing a term paper before she turned it in. Sam asked how that was possible. He said she asked him to look it over first, just to give her some pointers.

"Do you usually help students write their papers?" Sam asked.

"No."

Sam sank back into the sofa and drank her wine. The cold spot in the pit of her stomach warmed, traveled north, and lodged in her throat.

"So, you helped her with the paper. Did she write a good one?" she asked.

"Not particularly."

"And what grade did you give her?"

"For the paper, or the course?"

"I don't know. Both."

Steven said he gave the paper a C+ and the same for the course.

"But, since you had sex, she wanted something better, like a B+ or an A-."

"Something like that."

"So, she's mad she didn't get what she bargained for."

"Yes."

Steven said everything was consensual. He never pressured her.

Sam didn't believe that. When they became interested in each other, he wanted to have sex right away and she put him off because she was still involved with Timothy. She said it wasn't right. Steven said he understood. When they went to the conference last summer at Middlebury College he asked her again, and again she refused. At the time, she was flattered and took his insistence as proof of his growing affection for her. Now, in light of this, she wondered.

"How many students have you slept with?" she asked.

"I don't keep track."

"You should start. If this one made a complaint, others might, too. Christ, Steven, what were you thinking? Aren't there rules about this sort of thing?"

Rules came and went, he said. These days it wasn't strictly off-limits, only highly discouraged.

"Are you kidding? Haven't you ever heard of #MeToo?" she asked.

"Of course."

She said then he shouldn't have done something so dumb. He'd been teaching for a long time. Hadn't he figured out where the boundaries were?

"I guess not."

"You guess?"

"I understand the mistake I made, okay?"

She said nothing.

He extended his hand for her to take. If he sensed her momentary hesitation, he didn't show it.

Her phone rang, and she answered. It was Angie saying she was off the train and according to her phone was still six or seven blocks away. Sam said she must have gotten off at the wrong stop, and Angie said yeah, no doubt. Sam asked if she knew how to get here from where she was now. Angie said she did. Sam said they couldn't wait to see her.

Steven sighed and said he wished she weren't coming. They should have canceled when they still had the chance. Sam reminded him that she'd suggested it and he didn't want to.

"You don't have to rub it in," he said.

She asked what the next steps were where the complaint was concerned. He said he'd be told if the university wanted to formally investigate it. If they didn't, then that was that. But they probably would. They tended to believe any stupid young woman when she talked about being pressured sexually.

"Is she stupid?" Sam asked.

"No, not particularly."

"You just said she was."

"I said stupid young women make these kinds of complaints."

"Are you saying the complaints never have any merit?"

"Sam, please. Not now."

She got up and took their empty glasses into the kitchen. She stirred the sauce, then set the table. The dishes weren't as nice as Steven's back at home. Oh, she missed that house, and the quiet, pleasant life she'd had there! It was only the middle of January. The first of June was another four and a half months off.

She went to change her clothes. The wool dress she slipped on was cozy and gave her a sense of hope, but, of course, it was silly to feel that way. The situation they were in was not hopeful.

Jordan arrived. He was older than Sam thought he'd be, in his late fifties. And he was short. Sam had about four inches on him. Yet, he was dashing, with well-combed silver hair and a sweater vest. His loafers gleamed. When he sat on the sofa and crossed his legs, his argyle socks came into view.

"Well, Steven, congratulations! Well-deserved," he said.

"Why, thank you."

Steven's tone gave nothing away of his true mood.

"This isn't a bad place, is it?" Jordan asked as he took the glass of wine Sam handed him.

"We like it. Though, I miss the old house. Steven's house, that is," she said.

"Yes. It's a classic Maplehurst, isn't it?"

"I don't know what that is."

"The style of the house is called Maplehurst. You know, with the two peaks on the roofline and the rounded doorways and windows," Steven said.

"Right."

Sam went into the kitchen. Steven hadn't put out a pot of water to boil the pasta in, so she took care of that. Once the pot filled, she sprinkled a generous amount of salt into it and got it heating on the stove.

The doorbell rang, and Steven opened the door. Angie came in, and Steven took her coat. Angie put her shopping bag down next to the coat rack. Jordan came forward to shake her hand. She apologized for how cold her fingers were. She said her gloves were useless. Jordan took her hand and rubbed it vigorously between his to warm it. Angie stood for a minute, looking helplessly at Sam, then withdrew her hand.

"Thanks," she told Jordan.

Watching Jordan watch Angie, Sam realized Steven had told him that Angie had recently become single and was on the rebound. Jordan had accepted his dinner invitation with that in mind.

"You've been shopping," Jordan said to Angie.

"Yeah. I'm a good shopper."

"May I say that's a lovely scarf you're wearing."

Angie fingered the light-weight blue and gold scarf wrapped loosely around her throat.

"This old thing?" she asked. Jordan laughed. Angie looked at Sam again. Sam crossed the room and stood next to her. Jordan returned to the sofa and Steven poured Angie some wine.

"Did you ever find Timothy?" Sam asked her. Angie said no, then asked Sam if she needed help in the kitchen. Sam told Jordan and Steven they'd be right back. As Sam popped the bread into the oven to warm, Angie said Matt called her again on her way over here. Sam said she should block his number. Angie said she couldn't do that. In the living room, Jordan laughed at something Steven said, and Sam wondered how hard it was for him to pretend to be in good spirits. Sam told Angie not to think about Matt for a while, and to try to enjoy herself. For a moment, the mess Steven had landed himself in was on the tip of her tongue, but she said nothing.

Over dinner, Angie rose to the occasion and engaged Jordan by asking how he knew Steven. Jordan described a dreary winter day years before when Steven wandered into his bookstore in a rotten mood over a bad grade on a paper and began looking through first editions for sale. He found a T.S. Eliot in mint condition, Boni and Liveright's 1922 edition of *The Wasteland*. Of course, it was out of his price range, and Steven began a relentless attempt to barter for it. He offered to work for free as a salesclerk, and Jordan explained the store didn't do enough business to justify taking on someone else, even in an unpaid position. Then, Steven offered to give the place a good cleaning. As Jordan said this he laughed.

"It was pretty dusty," he said.

"Steven? Clean?" Sam said. She said it lightly, Angie and Jordan laughed, but Steven sat still.

Finally, Jordan softened and dropped the price. Steven wanted to buy the book on time, and there followed another long negotiation where Steven offered to rearrange the books for sale in a way that would be more inviting to buyers.

"The trouble was, he couldn't say just how he'd accomplish that. The poor guy just froze up when I asked for specifics," Jordan said. Angie laughed.

They enjoyed the pasta, and when Sam served the pie for dessert, Jordan had a second slice. Jordan offered to drive Angie back to the apartment, and she accepted. Sam made her promise to call her as soon as she was up in the morning so they could have a good long talk.

Sam did the dishes while Steven sat in the living room, staring into space. When she joined him, he apologized for not offering to help. She said she could tell the evening had been hard for him to get through, and she wished there were something she could do.

"You're already doing it," he said and reached for her hand.

They went to bed, and he wanted to make love. She didn't but did anyway. Later, as she lay awake, she wondered if Edith ever had sex when she didn't want to out of kindness or sympathy. She thought not. Edith was too tough for that.

Chapter Nine

As promised, Angie called bright and early. She said Timothy came in late but sober, and when she asked what he'd been doing, he said he went to the movies. Twice. Who goes to Boston to sit in a movie theater? Sam said it was a warm place to be. Then Angie said she was going home tomorrow.

"What? Why? You've only been here three days," Sam said.

"Matt needs me."

"Oh, God, Angie. No."

Angie said that woman had sent her a text message swearing they weren't involved. She had no reason not to believe her. Okay, Matt probably put her up to it, and it was just an elaborate ruse to let Matt get back in Angie's good graces, but for the moment she was going to believe it.

Sam said that even if he weren't involved with her, what about all the other problems?

"What other problems?" Angie asked.

"The fact that you don't trust him."

"Well, I'm working on that."

Sam got the uncomfortable feeling that Angie had exaggerated the extent of Matt's recent bad behavior. She might have just needed a break from things, and took a small, nagging suspicion and turned it into a crisis. Without Sam in town, she would have been lonely, even at loose ends. That was a pretty roundabout way of doing things, though, wasn't it?

"Timothy said Potter and Lavinia were talking about buying Matt's share of the bar back from him. Is that still going forward?" Sam asked.

"They were talking about that before this happened."

"Really, why?"

"I don't think he wants the financial responsibility."

"But he borrowed all that money to invest in the place."

"I know, I know. Look, Matt has his reasons for wanting out."

I bet.

Sam said she'd come by around lunchtime. They could go out somewhere.

Over coffee, Steven complained about his coffee being cold, that the dishwasher hadn't been turned on and was now running and making noise. At first, Sam thought he was worrying about the complaint, but he said he was unhappy with how she'd behaved at dinner. She asked him to specify. He said when Jordan asked how she liked the book Steven got her for Christmas, *You, Forever,* she said she hadn't read it yet.

"I haven't," she said.

"You didn't have to say so. It looks like you didn't care about it."

"You wanted me to lie to him to make you look better?"

"Well, if you put it that way, it does sound pretty silly."

Sam gave him a quick massage on his shoulders. She told him about Angie wanting to go home early, and that she and Matt were getting back together, not that they'd ever really been apart. He looked at her. He was miles away. He said he was scheduled to have a phone call with the chairperson of the department and someone from the ombudsman's office.

He said Gail hadn't answered his email yet. Sam asked who Gail was.

"My student, of course," Steven said.

"The one who went to the dean? Why on earth did you send her an email?"

"To say we could clear this whole thing up, of course."

"Clear up how?"

Steven said he thought he could persuade her to drop the complaint. If he recalled correctly, she wanted to apply to graduate school. He would offer to write one of her letters of recommendation. A glowing one.

"That would be seen as a further attempt by you to influence her. Don't offer her anything," she said.

Steven stared into his coffee cup. He said the truth was, he felt bad about what had happened.

"I think I was a little in love with her," he said.

"Okay."

"And, well, maybe I still am."

Sam sat down. She wanted to know how long he'd felt this way. He said all along, he never stopped feeling it, if that's what she were asking.

"How long were you involved?" she asked.

"Not long, only a few months."

"Were you still together when she asked you to change her grade?"

"It was winding down at that point."

"Who wanted out?" she asked.

"I did."

"Why?"

"I met you."

Sam said she was having a little trouble constructing his timeline. Did Molly come before, or after Gail? Steven waved his hand to signal he didn't want to talk about it anymore. He got up and went into his office.

Alone at the kitchen counter, the truth sat in her chest. She hadn't cared about Steven's past relationships when she met him. She saw him as a safe harbor, a place to recover from the bruising she'd taken for three years from Timothy. When doubts surfaced, she ignored them and told herself it was normal to be uncertain, even jittery, in a new relationship. But the idea of motherhood, or the loss of its appeal, should have told her something. Deep down, below words and logic, her heart knew it would be a bad idea with Steven. And then there was all his talk about the future, needing permanence, which at the time she welcomed, but was merely the safe harbor *he* was looking for.

His voice reached her through the closed door of his office. It rose and fell. Then there was a long silence, and his voice resumed. She couldn't make out the words.

She got dressed without showering and sent a quick text to Steven's phone saying they were out of half-and-half for their coffee, and she was desperate for some. Then she added a heart emoji.

She didn't know her father's appointment schedule and figured if he were with a patient, she'd go straight to voicemail, which she did. Her message said she was mulling something over and would appreciate a call. She added that she hoped he didn't mind her hitting him up for some free therapy. He called her right back. He was doing some paperwork, he said, and was screening calls because he needed to get caught up.

He asked how things were going in Boston, and she said fine, just fine. She apologized for not stopping by before they left, then felt guilty because he lived not far from her and Steven, yet she rarely saw him. That was on her. He invited her over a couple of times a year, and she'd only gone to his home once.

She walked and talked, and quickly worked up a sweat. She explained that she was finding out things about Steven she didn't care for. Then she mentioned Gail's complaint.

"That kind of thing happens more than you think, these days," her father said.

"I know, I know."

"Did he do it?"

"It's a gray area."

"So, yes he did, and he didn't mean to, or didn't think she would take it the way she did."

Sam came to an intersection she didn't recognize and realized she was lost. She couldn't pull up the map on her phone while she was still talking. It didn't matter. The winter sky had taken on a tender blue. A man scraped the ice off the windshield of his parked car. His methodical rhythm was oddly comforting. Her father was talking. He said it sounded to him as if the issue were with Sam, more than with Steven. What he meant was that she needed to take a good look at herself and decide what she wanted. She also had to understand why Steven seemed like a good option at the time.

"Oh, I was on the rebound, I think. And felt like a failure," she said.

"Because?"

"Well, I've told you about Timothy and his drinking. He wasn't able to get it together, and I assumed it was my fault."

"Do you still feel that way?"

"Not really. But I still feel attached."

"That might always be so. You shouldn't expect otherwise."

The man finished his scraping, got behind the wheel, and started the motor. Then he got out and went into the building and returned a few moments later. Sam thought he must be a trusting person, or he was just careless. She walked along a broad street with antique shops and restaurants that were all closed, though in one, people could be seen through the window taking down chairs that had been put on the tables the evening before. Her phone buzzed to indicate she had another call coming in. She ignored it.

"I'm sorry this is hard for you," her father said.

"I appreciate that."

"Go and collect your thoughts. Write down what you want from this relationship. Then, tell Steven what's on that list."

"If I can get him to listen."

Her father's pause said that was a problem, too. Which she already knew. She promised to be in touch soon and thanked him for talking to her.

"Remember, I'm always here. We have a lot of time to make up for," he said.

"I know."

When they hung up, Sam consulted the map and saw she'd been walking in a wider and wider square. But home wasn't far, and she headed that way. The message that interrupted her conversation with her father was from Steven asking where the hell she was. Things must have gone badly on his phone call. Then again, how could they go well?

She slipped off her glove to unlock the door just as he opened it.

"Hi," she said.

"Please don't just take off like that again."

"I send you a text explaining."

"Where's the half-and-half you had to rush out and buy?"

"I don't have it, obviously. Stop grilling me. Tell me about your call."

He ran his hand through his hair, then brushed his fingers along the lower lid of his eye where another stye was developing.

"I have to go back and meet with them in person," he said.

"When?"

"Now. Today. As soon as I can make arrangements."

"Where will you stay?"

"In a hotel."

"I can come with you."

"You don't want to do that."

"It might be fun, a few nights in a hotel."

"Another time."

Sam sat down at the kitchen counter. She hadn't removed her coat. She asked him to bring her a fresh cup of coffee. He got one for himself, too, and sat beside her. He said Gail called and he told her he'd be in town. She wanted to see him.

"About your offer to write a letter of recommendation?" Sam asked.

He said his best guess was that she wanted him to break up with Sam and resume his relationship with her.

"But she lodged a complaint against you! That's not how you get someone interested in you again."

"I know. She's a little mixed up."

"If you want my advice, and I know you don't, I'd avoid her like the plague."

He reached out and touched her leg. Sam looked at him as objectively as possible. He wasn't the kind of man women lost their minds over. Not like Timothy. But who knew? Maybe Steven reminded Gail of her father, or something similarly Freudian.

Steven said he needed to jump on his computer and see about a train, or he could fly. He went into his office, and she went into hers.

At her desk:

Why can't I be two inches tall with pearl hands & yellow silk hair?
A better, prettier self in a house on a table,
In a room people walk past & don't touch

Gail's hair could be yellow. She might be petite, too.
Like Melissa.

She hadn't cried since the end of Timothy and here she was, carrying on like a child. She wiped her eyes with her sleeve and remembered she hadn't showered. The whole day was upside down. If she looked out the window, the sky would be black.

The door opened and Steven entered the room, his eyes dark. He pulled her up from her chair and held onto her as she continued to weep. His voice flowed over her, though she didn't understand anything he said. Eventually, she calmed.

She wriggled free of him and sat down. She closed her journal when she saw him looking at it.

"Is it because of me?" he asked.

"Because of everything."

"I'm sorry," he said.

"Just go fix it if you can. If you can't, I guess we'll deal with that later."

"You're exhausted."

"I'm fine. I'm going to wash up and go over to Angie's. When are you leaving?"

"This evening."

"I can be back in time to make dinner if you'd like."

"You know I'd love it."

She looked up into his face.

"Steven?" she asked.

"What?"

The more she looked, the more his face remained the same.

"Nothing," she said.

"I wish I didn't have to leave you alone when you're so upset."

"I'll be okay."

He said he'd be gone only for a day or two. She told him to stay long enough to see it through, whatever it was.

Steven was back in his office with the door closed when she left. She didn't look in or call out that she was on her way. Not taking time to dry her hair after her shower meant her head was freezing as she drove to the apartment. Angie met her at the front door and said she was just about ready to go. Sam said she couldn't face going out, not yet. She suggested they eat in if there were any food around.

Angie asked what the matter was, and Sam told her. Angie led her into the living room where Timothy was lying on the sofa with a book. Angie told him to beat it, they needed some privacy, and Sam said no, he could stay. Timothy sat up to give Sam room on the end of the sofa. Angie took the chair by the fireplace.

"You look like crap, if you'll pardon my saying so," Timothy told Sam.

"Leave her alone," Angie said.

"It's okay," Sam said.

"Is anyone going to tell me why the sky is falling, or do I have to figure it out for myself?" Timothy asked.

Sam told him about Gail, her complaint, and Steven's guess that she wanted to resume their relationship. Timothy closed his book and put it on the coffee table. It was a biography of Ulysses S. Grant. He asked where Steven was and Sam said at home, getting ready for his trip.

"Well, the first thing I'd say is that he's obviously still attached to what's-her-name," Timothy said.

"He said as much. He wasn't trying to hide it," Sam said.

A tear formed and she wiped it away before the others could see.

"Let me ask you this. What bothers you more? That this student wants him to ditch you, or that Steven wasn't candid about his past affairs?" Timothy asked her.

"Both."

Sam said that on the other hand, she hadn't asked him anything. Okay, he might have volunteered it, but that was his business, wasn't it? He wanted time to get to know her better, to see if she were worth trusting.

"Whoa, hold the phone. You're making excuses for him," Angie said.

"You are," Timothy said.

"Well, I guess I'm good at that. After all, you should know," Sam said. Then she apologized. Timothy said not to worry. She was allowed to be brutally honest, especially now that they were no longer together.

Her heart sank as she realized how much she missed being close to him. She supposed it made sense. It was exactly as her father had suggested.

"Do you love him?" Angie asked.

"Yes." Then in another psychic jolt, she realized Angie was asking about Steven.

The tears came again. Angie was instantly by her side. Timothy said he'd make up a pot of tea. Sam asked him not to, to please just sit back down, and Angie, too. She pulled herself together. She said she'd come to take Angie to lunch, and that's just what they'd do.

"Oh, forget lunch. Timothy can get us some sandwiches. We'll hang out here," Angie said.

"When are you leaving?" Sam asked her.

"Well, about that."

"What?"

"Seems like Matt thinks they need a little more time apart to think about things," Timothy said.

"But that woman texted you and said they weren't seeing each other," Sam said.

"I know. But Matt is mad I didn't believe him, so I'm going to roost here for the rest of the week as planned."

"Didn't he ask you to come back?" Sam asked.

Angie shrugged.

Why was it always so difficult, what went on between men and women? Sam leaned back. They weren't insurmountable, the issues between her and Steven, despite what he'd done and what she now understood about where her heart lay, in the beginning. A future with him remained an option. Gradually, a gentle peace descended which reminded her of times in her childhood, after being hurt by her grandmother, or teased at school, when she found a place in her mind where she could stand and not be scared. She closed her eyes. When she opened them, she was alone in the room lying on the sofa with a blanket over her. The weak daylight had shifted. Faint country music leaked from the overhead speakers in the coffered ceiling. Angie must have figured out how to use the built-in sound system. Sam peeled off the blanket and got up. She smelled something cooking in the kitchen and when she entered, Angie was chopping carrots on a cutting board.

"What's all this?" Sam asked.

"There you are. You fell asleep."

"Yeah."

"I'm making us dinner."

"Oh, no. I told Steven I'd be back to make his."

"Tell him your plans changed. Or, better yet, invite him over."

Sam drank a glass of water and went to the powder room. In the mirror, she found her face calm and smooth. But the eyes gave it all away, didn't they? Their light was too bright.

Back in the living room she dug out her phone and called Steven. He answered right away. She told him she was having dinner at the apartment and that he could join them if he wanted to. He asked her if she wanted him to.

"If you don't mind taking the train. I don't imagine you're bringing a ton of luggage. Should be easy enough," she said.

"Okay. What time?"

"Five-thirty. Bring wine."

"I'll have to go from there to the airport."

"I can drive you."

"Sam?"

"What?"

"I wish I could see you alone before I leave."

"Well, if I drive you, we'll be alone then."

"You know what I mean."

She told him she'd see him later.

Suddenly, the idea of having the townhome to herself felt liberating. She could focus on her work and come here whenever she liked. Whatever happened between Steven and the university wouldn't change that, unless he got fired. Oh, lord! That hadn't occurred to her.

She went into Edith's room and called Martin's number. When he answered, she laid out the situation and asked if a tenured professor could lose his job over something like that. Martin said he'd have to read Steven's employment contract, but he was pretty sure there would be circumstances when someone could be let go, and clear sexual harassment was one of them. He asked how she was holding up, and she said not all that great, but her friends had come up and were settled in the apartment, and that helped a lot. Martin said he thought only one friend was coming, not that it mattered. Sam said the friend brought her brother, who just happened to be Sam's ex.

"Oh, my goodness. The plot thickens," Martin said.

"Yes."

"Well, you have my best wishes. If you need more formal legal advice, call me."

Sam said she would, and also that she hoped he was enjoying the Bahamas. He said it was lovely, the politics were terrible, and retirees were everywhere, making restaurants slow and highly inefficient. He had to wait over forty-five minutes for a meal just the other day. People there could learn a thing or two about how to hustle from the good folks of Boston.

She told him everything was fine with the apartment, and how grateful she was to have the use of it. Then they hung up.

Her neck was stiff from sleeping on the sofa. She stretched out on the floor and did a muscle-relaxing exercise she learned years ago. She combined it with a meditation routine she used to rely on, where she focused on her breathing, then allowed her mind to wander. Her thoughts were squarely on Steven.

She forced herself to list five of his best traits:

—He respected her artistic aspirations.

Did he, though? Only to the extent that they didn't interfere with his plans and advancement.

—He liked to cook.

But how great was that? A lot of men cooked, and except for the dinner for Jordan, which she had to take over, he hadn't cooked much since coming to Boston.

—He liked her a lot.

That was indisputable, but also irrelevant.

She looked for numbers four and five and came up short.

She wandered into the kitchen and told Angie she realized she'd missed lunch. Angie wiped her hands on her apron and said she could slap together a nice plate of cheese and crackers. There was some fresh fruit, too. Timothy found a great high-end food store not far away and decided to stock them up with healthy fare.

As she put the plate in front of her, Sam said she was glad to see Angie discovering her inner chef. Angie said she always liked to cook but since Matt moved in, she lost the urge. She poured herself a glass of wine, then one for Sam, too. Then she took the chair across from Sam.

Sam sipped her wine. Another top-notch French. She could spend a week doing nothing but reading and drinking good labels.

"Are you really letting Matt off the hook?" Sam asked.

"I suppose I'm hopeless."

"I wouldn't say that. I think I'm hopeless."

Angie seemed thoughtful. After a moment, she said the worse thing about getting mad at Matt was she always felt like she had to apologize afterward. In this most recent situation, she was dead certain she overheard him on the phone with Sharon, and later, when he was showering and she checked his phone for herself, she was right. He said it was about some money she owed him, and that could have been true, but with his history of not being completely honest, it was hard to know. Then, Sharon contacted Angie to say they weren't involved. Naturally, she ended up feeling at fault, as if the whole thing were her mistake, instead of Matt's.

"You're saying he manipulated you," Sam said. The wine had brought a pleasant glow to her face.

"Let's just say he played the injured party a little too well."

"Yet, you're ready to go back to him and pick up where you left off."

"I didn't say it was logical."

"Love never is."

Sam asked Angie what Matt's plans were if he sold his share of the bar to Angie's parents. Angie had no idea. He'd have to find something to do with himself.

"He wanted to get back into music, didn't he?" Sam asked.

"I guess."

Angie's expression turned grim. Sam said she hoped she didn't think she was being critical of her situation, especially given what was going on with Steven at the moment.

"Steven's mess predated you, though," Angie said. She asked if Steven were coming for dinner. Sam said he was and asked if Timothy would be joining them.

"I have no idea. He comes and goes. He went to a museum, I think," Angie said.

Sam asked what she thought of Steven's friend, Jordan.

"He was fine. Overeager, of course, but a gentleman," Angie said.

"You mean, he didn't try to kiss you."

"He tried. I let him. Why not?"

Sam was about to say something until she remembered Timothy kissing her in the elevator.

"Did you give him your number?" she asked.

"Of course not."

Sam said she was going to read some more of Edith's diaries unless Angie needed help with anything. Angie said she had everything under control, but she wouldn't do the dishes, afterward. Sam and Timothy could handle that, assuming Timothy returned by then.

March 4, 1964.

Not long now, poor Mama. Just let yourself go and don't worry about a thing. Edie's here.

Sam's eyes welled.

August 17, 1964

Everyone's gone, now. Papa, Betty, Mama. Malcolm has been sweetness itself. Even Marty has been kind, though he hates being uprooted again. I think he made some friends in Urbana. I'm glad to be home, though. The apartment has been empty and needs a complete airing. The cleaners came yesterday and did a poor job, so they're coming back. Malcolm tells me he wants to take a class at Boston College. Accounting, he says. Well, there are worse things for a man to study, God knows.

Sam calculated. Edith was forty-two years old when she wrote that. Nine years older than Sam was now. And her husband would have been sixty-eight, with a fourteen-year-old son. No wonder there was conflict. The age difference was hard.

Edith was trapped in a life she didn't want. No doubt, she tried to make the best of it. What about people who chose their own traps? Like Flora, her mother?

Had Sam walked into a trap with Steven? How could she have known that some former lover would turn up and cause trouble? Unless she weren't so former, after all.

Late night faculty meetings, he said. Holding office hours after dinner for students who had late classes, he said. The notifications on his cell phone that made him look at it, silence it, and slide it into his pocket.

Sam closed the diary, pulled out her poetry journal she grabbed on her way out of the townhome and wrote:

You're a candle in a glass lantern
And when I light you, you burn, then slowly
Slowly
Go out

The image of a flame dropping to the wick, smaller each second, until it was gone haunted her.

Better to be haunted by that, she thought, than by the doubts that rushed in when she summoned the future.

Chapter Ten

Twenty minutes before he was due, Steven phoned to say a big snowstorm was on the way and he'd booked an earlier flight. In fact, he was already at the airport. It looked like his plane would get off on time. He apologized for not being able to make it for dinner.

"No problem. I mean, you don't want to get snowed in, right?" Sam asked.

"Exactly. And, this way, I might be able to get back sooner. They've agreed to meet with me first thing in the morning."

They paused. Sam looked out the window of Edith's study. A few snowflakes drifted down.

She told him to take care, and to keep her posted. He said, of course, he would. They hung up.

She went to the kitchen to tell Angie it would just be the three of them, assuming Timothy returned in time. She also said there was a snowstorm on the way, and it looked like it had already started.

Angie said they would hunker down and watch the snow pile up. Sam said she didn't have a change of clothes if she wanted to stay over, and Angie said not to worry, she could borrow something from Timothy, like a pair of long underwear she could pad around in.

"We'll have a slumber party!" Angie was instantly animated by the idea.

"And watch old movies?"

"The only TV in this place is in my room, but I don't mind hosting."

Timothy appeared in the kitchen, still in his jacket and scarf. There were snowflakes in his hair. He put two bottles of wine on the counter.

"What's all this?" Sam asked.

"To go with dinner. Though I suppose, technically speaking, chicken calls for white, but who's going to drink white in the dead of winter?"

"I didn't think you liked wine."

"I don't. It's for you, Angie, and what's-his-name. Thought it was the least I could do when Angie texted he was coming. As for me, in honor of hosting our first and only dinner party here, I bought myself a single can of beer." He produced it from the same brown bag the wine had been in. He asked when Steven would arrive. Sam explained about the change of plans.

"Shame," Timothy said with a grin. He went to hang up his jacket and scarf. Sam opened the oven and inspected the chicken. She said she thought it was ready. Angie grabbed the oven mitts and lifted it out. She set the pan on the stove. Sam asked if she wanted her to make gravy, and Angie said she'd do it.

Sam brought the wine into the dining room, then thought she'd set the table. Martin kept his good china in a cabinet against the wall and after some searching, she discovered the silver in one of the sideboard's drawers. The table was huge, with ten upholstered chairs around it. It hadn't seemed so large when they ate there the other day, nor had she noticed then that the silver candelabra on it in needed polishing. The candles looked like they'd only been used once. She lit them with a book of matches she found in a different drawer. Then she used the rheostat on the wall to dim the overhead chandelier. The effect was charming and elegant. She opened the curtains. The view of the river wasn't as wide as in the library and living room, but was still powerful, even in the twilight.

Angie came in with the chicken. She set it on the sideboard, left, and returned with the bowl of vegetables. She said she'd burned the carrots. Then, as she carved the chicken, she said it was dry. Sam didn't care. She was hungry. Timothy appeared with his can of beer and said he felt like a slob drinking it in such a fancy dining room.

"Well, to us," Sam said and lifted her glass.

She wondered if Steven got off all right. He'd call if not, she supposed. Her phone was in the other room, and he'd be disappointed if she didn't answer. She didn't go get it. She worked through her overcooked chicken and burned carrots and enjoyed them both, despite their shortcomings. The potatoes were better. But then, it was hard to ruin potatoes.

Angie wanted more wine and Timothy poured it for her. He said he noticed she was drinking more than usual, and she said he wasn't one to criticize. In an instant they were arguing, not shouting, just poking each other with reminders of past faults and failings. Sam supposed siblings did this from time to time, but even so, she wished they'd shut the hell up. She told them to, in those exact words.

A startled silence fell, then everyone was laughing.

Timothy did the dishes, and Angie said she was going to get her phone and see what was on TV. She'd determined that Martin had cable service but none of the popular streaming channels, so they'd be limited in what they could watch. Soon, she and Sam were installed on the king-sized bed, propped up by extra pillows, with more wine and *Laura* on the television. Timothy pulled up a chair and watched for a while, then said he'd seen it several times and wanted to go read. It was Sam's first time, and she was enchanted by the noir atmosphere. The movie was made in 1944 and Sam realized that Edith was alive then, as a young woman, just like the one portrayed by Gene Tierney on screen, though she no doubt had less money and occupied plainer surroundings. When it ended, *Out of the Past*, another period noir, came on and after about twenty minutes, Angie fell asleep.

Sam left the room and went to the one where she'd made up the bed for herself. It was small, with only one window. Built for a former servant, if she had to guess. She hoped the double bed would be comfortable. She lay down and did her calm breathing exercise again. Steven hadn't texted to say he'd reached Dunston. He might not have charged his phone, or the plane had been late leaving and they'd already told everyone to turn off their phones for takeoff.

She told herself to stop speculating, then wondered what Edith might have done, in a situation like this.

Sam suspected she'd tell Steven to go straight to hell.

When it was clear she couldn't relax, she got up and went into the library. The apartment was silent, but she could sense Timothy's presence nearby. For a few minutes, she stood with the lights off and the curtains open and watched the snow rage. The world blurred, and all boundaries softened. She thought again of that poem by Abigail Lois Pratt, and wanted desperately to read it again. Martin probably hadn't taken her volume with him on vacation, so she turned the light on and looked through the bookshelves. The upper ones could be reached only with the attached sliding ladder. After reading the spines, some embossed with gold, some with a paper dust jacket, she found it next to a treatise on dog training. She reviewed the table of contents and went to the page she needed.

To look at that blanketed yard / street / town / state / country / world /

And realize / remember / that every falling flake is / unique / distinct / sole /

You wonder, during that / three-day storm / if you somehow / witnessed an /

Allegory of the human race

A beautiful sentiment.

She put the volume back and took down the one next to it, a collection by Carl Sandberg. As she flipped through the pages, she saw that someone had underlined passages in pencil, and made brief remarks in the margins. Next to the beginning of "Autumn Moment," there were the words, If you know nothing beautiful lasts, what's the point of crying? Sam looked in the front of the book and found the previous owner's name: Edith Sloan.

Edith loved poetry so much she found a way to publish it, yet here she was, bashing Sandburg for being sentimental.

There were other books that had been written in, not all by Edith. Sam could detect different handwriting. When Edith turned up again, it was on a blank page at the end of a novel by Graham Greene, *The End of the Affair*, where she said, Stupid woman! As if God, or anyone else, cares who you sleep with.

Here was Edith, angry again, yet she turned away women poets for being the same way. Was this her way of managing her own discontent? Of making the best of constant disappointment? After so many of years of looking at things straight on, she didn't have the strength to do it anymore. Her mother had died, her marriage wasn't particularly happy, and there was that thread of regret running through the pages of her diaries about that man, Philip. Edith lost something in herself, Sam felt.

She slept surprisingly well and woke when light rimmed the curtain in the narrow window. The long underwear Timothy had lent her was comfortable, and so were her thick socks from the day before. She reached for her phone and found a text message from Steven left the night before, Flight went okay, at the hotel in Dunston, dreading tomorrow, wish you'd come with me. Sorry I didn't take you up on the offer!

It was still early; Steven hadn't had his meeting yet. Should she call and give him courage? He'd feel funny, waking up alone. Assuming he was alone. Did she feel strange, there by herself? Not at all. She felt marvelous, not quite free, just more open to whatever possibilities the day might offer.

She got up and pulled back the curtain. The snow had stopped. She reckoned almost eight inches had fallen since dinnertime. The streets below weren't plowed and showed tire tracks left by brave drivers who just had to get somewhere. A man was gliding slowly along on a pair of cross-country skis. Sam had the good sense to wear heavy boots yesterday, so she'd be able to walk back to the townhome if the trains weren't running. But what would she do when she got there? The idea of having it all to herself didn't have the same appeal it had while Steven was grumping around about Gail and, before that, his stupid grant.

She noted her hostility as the sunlight was obscured by a cloud bank. There would be more snow. She padded into the kitchen where Timothy was buttering a piece of toast. He looked rested but his attitude was grim, and she knew it meant he was thinking something unpleasant. She asked if he'd heard a weather forecast. He said he hadn't, then told her there was coffee in the pot.

"Angie's not up?" Sam asked.

"It's too early for her."

"Shouldn't be. She fell asleep early."

Timothy's expression said he didn't care what time Angie had fallen asleep. He was looking at his phone.

She asked if everything were all right. He said Mark got in trouble at school and Melissa wasn't clear about the details. Sam asked if he wanted her to find out what was going on.

"How?" he asked.

"We're friends. She might find it easier to talk to me about it."

"When was the last time you heard from her?"

"It's been a while, but I don't see what difference that makes."

Timothy shrugged. Then he said he'd ask Mark and hope for a straight answer.

Sam drank her coffee at the table with him. They didn't talk and it felt fine. She liked not having to keep a conversation going, and she liked not having to worry about his mood.

Her phone buzzed. It was a text from Steven, Wish me luck! Heading to campus now!

When she put her phone down on the table, she discovered Timothy looking at her.

"What are you going to do when they nail him?" he asked.

"Be supportive. Help him find his way."

"What about your way?"

"What do you mean?"

"Oh, I don't know. Don't listen to me. I'm in a bad mood this morning."

"I can tell."

He stared into his empty cup. He said he just wondered what she was doing with her life, and if it felt right.

"Are you still worried about my leaving school?" she asked.

"Not really."

"What, then? Are you asking if I'm committed to Steven?"

"I'm asking if you're committed to yourself."

She stared at him. His thoughts were hidden.

She asked him to continue. He said she was always so concerned about other people's welfare that she overlooked her own. He didn't mean to suggest she neglected herself, or anything like that, but it looked to him as if she'd transferred her mothering instinct from him onto Steven.

"I'm not mothering him. I'm trying to be there for him," she said. Her face was hot.

"Is that what you want? Always to be there for someone else?"

She said that's what caring meant to her—showing up and helping out.

He asked what caring meant to Steven. She said that was none of his business, then she asked what caring meant to *him*.

"I don't have a good handle on that," he said. She was taken aback by his candor, and it must have shown because he added that it took him a while to see that. When they were together, he had trouble accessing his feelings and stuffed them inside a few gallons of booze.

"Are you sure you haven't been seeing a therapist?" she asked.

He laughed, and the change in his face and the whole way he sat in his chair pulled at her hard. They watched each other for a moment, and he said he guessed she was wondering why he couldn't have been this way before.

"Something like that," she said.

"It took you leaving me to wake me up."

"I'm sorry."

"For what?"

"I don't know."

"See, that's another thing you do, feel sorry when there's nothing to feel sorry about."

She went to shower and as she enjoyed the hot water on her skin, she wondered what bothered her more—Timothy's smug attitude, or what he said. Of course, she had a way of covering for other people. When you grow up making excuses for the bad behavior you see around you every day, it's a hard habit to break. And that question about what she wanted to do with herself? She was doing it, wasn't she? Her poetry was a river running through her, and she was riding it the best she could.

She dressed in what she'd worn the day before. She could get one more day out of the shirt, socks, and underwear, then she'd have to wash them or switch them out. The storm might be over by then.

She went into Edith's study with her backpack, cleared some space on the desk, pulled out her journal, and wrote:

Even in the timeless hours, seconds pass
Nothing stops, nothing rests
Dreams open & close like gentle hands
Which in anger turn to fists
Battering flesh & stone

Who was she angry at? Steven, of course, but she could bet money a lot of professors had relationships with their students. He just had the bad luck to get involved with one who was greedy and manipulative. Okay, Gail's feelings might be genuine, fine, and worthy, but she was making trouble for him, and if you really cared for someone, you didn't do that.

As she held her pencil above the page and struggled for more words, she thought how hard it must be for Steven to be distracted from his work, on top of all the worry the complaint was causing. Sam could reassure him all she liked, but she wanted to be useful. What if she looked through all the boxes Martin had brought up from the storeroom, and pulled out anything that bore on the operations of The Hedgerow Press? Then she could organize them and even draw up an index of the materials. She might not get everything done before he returned, but it would still be a nice surprise.

She sat on the floor and upended one box.

There was a quiet knock, then Angie came in with a mug of coffee in her hand. She looked rested and peaceful. She said she was hungry and was going to make some breakfast.

"Have you eaten?" Angie asked Sam.

"I will later."

"What are you doing?"

"Sorting this for Steven."

"You're so thoughtful."

Angie's tone was wry. Sam asked how she was doing today with the whole Matt thing. Angie said a little better. She had no idea what was going to happen to them as a couple and for the moment, it was okay not to know.

Angie went on her way and Sam dumped out the contents of another box. There were photographs among the papers. Some had scalloped edges and were in black-and-white. Newer ones were in color. Martin as a teenager appeared next to his much taller and plumper father. Malcolm Alistair had a grim expression through which happiness wanted to show, at least that's how Sam interpreted the look in his eyes. Every picture of Edith was stunning. She was slim, well-dressed, and held herself proudly, with a sophisticated air. Her expression was always impossible to read, though in some her eyes were cast down, as if studying something on the ground. Here was a woman who didn't want to be where she was, with the people she was with, yet she remained. She might not have felt she could begin again, or that she owed Malcolm her company for reasons Sam would never know.

What did she want here, among these tokens of someone else's life? An answer to the problems in her own?

She tossed the pictures back in the box they'd come from and examined a stash of letters, many of which had become separated from their envelopes. Then, over the next hour and a half, she sorted them into a personal pile and a business pile, though for some, it was hard to distinguish if the subject were the press, or someone's book, or to an author about a manuscript under consideration. Eventually, she combined them back into one stack, arranged chronologically, with the most recent on top and the oldest on the bottom. Empty envelopes she didn't bother with.

The letters were mostly typed, but there were a few written in faded ink. Edith's hand was neater there than in her diary. Some letters to her were also handwritten. One was from Philip Green, and this one Sam set aside.

November 19, 1961

New York, New York

Edith –

Of course, I remember you. I think of you every day. And, over the course of thirteen years, that's a lot of days.

Suddenly, she felt as if she were intruding on something not meant for her, invading a privacy that should remain quietly intact.

She went into the kitchen to find everything put away and the counters clean. She slid a piece of whole wheat bread into the toaster, did a quick scan of the fridge and pantry to see how they were fixed for food, and, when the toast popped up, she buttered it thickly and took it into the living room where Angie and Timothy sat on either end of the sofa, each reading a book. She ate standing at the window. It was snowing again, and any earlier tire tracks were filled in. Despite the size of the room, and the high ceilings, she felt shut in and restless. She said she was going to go out and see about getting some groceries, and Timothy offered to go with her. They both looked at Angie, who clearly had no intention of moving.

As they trudged along the deeply covered sidewalk, Timothy said Angie was enjoying not having to be on her feet all day at the bar. In fact, she was enjoying it a little too much.

"What do you mean?" Sam asked.

"I think she's putting on a little weight."

"So what?"

"It's not a good look on anyone."

Sam stopped walking. "Did you feel that way when I was heavy?" she asked him.

Timothy stopped, too, and turned to look at her. His wool cap had collected so much snow, it was white all over. His nose was red, and his eyes teared in the cold. His cheeks looked raw as if he went in too close with his razor that morning.

"Of course not."

"But I was heavy. Way more than Angie is now."

"You weren't.

"God, Timothy, you lived with me every day! I lost over forty pounds! Don't you remember that? Or what my body was like before?"

It was clear he didn't want to think about it, but Sam was on the rise now. She said she knew he hated how she looked and just never said. She supposed she should appreciate his sparing her feelings, but it was hard now to realize she repulsed him.

"So, why did we have sex so often, if I thought you were physically disgusting?" he asked. His voice was loud and carried down the street where a woman brushing snow off the windshield of her parked car paused and stared at him.

"It was convenient, that's why. I was convenient. I was there," she said, not shouting.

He took a step toward her, then stopped. His breath plumed silver.

"You never thought I loved you. That's it, isn't it?" he asked.

"Of course not."

"No, no. You think I wanted sex so badly that I put up with someone I wasn't attracted to. It never occurred to you that I didn't care about your weight. I didn't fall in love with a number on a scale, I fell in love with a brilliant, sensitive, deeply harmed young woman."

"What do you mean, deeply harmed?"

He shook his head to say he wasn't going to go into all that again. He said the store was right around the corner, they were almost there, and they should get out of the cold and buy their damn groceries.

The heat inside was a welcome relief, then soon was too much, so Sam removed her jacket. She focused on what to buy. The produce looked wonderful. She asked Timothy how he felt about a hearty beef stew, and he said that sounded good. Soon, her basket was full of carrots, an onion, parsley, a couple parsnips, frozen peas. The meat counter offered both beef chuck and beef round. She chose a large package of chuck. She couldn't decide between noodles and freshly baked bread, and when she looked for Timothy to ask his opinion, she found him in the liquor aisle, removing a bottle of vodka from the shelf. She went to him and put her free hand on his arm.

"Don't do that," she said.

"Why not?"

She said nothing. He stared at the floor, then put the bottle back on the shelf. She looked at the items in her basket and realized she didn't want to cook anything. She told Timothy that, and he offered to make the stew himself. He'd seen her do it before, it couldn't be that hard, and besides, Angie was pretty handy in the kitchen. He'd ask for her help.

Sam went on standing, not feeling able to move, and he asked what else she wanted to buy. His backpack could hold a fair amount, and who knew how long the snow was going to fall? She said to get a fresh carton of eggs and more bacon, also more bread, a package of salami, and one of sliced cheddar cheese. Mayonnaise, too, and another bag of coffee. She hadn't checked how much laundry soap they had, and Timothy said they were fine on that.

He took the basket from her, put the contents in a small, wheeled cart, and went on his way to find what she asked for. Sam stood by the magazine rack and looked through the window at a man on snowshoes trudging up the street. How could he assume a car wouldn't come along? But there weren't any cars out, only people trying to somewhere on their own steam. Heavy snow was beautiful but also an obstacle, and hard to overcome. Were all beautiful things that way?

Timothy returned. He hadn't paid for the groceries yet, and Sam was about to ask why when he said Angie had just called. Sam had left her phone in the apartment and Steven was trying to reach her.

"Oh, no. Why did I do that?" Sam asked.

"Doesn't matter. Let me go through the line, pack up, and we'll get out of here."

Sam went on standing where she was. For a moment, she considered asking Timothy if she could use his phone to call Steven back, then thought he wouldn't appreciate seeing Timothy's number on his screen.

Timothy approached, laboring under the weight of his loaded pack. Sam put on her coat and when they stepped outside, she was stunned to see the snow had stopped and blinding sunlight washed over everything. Timothy whipped out a pair of sunglasses from an interior pocket of his jacket. Sam was left to squint. It was hard to walk, and Timothy pulled ahead of her, then realized he needed to wait for her to catch up. He took off his pack, dropped it on the ground, rearranged the contents and put it back on. He explained a can had been digging into his shoulder blade. Sam said she should have brought her pack, too.

"Another thing I forgot," she said.

"Don't worry about it. You'll call him when we're back."

Sam shuffled along behind Timothy, feeling the snow give under the weight of each step. She quickly worked up a sweat that brought an unpleasant chill when the freezing air found its way inside her coat. Their progress was slow, and it felt as if they'd been gone for ages by the time they made it back to the apartment, but a glance at the small, elegantly carved wooden clock on the table by the door said they were only out for about an hour.

Timothy went straight to the kitchen to unload the groceries, and Sam removed her snowy boots and coat. Angie was in the kitchen with Timothy, putting things away. Sam's phone was on the table. She stared at it as if were a lump of coal.

"Oh, hey, sorry I answered it," Angie said.

"How did he sound?"

"Steven? Fine, I guess."

"Did he say anything about how the meeting went?"

"What meeting?"

"Don't worry about it."

Sam dropped into a chair while Timothy and Angie finished up. Then, they left her alone. She picked up the phone and looked at it. There were three text messages:

Call me when you see this
Where are you?
Never mind, I can guess

Sam went on holding the phone for a moment, then put it back on the table. She filled the kettle with water and lit the flame on the stove. Tea was what she needed. Only they hadn't replaced the box of English Breakfast Tea they used up that first night.

Why on earth did that make her cry?

She found a box of green tea and pulled out a bag.

Her phone rang.

"Hello?"

"Finally!"

Steven said the meeting went well, Gail had withdrawn the complaint, saying there'd been a misunderstanding. The woman from the Ombudsman's office thought Steven had pressured her to retract it, which ticked him off to no end. Billings, the department Chair, defended Steven and said he was certain he wouldn't pressure a student into anything. Gail's written statement cited academic stress and family issues. The thing was, she might now get in trouble for making a false claim, though he suspected she could get out of it.

"All she has to do is keep saying she was working too hard, then her mother got sick, and so on," Steven said.

"Did her mother get sick?"

"What? I have no idea."

The kettle steamed silently. Sam wondered why it wasn't whistling.

Steven said he was going to take another day in Dunston and drop in on Lyall and Claire. They still had some issues with the house, and he hoped he could get those taken care of. But he planned to be back tomorrow evening or the morning of the next day if the weather let up. It was snowing there, too, and when he got up that morning he wondered if they were going to cancel the meeting. Of course, they could have done it over Zoom, but from what he knew of the morons in the Ombudsman's Office, they weren't exactly tech-savvy.

"Okay," Sam said.

"You sound funny. What's wrong?"

"I'm sorry I left my phone here when I went out for groceries."

"It's okay."

He asked if she were planning to camp out at Martin's until he got back. He didn't mind if she did. He'd rather she were around people than in the townhome alone. Though, of course, it was safe. Who was going to go out breaking into houses in a snowstorm?

"A bear?" Sam asked.

"I miss you."

"I miss you, too."

"I'm sorry this happened, but I knew it would all work out, in the end."

"Did you?"

"No, not really."

She watched the steam rise and rush along the ceiling.

She told him about organizing all of Edith's letters, both business and personal. He paused, clearly surprised, then said it was great of her to do that, but what about her work? She said not to worry about that.

"This has been upsetting for you," he said.

"That, and everything else."

Steven paused. Then he asked if, by everything else, she meant Timothy. Sam said it was weird to see him, how he changed, and how he hadn't.

"He was going to buy a bottle of vodka at the store today," she said.

"Yeah?"

"I told him not to, and he put it back. He never did that when we were together."

"He might just be trying to impress you."

"He was never interested in impressing me before."

Steven reminded her of his theory, that Timothy was trying to get her back.

Sam said he wasn't. Steven said he didn't trust him.

"Well, I don't trust Gail. How about that?" she asked.

"All right, all right."

"Are you going to see her?"

"There's no reason to, now."

She said she had to go and hung up.

Angie came into the kitchen and said she'd tackle making the stew. Sam made her cup of tea and took it into the living room, which she found empty, added fresh logs to the fireplace, and lit a match. They had enough for a couple more fires. She wondered what day the service delivered new logs, and if they also cleaned out the fireplace. She'd have to ask Martin. After a while Angie appeared to ask if she needed anything. Sam apologized for just sitting there.

"I was supposed to be taking care of you. That's why you came up here," Sam said.

"Oh, don't worry about it. I'm doing fine. Matt was right. Time apart is just what we needed."

"And when enough time has passed?"

"I don't know. Either we forgive each other, or we don't."

After Angie left, Sam sat so long her tea got cold and the fire died down. She reflected on the difference between forgiveness and enabling. The two were tightly bound. Sometimes you couldn't have one without the other and in some situations, with some people, they were the same thing.

Chapter Eleven

Flora was alarmed to see Sam's name on her phone and asked what was wrong the minute she answered. Sam said she needed to talk and asked if this were a good time. There was music in the background, and the sound of laughter. Her mother never socialized. Had Chuck developed that part of her? Flora said they had people over, but she could take a couple of minutes. She asked again what was wrong. Sam said nothing in particular and everything in general. Flora told Chuck it was her daughter and she'd be a minute.

The background noise quieted, which meant Flora must have taken herself into another room.

"Okay, shoot," she said.

Sam didn't know what to say or where to begin. Then, it all came out. She had broken up with Timothy the summer before and moved in with her former professor, Steven. Now she was in Cambridge.

"England?" Flora asked.

"No! Boston. Just listen, okay?"

Steven got a grant to study this poet and the press that published her. Sam was staying in the apartment the publisher's son grew up in. Angie was there for a few days, and Timothy, too. She didn't know Timothy was coming, Angie hadn't told her beforehand, but it hadn't worked out too badly.

"Where's the new guy, what's-his-name?" Flora asked.

"Steven. Back in Dunston. He had to go to a meeting at the university."

"Okay."

Sam paused. Flora asked if she were still there. Sam said Steven had been involved with one of his students and she made a complaint about him, then dropped it. That's why he went back, to meet with the people at the university who were looking into it.

"You're talking about everyone except yourself," Flora said.

"I do that, don't I?"

Sam said she was wrong about things, about the past, about the hold the past can have and how it traps you and keeps you from moving forward. All the awful things she grew up with had ruined something in her, and made her put up defenses, which she supposed was a normal thing to happen, but in her case, the problem was that she made excuses for people and tried to smother them with understanding and love.

"Why is that a problem? I mean, the smothering part I get, but understanding and love aren't bad, are they?" Flora asked.

Sam didn't expect her mother to speak plainly. For years, she talked in circles and was impossible to pin down. Again, this might be Chuck's influence. Or her mother had finally grown up.

Sam said when she was young, she felt like she was an adult and her mother a child. Did that make sense? Flora said it did, and she wished it hadn't been that way, but she couldn't help things back then. She wasn't sure how well she could help things now, but that was beside the point. She asked Sam to continue and to try to explain why she called.

Sam said she felt like she was about to fall apart and couldn't let herself because no one would take care of her, not even Steven, especially not Steven. He seemed to nurture, at first, but fell into himself and his issues. People did that, of course, that was human nature. You couldn't fight it or change it. You just had to accept it.

"You don't need anyone to take care of you. You can take care of yourself," Flora said. She reminded Sam how tough she was, how she picked up and moved to LA all those years before. That took guts and wasn't something a weak, scared person did.

"But what if I *am* weak?"

"You're not. You were together with Timothy for a long time, then you got out. He's a drinker, right? They never change, not until they want to, and you must have seen that. So, you left. That took guts. Don't sell yourself short."

Flora suggested she talk to her father. He was a smart, solid guy.

"I thought you hated him," Sam said.

"No, no. I just couldn't let him in my life, way back when. But I reached out a couple of years ago. And no, it wasn't to ask for money. I owed him an apology, or at least an explanation for what I did."

"How did he take that?"

"I think he took it well."

Sam said she called him just the other day, in fact. He tried to get her to focus on what she wanted out of her relationship with Steven. That was easier said than done.

"Sometimes the best thing is to do nothing and focus on staying calm," Flora said. She said she was sorry she hadn't been more help, but right then she needed to get going. Chuck was waiting for her.

"Call me again, if you want to," Flora said.

"Okay. Thanks."

Angie appeared in the living room where Sam had made her call. She said she'd come by a few minutes ago and heard her on the phone. Sam said she was talking to her mother.

"You're kidding," Angie said.

"I needed to tell her things."

"I thought you didn't want anything to do with her. Didn't you tell her to leave you alone?"

Sam said she had, last year. She never meant for it to be permanent, and Flora didn't take it that way either, given how willing she was to talk.

"What did you talk about?" Angie asked.

Sam explained about feeling trapped and wanting to do nothing for a while.

Angie said she should do exactly that. She and Timothy could run things.

"Don't be silly. I'm fine," Sam said.

An hour later Steven texted to say he was booked on the first flight out in the morning.

Great! she texted back.

She was on the sofa with a volume of Emily Dickinson, her favorite whenever she felt down. The snow fell lightly. The storm would be over soon.

Her phone rang. It was Martin. He said he heard the weather was wild there and he wanted to make sure everyone was all right. Sam said they were, that Steven was in Dunston dealing with that student's accusations which she dropped and was due back tomorrow.

"Glad it all worked out," he said.

Sam said nothing. Then, "I have a weird question for you. Did your mother make excuses for people? I mean, did she overlook the lousy things they did just for the sake of keeping the peace?"

Martin paused. He said he supposed most people did that, at one time or another. He certainly had, during his marriage. As to his mother, well, she could be pretty crusty and cold if she didn't get what she wanted. She didn't accommodate people so much as get out of their way. Or rather, she moved them out of her way.

"Why do you ask?" he asked.

"I don't know. I'm just trying to get to know her. Posthumously, of course."

"I think you've got a bit of a crush."

"I just wish I were more like her."

Martin seemed not to know what to say to that. He told her to let him know if she needed anything. She promised to and thanked him for checking in.

"Try not to worry so much," he said.

"About what?"

"Everything."

"Okay."

They hung up.

The time she spent with Dickinson made her feel better, and Angie's stew was delicious. Timothy said he was going to head back to Dunston tomorrow night. That was the earliest he could get a plane. The trains were delayed by the weather, too, so he was stuck for the moment. He'd talked to Mark who said he got in a fight with a kid at school. Mark said he didn't start it, a teacher said he did. Mark punched the other kid and sent him home with a bloody nose. Timothy had been trying to find out what happened, what caused it, that is, and Mark clammed up at that point. So, he was going to see him in person and try to sort it out. He didn't care what Melissa thought of that. He was the kid's father, and that's what he was going to do.

"Hear, hear," Angie said.

Sam did the dishes, then said she was going to pack up and take her stuff back to the town home. She thought the roads were clear enough.

Angie looked disappointed for a moment, then said she was glad they'd hung out.

Sam told Timothy she'd wash the long underwear and shirt she borrowed and send them home with Angie if that were all right. He said sure, no problem.

She organized her things, and Angie came to see her off. She said Timothy was holed up in his room.

"Tell him I hope everything works out with Mark," Sam said.

"I'll call you tomorrow."

"Good deal."

The roads were slick and treacherous. What should have been a twenty-minute drive took twice as long because, although there were few cars out, the drivers all seemed petrified and crawled along at about twenty miles an hour. Steven was right about the general state of snow removal there. It was handled much better in Dunston.

She parked, took her things, locked the Jeep and found a note on the door saying a pipe had burst, the water was shut off, and someone was on the way to fix it. Inside, the kitchen floor was wet.

"Oh, crap," she said. Her first thought was it was her fault for not being there when it happened and realized that was ridiculous. Steven would find a way to blame her, though she had no specific reason to think so.

She hung up her coat, dropped her pack on the sofa and went next door. A short man with a long ponytail answered her knock.

"Hi, neighbor!" he said.

"Hi. I don't suppose you have a wet vac, do you? There's water all over my kitchen floor."

"Come in."

His place was bigger and nicer than theirs. His living room windows looked into the greenspace behind the building. Sam's view was of the alley.

"Dave," he said.

"I'm Sam."

He looked up at her. He was in his mid-forties, judging from the gray streaks in his hair. He wore a flannel shirt and jeans.

"Short for Samantha," she said.

"Like the character in that sixties show."

Sam didn't know what he was talking about.

He said the plumber would bring the wet vac. At least, he assumed he would. He could call and confirm if she wanted, but then two guys were at the door, saying they'd come for the pipe. Dave didn't know where it was, exactly. He heard the water running and thought the people next door were taking a bath or something, but it went on too long, so he checked the water heaters in the garage to see if one had rusted out and they were both fine. That's when he found the master valve and closed it. Sam said there was water in her kitchen, then took them over so they could check it out. They put down a plastic sheet so they could come and go without getting the rest of the floor wet.

After letting them in, she wasn't sure what to do, so she picked up her pack, returned to Dave's and thanked him for calling the plumber.

He offered her a cup of tea and said the kettle was already full. When she said nothing, he explained that was a lucky thing because the water was off. She said tea was fine. He asked her to take a seat at his kitchen counter. It was covered with glossy, colorful travel brochures. She asked if he were planning a trip.

"It's my parents' fiftieth wedding anniversary, and I'm surprising them. I haven't decided where they want to go yet," he said. She realized his accent wasn't local and remarked on it.

"Indiana, by way of Ohio," he said. "You?"

"Dunston, New York."

"Oh, right. Thompson told me that."

Thompson was the man Sam and Steven rented the townhome from. He was a professor at MIT and was on his own sabbatical somewhere in Europe.

Dave said, anyway, his folks were hard-working types, never traveled much, and he wanted to thank them for their support. Sam asked what support he meant.

"I own couple of galleries that specialize in Native American pottery. After art school I had trouble finding my way, and my dad suggested I get into the retail end of the art world. It took a long time, but it worked out," he said.

He told her it was fascinating stuff. The tribes in New Mexico were arranged in pueblos, not reservations, because they were traditionally farming and ranching communities. They were settled, not itinerant, in other words. Sam said she didn't know anything about New Mexico and would like to visit one day. Dave took down a couple of mugs from a cabinet and a box of citrus-spiced black tea. He asked Sam if that were all right. She said it sounded perfect.

He asked what she did.

"I'm a poet. Or, trying to become one," she said.

"Which is it?"

"I guess I'm a poet."

He asked if she'd just returned from a trip because he noticed their car had been gone. Sam explained about Steven needing to be back in Dunston and staying over at Martin's apartment.

"The Sewell? I know that building. It's a classic," Dave said.

The sound of hammering reached them through the wall. Sam said she hoped they weren't making too much of a mess over there. She wasn't in the mood to clean up after people. Then she wondered aloud if she should let Thompson know what had happened. It was strange not to have met him, since they were living there, with his things all around. Well, with their own things, too, of course.

"He'd want to be told," Dave said.

"I suppose we have to pay for it."

"He'll reimburse you, I'm sure."

She removed her teabag and put it in the saucer Dave had set on the counter between them. Her shoulders hurt from that narrow bed she slept in, though it had felt quite comfortable at the time.

"They'll be charging overtime for this," Sam said.

"I expect they will."

She sipped her tea. It had an overlay of orange and cinnamon that reminded her of fall holidays she looked forward to and was always disappointed by. She shivered, though the room was warm. Dave noticed and asked if she wanted to borrow a sweater.

"No, thanks, I'm fine. You know, it's funny, I was just thinking. My mother lives in Florida now, and the man who owns the apartment I was staying at is vacationing in the Bahamas."

Dave waited for her to say more and when she didn't, he said both places sounded tempting in the middle of a Boston winter.

"I've never been to either," Sam said. "I've never been anywhere, except LA."

"That's quite a distance from upstate New York."

"In some ways, it wasn't far enough."

The mechanical sounds next door paused, resumed, then paused.

When her phone rang deep inside her backpack, she didn't move. Dave said nothing at first, then asked if that were hers or his. Sam said unless they had the same ringtone it was hers. The muffled William Tell overture continued to trill cheerfully. Sam got off the kitchen stool and pulled out the phone.

"Steven," she said.

"Hey, thought I'd call and check in."

"Hi."

He said he was having a dull evening on his own. She asked if he'd seen Lyall and Claire yet. He said he was due there first thing in the morning. She said she thought he was getting an early flight, and he said he pushed it back until just before noon. He asked what she was doing. She explained about the broken pipe and being over at the neighbor's townhome while it was getting fixed. Steven said she shouldn't pay the plumbers but ask them to contact Thompson about it directly, or Bethany, the property manager. That was even better. He'd text Sam her contact information.

"I hadn't taken my boots off yet. Can you imagine how nasty it would have been to walk into cold water in my stocking feet?" she asked.

He asked how Timothy and Angie were. Sam said they were fine, and that Timothy was heading back to Dunston tomorrow. His son got in trouble in school, and he had to get to the bottom of it.

"Did I know he had a son?" Steven asked.

Sam couldn't remember if she told him. She said Mark was twelve or thirteen, an iffy age for boys. Steven agreed. He said he hoped things worked out okay. Then she said she'd called her mother.

"Really?" Steven asked.

"Yup."

"Where does she live, again?"

"Florida."

"How is she?"

"Fine. Smarter. The sun must be good for her brain."

"I thought you didn't talk to her."

"Well, I don't usually, but I did today."

Steven said he was glad she did. That is, if she were glad she did.

Dave had discreetly left the kitchen during their phone conversation, but was back then, trying to get her attention. Sam told Steven she had to go and to call her in the morning if he wanted.

She put her phone away. Dave said the plumbers were replacing the broken pipe and that the wet vac was on the way. Sam took her pack and went over with him in tow. She dropped her pack back on the sofa and stared forlornly at a wide, ragged-edged hole in the kitchen wall. One of the plumbers approached Sam.

"Pipe wasn't insulated properly. I put that on the builder. Anyhow, we replaced the broken section, then wrapped what we could reach. Your best bet would be to have us come back and wrap everything, but that's on the pricey side," he said.

Sam said she was just the tenant, but she'd pass along his recommendation. Then she asked when the wet vac was due. The plumber checked his cell phone. He said it wouldn't be too long, and that he and his buddy were going to go to the take-out place a block away. They hadn't had dinner yet. He'd get the water on before they left. If she noticed the pipe leaking, she should text him right away. Her neighbor had the number. When they left, she told Dave it was her turn to offer him something, but she couldn't get into the kitchen. He mentioned the wine bottles and glasses on the sideboard in the dining room, and Sam said, why not?

Dave inspected the bottles and said someone had good taste. Sam explained that Martin, the man who owned the apartment in the Sewell, had been thoughtful enough to stock his kitchen and pantry for her friends who'd come to visit, and she'd taken a couple of bottles home with her.

He opened a Beaujolais and poured them each a generous glass. Sam gestured to the living room. He helped himself to one end of the sofa. She rearranged the logs in the fireplace, added some kindling from the basket on the hearth, and lit a match.

Living in the glow of fire

That could be the first line of a new poem about a time when all people had was fire to keep them warm, sit and read by. She watched the flames rise and considered.

Flames dance with rage or hope,

Depending on how sore the heart

Dave asked if she were all right. She said she was formulating something and apologized for being rude.

"Not at all. I'm the one who should apologize for taking up your time. I appreciate you letting me keep you company. I should have stopped by before to introduce myself, but I never found the right moment," he said. She sat on the other end of the sofa.

She asked him to tell her more about New Mexico. He said it was a wonderful place, different from New England, dry, high altitude, and sunny most of the time. He took a trip there in college with a friend whose family had been in Taos for generations. One day he hoped to move down, buy a home, and work more closely with the artists he represented. His parents were still in Ohio, and New Mexico felt particularly far from there. They wouldn't be around forever, of course. But he didn't like to think about that.

"You're close," Sam said.

"Yes."

"Siblings?"

There was only a sister, and they didn't talk. She was older and treated him badly when he was young. She lived in Michigan, and so was closer to his parents, but didn't see them much. Her disaffection was particularly hard for his mother. He supposed his father suffered from it, too, but he never spoke of it. Dave always felt it was his job to make up for his sister's failings, though, at the end of the day, he supposed that didn't make much sense.

"It makes perfect sense," Sam said. She asked if he had ever married, and then said he didn't have to answer that, if he didn't want to. It wasn't any of her business.

"Briefly, when I was young. It didn't last long. I loved her very much, but it was too hard to share myself, I guess. I know you must think I'm quite a talker, but in those days, I had much less to say, and she wanted to talk about everything. Listening wasn't enough. She said I made her feel lonely."

Sam nodded.

Flames drop, the log burns slowly through the night

"And you?" Dave asked.

"Me, what? Married? No, though my last boyfriend proposed to me a few weeks before we broke up."

"Bad timing."

"Yes."

Dave asked if she minded if he helped himself to a bit more wine. She said to go ahead. She turned around and looked again at the hole in the wall. Steven might be able to patch it himself. But then, he wasn't handy.

The text from Steven with the property manager's number had come in some time before, and Sam wrote her a note about the situation.

She closed with, Waiting on the wet vac. Will look into repairing the wall tomorrow. Can you contact Thompson, or should I?

Before she could put the phone down a call came.

"What do you mean, broken pipe? Are you kidding me?" Bethany asked.

"They fixed it."

"And there's a giant hole in the wall?"

"It's pretty big, yeah."

Dave answered the knock on the door and two different plumbers wheeled the wet vac in. Sam said it was about to get noisy where she was, and asked if they could talk again in the morning.

"He's going to kill me," Bethany said.

"Who? Thompson? Why?" Sam asked.

"He's my ex and only hired me to manage the place because I begged him."

"It's not your fault the pipe burst. The plumber said it wasn't insulated properly in the first place. It must have happened when the place was being built."

"Well, the fact that it broke on my watch will be an issue."

Thompson sounded like a jerk.

Sam asked about getting reimbursed. Bethany said to text her all the figures and she'd take care of it. They hung up.

The wet vac started up, and Dave said he was heading home. He handed her his glass, which still had wine in it, and Sam put it on the coffee table. The plumber running the wet vac steered it around the kitchen. It rolled along slowly, as he pushed the hose and attachment along the base molding. Sam put her pack in her office and turned on her laptop in case she needed to use it later. She went into the bedroom to change into a pair of sweatpants. She brushed her hair and remembered what it was like when it was still long and wild. On the bed was a small pile of clean laundry Steven had left. Sam folded it and put it away. The wet vac shut off and she went into the kitchen to check the floor. It was still damp around the edges. She got some paper towels and dabbed up what was left. The guy who'd been using the machine wheeled it back out, and his partner picked up the clipboard from where he dropped it on the kitchen counter. He wrote slowly. Sam checked the tile for any sign of buckling. She peered underneath the Viking range and discovered a ping-pong ball. She wondered about finding something to nudge it free and didn't want to bother.

The plumber broke off writing and stared down at her. He seemed surprised to see her there, on all fours. He said he needed her signature and asked how she would like to pay. She stood up, looked at the total, and signed her name.

"I'm in the wrong business," she said.

"What business are you in?"

"Poetry."

"Can't imaging you're rolling in it."

"No."

She went into her office for her wallet, came back and gave him her credit card. He said he didn't have a card reader, so he'd write down the number, and the girl in the office would run it in the morning.

"Okay," Sam said.

He said he could recommend a good drywaller if she wanted. She thought for a moment and said she wanted to wait until her boyfriend got back. He might have some ideas of his own.

"Sure," the plumber said. He folded up the plastic sheet and took it away with him.

Alone again, Sam returned to the living room, turned off the light, sat on the sofa, and gazed into the fire. She pictured Steven, bored in his hotel room. He might be on the bed, propped up with a book and his ankles crossed. His shoes were probably on. Did he feel relieved that Gail let him off the hook? Was he angry that she made the complaint in the first place?

Steven had traits he was unaware of, like how much he flirted. To him, it just seemed normal, something all men—and women— did most of the time. Sam didn't flirt, of that, she was sure. Both Timothy and Steven even said so. She never saw the point. If you were attracted to someone, then you found a way to be around them. Making suggestive remarks was an unnecessary distraction. It was also aggressive and demeaning. It made you an object, not a person. Only love made you a person.

It was the nineteenth of January, and they'd been in Boston for exactly two and a half weeks. The biggest frustration facing her before they came here was telling Steven she'd dropped out of school. Now she had his untold past to deal with, and her articulated one, namely Timothy.

Okay, so she was still in love with him. She could live with that. What upset her was seeing how much he'd changed and wishing—again—that had happened about six months ago.

Sam didn't realize it was after ten when she punched in Lavinia's number. Lavinia was awake and immediately concerned that something had happened to Timothy. Sam assured her he was fine, or he was when she last saw him, which was earlier that day and that in any case, he was returning home tomorrow to deal with his son.

"What about his son?" Lavinia asked.

"He got in trouble at school. Didn't he tell you?"

"He never tells me anything. Anyway, what's going on with you?"

Sam said she was sorting things out, something she'd never been good at. Lavinia said seeing Timothy again wouldn't have been easy, and, frankly, she'd advised him not to go up there with Angie and to let Sam have her space. Sam said she appreciated that, but it wasn't just Timothy. Steven got himself into a mess with a former student and was in Dunston, dealing with it.

"Mess? What sort of mess?" Lavinia asked. She was walking through her house; Sam could tell from the way her voice faded in and out depending on the strength of the cell signal.

Sam told her about the complaint. Lavinia asked how she felt about it. Sam said it happened before they met, and since then, as far as she knew, he'd been on the up and up.

"So, you trust him," Lavinia said.

"Honestly, I don't know."

Sam said another problem was that Steven worried so much about his career. He had mood swings and got upset easily when he was under pressure.

"The world gets handed to them on a silver platter, and they still wring their hands like old women," Lavinia said.

A spark flew from the burning log in the fireplace.

"I think in this case, with the complaint and all, Steven had a right to be worried. But he worries too much in general, and I can't seem to help him with that," Sam said.

"Maybe that's not your job."

"Maybe not."

Sam thanked her for her time and said she was sorry to call so late. Lavinia said it was no bother, she tended to stay up to all hours these days. Sam promised to call again when things were easier.

After they hung up, Sam sat while the fire gradually died down.

Tomorrow, she thought. Things will be better then.

Chapter Twelve

Sam was having lunch with Angie when Steven returned from Dunston. She hadn't said she'd be out, nor had she promised to be home waiting. She didn't return his text. After eating, Sam took Angie to the boutique that had once been The Turned Page, where she'd gotten the turquoise ring for herself just after arriving in town. Angie was enchanted and gave everything a close inspection. She chose a silk blouse whose pale gold color didn't suit her at all. She realized her mistake when she tried it on. Sam was tactful and said a scarf would help, but the salesclerk, the same one who sold Sam the ring said it was the wrong shade entirely. Angie's mood sagged after that, and to cheer her up, Sam bought her a slim silver bracelet Angie admired on their way out.

The day was clear and less cold than it had been since Sam moved there, or perhaps she was just acclimating. They walked arm-in-arm along the icy sidewalks that were salted only in places. The chill on her face seemed to improve Angie's spirits and she announced that she was breaking up with Matt permanently.

They stopped walking.

"I thought he asked you to come back, you said you would, then he wanted more time to think about things, and you thought you did too," Sam said.

"I know, and what I realized is that is that I don't trust him and never did, even when we moved in together. Oh, I wanted to and told myself I did. But the bottom line is he can't help himself where this woman is concerned and I'm sick of it."

They were in front of a bar that had a brick fireplace on one wall. Sam suggested they go in and get out of the cold. A glass of wine was what they needed. Angie said to make it a bottle, and she had herself a deal.

When they were half a bottle down, Angie's fortitude vanished, and she began to weep. Sam squeezed her hand. The server, a thin young man with acne, approached and asked if there were anything he could do. Sam said quietly that her friend was in the middle of a bad breakup, and she was sorry if she were causing a scene. The server said not to worry, sometimes it was best to cry it out.

Angie drew sympathetic glances from a pair of young women a few tables away. Even the bartender looked sad for her. Angie wound down and asked Sam to pour her another glass. Sam thought it wasn't a good idea but poured it anyway.

Another text from Steven came in asking where she was and if everything were all right. For a moment, Sam thought it was fair that he worry about her, but then she felt bad. She told Angie to give her a second, she had to make a quick call.

Steven didn't answer until the fifth ring, and Sam grew annoyed.

"Hello?" he said.

"Hi, welcome home."

"Where are you?"

"Out with Angie."

"You didn't take the car."

"I didn't want to deal with parking in Harvard Square."

They paused.

"When are you coming back?" he asked.

"In a bit. Angie's having a moment. I need to get her through it first."

"What happened?"

"I'll tell you later."

A group of students came into the bar, talking loudly.

"Sam, I want you to come home. I need to talk to you," Steven said.

"Soon."

"All right."

She hung up. Angie blew her nose and wondered if they should have something to eat. As Sam reminded her that they'd had lunch not long ago, she realized she'd been cruel to Steven, and rather than be flooded with remorse, she just felt numb. Angie noticed that she wasn't saying anything and asked her what was wrong.

Sam said she couldn't remember ever feeling this unclear about things. She always knew what she wanted, though not always how to get it. Angie asked her if she thought she made a mistake leaving Timothy. Sam sipped her wine and took a moment to answer.

"No. It wasn't bearable, the way things were. He was out of control, and I was caught up in the chaos," she said.

"Fair enough."

Sam realized that Angie was studying her.

"Do they all hate me? The family?" Sam asked.

"Of course not."

Angie said everyone had hoped for so long that Timothy would get it together and that Sam would help him. They never sat as a group and talked about it in those terms, but it was obvious.

When Sam moved out, they were worried that Timothy would go into a tailspin, which he more or less did, but they all understood that Sam had had enough. Now, he was doing better, and everyone was relieved.

"You don't sound relieved," Sam said.

"I am, sometimes, but other times I realized it's just a matter of time before he hits the wall again. That's how it is with addicts. He's got a lot more to do to put alcohol behind him, and he hasn't done it yet."

Sam said she didn't want to talk about it anymore. She asked Angie if she were ready to go and Angie said sure. Angie asked if they could cork the wine so she could bring it back with her.

The server brought them a paper bag for the wine and their bill. Angie paid. She said it was the least she could do. Outside the bar, she said she was pretty sure how to get back to the apartment. Sam said she dreaded seeing Steven, and Angie said it would be okay and that she should call later with an update.

When she returned, Steven was in the kitchen cooking. She removed her coat, hung it up, and went to him. There were circles below his eyes, and he was pale as if he were coming down with something. They embraced.

"You look tired," she said.

"I am."

"What are you making?"

"Vegetable soup."

"I can take over, if you like."

"It's okay."

She said she was sorry about the big hole in the wall. He thanked her for taking care of the broken pipe. He asked if she sent in her receipts to Bethany what's-her-name and she said no, not yet.

She'd do it promptly. He said he wasn't sure where to find a drywaller, and Sam said they could just look online.

She put the dirty dishes from the sink into the dishwasher. Steven chopped garlic on the cutting board.

"I've run into some trouble with the department," he said.

"What? You said Gail dropped the complaint!"

"There are other issues that have now come into focus as a result of that."

"Like what?"

"Some poor student evaluations."

"All professors must have a few of those from time to time."

"Mine carry more weight."

He dropped the chopped garlic into the pot.

"Why?" she asked.

"Because Baker wants me gone."

"Donald Baker?

"The very same."

Professor Baker and Steven were hired at the same time, he said. Two bright new Harvard PhDs. Steven got tenure first, and Baker was delayed a year. Steven got his pick of courses to teach, Baker got what he didn't want.

"That was a long time ago. Why does he still care?" Sam asked.

"He's got a lot of friends in high places, as it were. He's convinced them that I'm too hard on my students and that I rely on my teaching assistants too much."

Sam asked him to get to the point.

"They could make it clear I don't have a future there."

She was about to offer to speak on his behalf and say how important his support had been to her as an artist and stopped herself. She stared into his soup. It was brown and bubbling.

"He's got an axe to grind, for sure, but there must be something more to it. Find out what's behind it all, what his real issue is and see if you can fix it," she said.

"Oh, I know what his issue is."

"What?"

"He thinks I plagiarized part of my doctoral thesis."

"Did you?"

Steven looked out the window over the sink.

"Steven?"

"I improperly cited one of my sources. My committee didn't take exception to it."

"Did they even know?"

"I don't think so."

"But Baker knew."

"Obviously."

How petty, Sam thought, yet an academic career was built on words, and their origin was always scrutinized. She was glad everything she wrote belonged to her alone. One day scholars might quote or refer to her and she hoped they'd do it correctly but if not, their error wouldn't lessen her work one bit.

"He needs to put on his big boy pants," Sam said.

"I'd suggest it, but I don't think that would go over too well."

Sam asked how much time had gone by since the disagreement. Steven said almost ten years.

"So, he's just been waiting for a chance to mess you up?" she asked.

"Let's just say he's been keeping his eye on me."

Sam reiterated that he had to find a way to bring Baker around, or at least to lessen his influence. Build a coalition of support. Tap anyone and everyone who owed him a favor or who saw him as an asset to the department. Steven said his best shot was to write a compelling, thoroughly researched book about Clara Levy, Edith Alistair, and The Hedgerow Press. Women in the arts was a powerful topic these days. That's why he chose her, in part.

"But that will take months. What if they move against you now?" Sam asked.

"They'll wait until the fall, at least."

"Well, in that case, they might not do anything."

"I suppose you're right."

He asked about the papers she'd sorted for him, and she said they were at Martin's.

"What's the point of putting them together and then leaving them there?" he asked.

"I forgot, okay?"

She said she'd go get them, if he liked, but honestly if he could wait until tomorrow, she would appreciate it. He said tomorrow would be fine.

She asked how it went with Lyall and Claire. Were they taking good care of things? Steven said they seemed to be, but they moved the furniture around in the living room, which he found disorienting.

"The soup won't be ready for a while. Let's go sit and have a fire. I'll put on some music if you want," he said.

Sam said music would be lovely. They didn't listen to it much at home, but Thompson had a great sound system, though of course they'd been asked to handle it with extreme caution. Steven pulled out a Coltrane CD, Sam put fresh logs in the fire and lit them.

They sat on the sofa, and he put his arm around her. He said he was sorry for everything, and Sam said it was all right, he couldn't possibly have known about Gail. He asked her if she wanted him to tell her about Molly and she said no, she didn't.

Then, she said she had something to tell him.

"It's Timothy, isn't it?" he asked.

"What? No."

"Oh, okay."

"I want to talk about how I grew up. It's been on my mind a lot lately."

"What, now?"

"Yes, now."

Steven removed his arm from her shoulder. He said he was in a rocky headspace, and he wasn't going to be able to give her words his full attention. Could she hold off until things settled down? He promised he'd listen carefully to whatever she wanted to say then.

"Would you have listened if I wanted to talk about Timothy?" she asked.

"Yes."

"Why?"

"Because that affects me."

"So, if it's something important to me that doesn't affect you, you don't want to listen?"

"Well . . ."

The music played, upbeat yet jagged, intentionally uneven.

"Am I right?" she asked.

"Sam."

"Do you even see me here?"

Steven told her to be fair. She knew he was invested in her work. He asked about it often, or didn't she appreciate that?

She said, of course, she appreciated it. His encouragement meant a lot. But now *he* had to be fair and realize how things might look to her.

"What things?" he asked.

"I'm your little trophy. The promising student you took under your wing. Only, I dropped out, and I'm not so promising anymore. You're embarrassed by me now, where before, I reflected well on your skills as a mentor. I bet you're missing that ego boost now, after Gail and Baker. See, I'm the disappointment here, because I'm just an ordinary person, toiling away at my chosen art, writing things that never had anything to do with you and never will. Except to express rage."

"Come on."

She went into the bedroom. She stood, listening to the blood slam idiotically in her ears. The desire to flee was familiar and she wasn't sure she should yield to it. Yet she was exhausted by constantly being careful, measured, and steadfast. Her clothes were neatly arranged in the closet and dresser. Packing them took no time. Her office was easy to scoop up, too. Her laptop, journals, and handful of books fit easily in her backpack. While she worked, Steven sat on the sofa, with Coltrane still in the background. When she tried to meet his eye, she found him staring into the fire.

"Steven," she said.

The CD ended. Across the silence, the logs cracked. The music started over, just as sad and jaunty as before.

"I'm taking the car. You'll have to come get it at Martin's. I'll let you know when."

"Why?"

"Why will you need to get the car, or why am I leaving?"

"Don't be stupid."

"Oh, I'm not. Never have been."

After she wheeled her suitcase out and the door closed behind her, she thought he called her name.

As she drove, not one tear fell. Her phone stayed silent. Of course, he wouldn't try her now. He was too busy feeling sorry for himself.

She unlocked the door to the apartment, brought in her suitcase, then took off her coat and draped it over a chair in the foyer, though the closet was right there. She dropped her pack on the floor. The apartment was quiet. Then she heard music from the built-in speakers overhead, Nina Simone, if she had to guess. But why was it so faint? That kind of vocalist needed volume.

The living room, dining room, and library were empty. In the kitchen she found Angie and Timothy at the table, snacking on popcorn.

"What are you doing here?" Angie asked, her mouth full.

"Starting over."

"What?"

"I left him. I'm done."

"Oh, my God, Sam, why?"

Sam helped herself to a chair and said this whole time Steven looked on her as a prize to show off to his colleagues, the ignorant young woman taken under his wing and introduced to the ethereal world of poetry.

"You were writing before you met him," Timothy said.

"Yes, but I had no ambition."

"Bull. You were determined to make it as a poet. That was one of the first things you ever told me."

Sam didn't want to think about those days.

"And it's got nothing to do with that student who filed the complaint?" Angie asked.

"No. I mean, I didn't like finding out about her, and that he might still have feelings for her."

"So, it was a combination of things," Angie says.

"That all come down to one thing. I can't live with him."

Sam poured herself a glass of water and drank it at the sink. She returned to the table.

"God, what a week," Angie said. She picked something out of her teeth. She said she hadn't made any plans to get back to Dunston, and the more she thought about it, the less appealing it sounded. Her dad was managing the bar beautifully, from all accounts. Sam glanced at Timothy. He said his flight was in a couple of hours.

"Whoa, hey, don't do that," Timothy said, and handed Sam a napkin to dry her eyes.

"Don't worry about it. I always cry over big life changes."

"Did you cry when you left me?"

Angie asked him why it mattered now. Timothy said it didn't. He put his plate in the sink and said he was going to go pack up his stuff. When he was gone, Angie encouraged Sam to talk it out. Sam said there really wasn't anything to talk out. Angie said that in that case, she was going to go read in the library and asked if Sam wanted to come too. Sam said she might stay there and make herself a cup of tea. Angie said tea would be good for the soul.

When she was by herself, her mind fell into a soft, unfocused state, full of random images and pieces of conversations with Steven. Her temporary joy at moving into his place caused brief heartache. Regret over what she said back at the townhome overwhelmed any attempt to think clearly, so she let her mind go on wandering. It soon settled on her grandparents—her grandfather telling her about caterpillars and butterflies; her grandmother explaining how to tie her shoes. Not all their words were cross. They were gentle when she was young, then they changed. They became afraid of her, afraid she couldn't be cowed and terrorized, the way Flora was. Abuse kept someone close and prevented them from finding confidence to leave. When Flora got pregnant, instead of offering moral support, they condemned, because to be kind would be to foster hope for a better future. Their nutty religion, some bizarre Baptist offshoot, had something to do with it, but really, they didn't want to be alone.

She shivered, though the heat from the radiator was robust. The cold was everywhere, bearing down on her, pulling her into a tight ball of her own stupid mistakes.

Her phone rang. It was Steven. She didn't answer, then she listened to his message.

"I don't know what you think I've done or haven't done, but I want you to take time to think this all through." He sounded worn out. She didn't listen to the rest.

In the library, Angie was lying on the sofa with a book. Sam asked what she was reading.

"*Age of Innocence,*" Angie said.

"Since when are you a Wharton fan?"

"Is that who wrote it?" Angie looked at the cover.

"Is it just me, or is it cold in here?"

Angie said the place felt almost too warm to her and Sam might be coming down with something. Sam said no, she was getting out from under something.

"Good one," Angie said.

Timothy appeared with his pack to say goodbye. Sam asked if he wanted a ride to the airport and he said a cab was on the way.

"Any message for the clan?" he asked Angie.

"Just send my love. Tell them I don't know when I'll be back. Dad knows where to find me if he's got bar-related questions. If you see Matt, well, you know."

"Got it."

Timothy blew Sam a kiss and then he was gone.

Angie sat up and put her book on the table. She said she was sorry she brought Timothy up, and hoped it had nothing to do with what happened with Steven, though from the sound of it, it seems like she just woke up and realized she was with the wrong person.

"He wouldn't let me talk about myself," Sam said.

"You mean he talked about himself all the time?"

"No. I said I wanted to tell him about how I grew up and he said he was too distracted to listen closely."

"God."

Angie knew that story by heart. Sam had been open about everything when they became friends and often thought it might have been Angie's training in social work that made her such a good listener.

Beyond the window a single cloud held the dropping sun effortlessly. A moment later, its color had dulled. Sam's head hurt. She thought she should take something for it.

Focus on your breathing.

That helped, but she was still on edge. She told herself to think about Edith, and what she'd do in a situation like this. Just what Sam was doing, but she'd feel a lot better about it. Edith wouldn't look back.

Her phone rang.

"Not again," Sam said, but it was Melissa's number on the screen. Sam answered and Melissa apologized for bothering her, but she was trying to reach Timothy, and he wasn't answering his phone. She heard from Lavinia that he was up in Boston with Angie visiting. Sam asked if something had happened to Mark, Melissa said no, and Sam said Timothy was on his way to the airport and would be back home later tonight.

Sam asked if there were anything she could do. Melissa said no, not really, then paused. She said Mark got in trouble at school right after Winter Break and was suspended for a week. She had to work, which meant he was on his own. She got home today to find him out somewhere, without his phone. He came back not long after, and they had a huge fight about it, and, well, she was really hoping Timothy could talk to him or try to straighten him, though at the end of the day, he might not be able to do anything. And she was only getting him involved because she heard he quit drinking.

"He seems to have cut way back," Sam said.

"I'm sorry. I shouldn't have laid all that on you."

"No, it's fine. Timothy told us Mark had gotten in trouble at school. He didn't say anything about him getting suspended. I guess he didn't know about that."

"I'm sure Mark didn't tell him."

"Probably not."

"Anyhow, what's up with you?"

Sam said she'd just broken up with her boyfriend, but otherwise she was fine.

"Yikes! Sorry," Melissa said.

Sam said the shock hadn't hit her yet, though she had a weepy moment a little while ago. Melissa said whenever she broke up with someone it took forever to recover, so it was good that her boyfriend wanted to get married. Not that marriages didn't fail, that wasn't what she was saying. Only this seemed like a better bet than any of her past relationships.

"Wow. Congratulations," Sam said.

"Thanks."

"When's the wedding?"

"Oh, who knows? He just asked me the day before yesterday."

Sam wondered if the increased presence of the boyfriend in Melissa's life had anything to do with Mark acting up.

Melissa asked if she'd be moving back to Dunston now. Sam said she would but didn't know when. She needed a vacation first.

"Go somewhere warm," Melissa said. They promised to talk again soon and then hung up.

Angie asked who called. Sam told her. Angie said it was amazing that they were friends.

"She's a good person," Sam said. Then she added Timothy's obsession with her last summer can't have been easy.

"For whom? You, or her?" Angie asked.

"Both of us, but more so for her. And for him too, of course."

Sam said he fell for Melissa hard all those years ago, and whether it was all in his mind, or something well-thought out, didn't matter. He suffered for it.

"Is love ever well-thought out? Or just instinctive?" Angie asked. She was lounging comfortably on the sofa. Timothy's departure had loosened something in her.

"A combination. Or a sequence. You get attracted, don't think, then think a lot, then the other part of you takes over again. Like a seesaw."

Angie nodded. She asked how she was feeling about the Steven situation now.

"Stupid," Sam said.

"Why? How were you supposed to know what he was really like?"

"Not for that, but because I stayed down too long on the seesaw. I didn't take enough time to think anything through. I just wanted so much to end things with Timothy, and there was Steven, so eager to get something going with me. You know the old saying, 'too good to be true.' Or something like that."

"I don't think that applies here. If anything, it should be 'look before you leap.'"

"Yeah."

Angie said it wasn't like she got knocked up by the guy, or lent him a ton of money, or went into business with him. And it didn't sound like she'd fallen madly in love either, so she needed to chill, pull herself together, and move on.

Sam nodded.

"You're the long-term type. I know, because I am too," Angie said.

"Though forever is a fantasy, when you think about."

"Oh, I don't know. People stay together forever, don't they?"

"Sometimes. Even if they shouldn't."

Sam said she wondered how Steven was, if he were sad, or angry, or scared. Angie asked her to think about herself, for a change. What did she want out of life? What did she want right this minute?

"To be somewhere warm," Sam said.

"Man, that sounds good."

Sam realized the music wasn't playing anymore and asked Angie why not. Angie said Timothy turned it off. He didn't want it on in the first place. They'd argued about it, and Angie told him to stick it.

She said her twin sisters had texted, wanting to know why she was in Boston in the middle of winter. Sam asked how they were doing, and Angie said they were the same as ever, though Marta just got a new role as a housewife, which struck her as hilarious, given that she never cleaned a thing in her life. Sam thought being an actor would be wonderful—all those lives to wear for a while and hang up again at the end of the day.

Sam's phone rang and when she saw Steven's number, she went into Edith's office and picked up but didn't say hello. Steven didn't notice. He launched right in.

"I don't know how many times I have to say this: I'm sorry," he said.

"You didn't say it once."

"I'm saying it now."

He told her to come home. Then he asked her to. She said she didn't have a home except the place she was standing in then. She'd felt at home in Dunston, but there were other people in that house there. Claire and Lyall were lovely, well Claire was, so she didn't mind too much. Not that she had any right to mind anything. It wasn't her house.

"I'm sorry I've been so distracted with everything," he said.

"The grant delay you couldn't help. The complaint you brought on yourself. Where Baker is concerned, you have options, but I don't think you want to avail yourself of any of them. If I were to get psychiatric, I'd say you have a latent wish to get fired or start a new career or something. Maybe that's bull. All I know is, if someone tried to take something away from me, I'd fight like hell to keep it."

"That's how I feel about you."

"I took myself away. Because you won't listen to me."

"So, tell me whatever it was that was so important."

"No. Not over the phone. Maybe not ever. At least not until you figure out why my issues have no place in your life. I'm not some two-dimensional cardboard character you trot out when the stage set changes."

He talked some more, and she didn't listen. Then she said she had to go and hung up.

The box of papers she'd arranged for him was on the floor near where she stood. The urge to kick it over was strong, yet she resisted. She went back to the living room where Angie was on her phone. She sounded cheerful and upbeat. Sam worried that she was talking to Matt, and they'd somehow patched everything up, then Angie ended the call and with her phone still in her hand turned to Sam and said, "Guess what? We're going to Florida!"

"What?"

"I'd been thinking about it, so I called my mom to see if she wanted to come too."

"To Florida?"

"Yes, to Florida. I just said that. She's buying the tickets, and you know what that means. First class, baby!"

"For me too?"

"Yes. Aren't you listening to me?"

"Why Florida?"

"Are you kidding me right now? It's eighty degrees down there, or something."

"Where in Florida?"

"Oh, I don't know. Mom's keen to check out Miami, so probably there."

Angie stood up and did a brief victory dance.

"Sunshine. Beaches. Oh, I don't have a bathing suit!" Angie said.

"Buy one there."

"I need to lose five pounds first."

"When are we going?"

"The day after tomorrow."

"That's not a lot of time to lose five pounds."

"Yeah, forget that. I'm not looking to impress anyone anyway."

Sam sat down. Angie asked her what was wrong. Sam said she wasn't sure she should go.

"Why not?" Angie asked.

"Oh, I don't know. I won't be good company."

"I bet you cheer up in no time. Now come on, snap out of it!"

To be where you could go outside without a coat on sounded wonderful. Sam had never set foot in the ocean, even when she lived in LA, and now was her chance.

A list of tasks came into focus, most of them to do with closing up the apartment, since it would make sense for her to go back to Dunston, not Cambridge, after the trip. She'd ask Martin for guidance there. She'd call her mother, too, and say they should meet for coffee or one of those inane tropical drinks with the tiny paper umbrellas. Her mother might say it was an odd twist of fate that Lavinia chose a vacation spot that was a stone's throw from where she lived; she might say she didn't have time for Sam; she might resume asking for money.

It was a chance Sam was willing to take. What was that saying of her grandmother's? When God closes a door, He opens a window? Flora was the window, and Steven was the door.

Chapter Thirteen

Sam assumed that she and Angie would fly directly to Miami, but Lavinia insisted that they go via Newark, where she would meet them. She could handle the flight from Dunston on her own, but for the longer leg she needed company. She was terrified. Sam wasn't an experienced flyer either, the trip out and back from LA years before her only time in the air, but she wasn't nervous about it. Angie had only flown twice before, too, when she and Matt went out to Pittsburgh, and that plane was smaller, dinky, in fact, with no meal service. The flight down from Boston had only a beverage service, but that suited Angie just fine, thank you. She had two glasses of wine, then the flight attendant suggested she didn't have time for another. The next leg wouldn't board for three and half hours, and Lavinia wasn't due for another ninety minutes. This information caused Angie's mood to suffer. She complained about the arrangements, although she'd agreed to them. Sam reminded her they were traveling free of charge and Angie reminded her she had to pay for her drinks.

"Hardly a deal breaker," Sam said. They sat in a coffee shop where throngs of people came and went up the concourse.

Angie said the last communication from Matt had been harsh, and she was taken aback because anger wasn't something he usually expressed.

"He said I was a terrible person, and he wished he'd never met me," she said.

"Not too original, is he?"

Sam could tell Angie hoped she'd talk about Steven in the spirit of solidarity, but Sam couldn't share that space right now. For one thing, her situation was different in that she hadn't been desperately in love. Or, in love at all.

The worst part was knowing that at the time and not caring. She'd been too swept up in that lovely, brand-new life she was handed. She even loved being treated like a protégé. When she published a group of poems and then another, Steven seemed glad, then less glad. She went up the curve faster than he expected, rendering his guidance useless. That was hard to see at first. Now it was clear. As was his lack of interest in anything else about her, particularly what let her write in the first place—her childhood.

Lavinia called Angie and asked where the hell she was. Angie told her how to find them, and a few minutes later Lavinia sauntered into the coffee shop wearing a fur coat and a pair of smart, black boots. Sam and Angie stared at her as she sat down. She moved slowly and deliberately, and before either of them could say anything, she explained that her doctor had given her a mild sedative for the trip.

Sam asked how the flight had been. Lavinia removed her coat and fingered the lapis pendant which lay down the front of her green silk blouse and said the plane was small and the trip was bumpy. Timothy drove her to Dunston airport. She got the feeling he wanted to come along, and she told him it was a girls-only vacay.

Lavinia's phone rang. It was Potter.

"Yeah, I made it to Newark. What? I don't know. Ask her yourself." They talked for a few more minutes and hung up. Lavinia said he couldn't find his bowling shoes. The housekeeper must have put them away somewhere.

"Bowling?" Angie asked.

"He's joined a league. Isn't that hilarious?"

Sam's phone dinged. Steven had left a voice message saying he just brought in the mail and found an envelope from her with the key to Martin's apartment, plus the extra set he'd made for Angie. Naturally, he was curious, so he went by Martin's and found the place empty. There was more she didn't listen to. She put her phone away.

When they boarded the plane, Lavinia was confused about which seats were theirs, despite Angie repeating the numbers clearly. They were all in the same row, two window seats and one on the aisle. Lavinia took one of the window seats and before Sam could speak, Angie claimed the other. Sam settled in on the aisle next to Lavinia, enjoying the generous first-class legroom, and Lavinia took an eye mask from her purse, slipped it over her head, and pulled it neatly into place.

As they taxied and rose gracefully into the air, Sam promised herself not to think about Steven and thought about him the whole way south, except when the cloud banks visible through Lavinia's window gathered golden light. As a child she thought angels might live in clouds, or were clouds, and learning later in school the scientific descriptions of them was a letdown. The man next to Angie tried to engage her in conversation. Angie plugged in her earbuds and listened to podcasts on her phone. Even so, the man kept talking about his dry-cleaning business and a new option he was exploring in Miami.

Steven would have trouble adjusting to her absence. His work should become his focus, but he'd find it hard. There was no one to talk to about it. The times he openly shared his mind, which Sam delighted in, were now cast as something else—his need to hear his ideas flow out of his mouth. It made them real and legitimate. She'd never seen how insecure he was, especially after the way he commanded his classroom.

"Was Browning writing about an actual dog or what all dogs represent? Does it matter?"

That day Steven wore a sweater vest and a bow tie. His hair grew past his ears. Sam hated "Flush or Faunus," hated Browning in general and knew she shouldn't, because of how hard it was for women to publish in the nineteenth century. Or the twentieth. Perhaps it was a bit easier now, in the twenty-first. The students listened and took notes. It would make you feel powerful, seeing people do that when you spoke.

He brought it home. Even when he cooked, he was lecturing. And Sam took it in. Then she gave it back with a challenge now and then. They argued about Sylvia Plath. Anger was her fuel, Sam said, and while Steven couldn't deny it, he found it wearing. She asked him if he would find the work of an angry man just as wearing. He said no, because what made men angry were things he understood, like social injustice. Sam was taken aback. Didn't women advocate for social justice through their writing, or at least shed light on where justice was lacking? Steven thought women were more bound by the domestic than the political, and while Sam railed inwardly at that, she held her tongue. Recalling that now, as they began their descent into Miami, Sam thought he was bound to dislike what he read in Edith's diaries. There was enough anger and resentment there to tire even the sturdiest heart. But he wouldn't read those, they didn't count. Only her life as a publisher mattered. Why couldn't he see the two were inextricably linked?

Lavinia roused herself and asked where they were.

Sam said they were about to land. Across the aisle, Angie's seatmate looked pale. He must be one of those iffy flyers who was brash on the way up and terrified on the way down. Angie's ears were still plugged and when the flight attendant asked her to put her seat in the upright position, she didn't hear her the first time. She removed her earbuds and complied.

The moment they got off the aircraft they were met with warm, humid air. Sam had dressed for it in lightweight pants and a short-sleeved shirt. She carried her coat over her arm. Her beloved backpack bounced against her shoulders as they navigated the gangway to emerge into the terminal building. Lavinia needed to use the ladies' room and Angie went with her. While she waited for them, Sam checked her phone. There was nothing further from Steven. Timothy sent a text saying he hoped she was having fun down there in the sun.

They collected their checked bags and looked for the car service Lavinia hired to ferry them to the hotel. An old man in a black jacket, slacks, and chauffer's cap held a sign saying DUGAN. Next to him was an empty luggage cart for their bags. He said his name was Bonaparte.

"You're kidding," Lavinia said. A taut, non-medicated tone had returned to her voice. He said his mother was enamored of European history and that his sister barely escaped being named Josephine.

"I thought we were renting a car," Angie said. She was overdressed in a turtleneck top and jeans.

"We'll be at the resort most of the time, and if we want to go anywhere, we'll just call up Bonaparte," Lavinia said. She handed him her fur coat. He draped it across the stack of suitcases he arranged on the luggage cart.

"What if we want to go somewhere on our own?" Angie asked. Her tone was close to whining.

"Then you will," Lavinia said.

Bonapart led them to a parked minivan and Lavinia said she understood they were to be driven in a Lincoln Town car, not that it mattered. The minivan was just fine. As Bonaparte loaded their luggage into the back of the vehicle, Lavinia removed her leather boots and slipped on a pair of sandals she'd had in her large handbag. Then she handed the boots to Bonaparte who slid them in between Angie's suitcase and a flat of bottled water.

Their route took them over a bridge to South Beach. Lavinia sat in the front passenger seat, and Angie and Sam were behind her. The sky was blazing and the temperature on the dashboard showed eighty-two degrees. Angie said she'd have to get some new clothes or she was going to burn up in the heat.

Sam's impressions: white buildings with balconies, shiny cars, sidewalks lined with palm trees. The way their leaves fluttered especially drew her eye.

Palm trees sway in the breeze

Hearts flatten against the gale of deceit

She dug out her journal and pencil from her backpack. Jotting down the words was hard, given the motion of the van, so she waited until they stopped for a light. Angie asked what she was doing. Sam said she had an idea for a new poem and wanted to get it down before the muse carried it off.

"You're very industrious," Lavinia said.

Then they were pulling up at the hotel. An enormous fountain sent a plume of water into the air. It felt cooler than it had when they left the airport, no doubt because they were closer to the ocean. A valet trotted up and took over unloading the luggage and getting it onto a cart. Bonaparte gave Lavinia his business card and said he would be available if they needed him. He asked how long they were staying. Lavinia said she wasn't sure yet. She'd let him know about getting back to the airport, and if the girls wanted to be driven somewhere. Then she handed him a fifty-dollar bill. He stared at it for a moment before tucking it into his pocket.

"Are you serious?" Angie asked her. Lavinia waved her hand to say she wasn't going to discuss it.

The valet asked what name the reservation was under, and Lavinia told him. He steered the cart through the automatic glass doors into startlingly cold air conditioning. Lavinia wet to the desk to check them in. Angie took pictures of the lobby, especially of the exotic tropical birds of paradise. Sam sat in a rattan and linen chair and thought about the poem she started.

The wafered trunk is a miracle of strength

Truth is relative

There is your truth

Then there is my truth

Her phone dinged. A voice message had been left. Sam wondered why she hadn't heard the call itself, then thought she might have been in a cell pocket on the way from the airport to the hotel.

It was Martin. He had just landed in Boston. His ex was still in the hospital and asked him to come back from the Bahamas to hold his hand, more or less. But that's not why he called. He said the apartment was in great shape and thanked her so much for leaving it that way, but he wondered about the keys. Did she have them, or were they with Steven? Sam texted back that they were with Steven, they had broken up, and she was out of town at the moment.

"Girls," Lavinia said.

The valet went with them into an elevator with their luggage. They rode up to the eleventh floor—the top—and got out. Sam thought that she and Angie would have to share a room, so when the valet opened the door to what he said was their loveliest three-bedroom suite she was elated. The view of the ocean was unobstructed. Lavinia told him where to put the luggage, then followed him to supervise.

"Holy crap, can you believe this place?" Angie asked.

The suite had a kitchen and a dining table, plus a living room area with a sofa, loveseat, and two chairs. There were snacks in a basket on the kitchen counter and Angie began digging through it. She took a small bag of potato chips and opened it. Lavinia and the valet returned. She gave him a twenty-dollar bill and he thanked her effusively.

"Who's where?" Angie asked. Lavinia said she'd taken the bedroom with the king bed. The other two had queen beds.

Angie and Sam went down the hall Lavinia had just come up to find one room with a city view, and the other facing the ocean. Sam said Angie should take the ocean view one because her mother was paying for everything. Lavinia had told the valet to put Angie's suitcase in the other room and Sam's in here, so they switched. Sam's room had its own adjoining bathroom with a sunken tub. She unpacked her toiletries and brushed her hair. She changed into a cotton sleeveless dress and pulled out a sweater against the overwhelming air conditioning. She left her room and went back into the common area. Lavinia was on the porch, stretched out on a lounge chair talking on her phone. Sam joined her and needed to remove her sweater right away. The air conditioning didn't reach out there.

Lavina ended her conversation and explained that Potter still couldn't find his damn bowling shoes. She should buy him a new pair while they were down here. She asked Sam if she wanted to visit the pool or go to the beach, and Sam said anything was fine, whatever Lavinia wanted.

"Me? I'm going to lie here and ponder the infinite. Until I get hungry, that is."

Angie appeared in a short-sleeved blouse and ankle-length skirt.

"I thought you didn't bring any summer weight clothes," Lavinia said.

"I said I didn't have enough."

She had another snack bag in her hand. Cookies, from the look of it. She offered the bag to Lavinia who didn't want any. Sam didn't either. Lavinia said when the time came, they could order dinner in the room or go downstairs. There were at least two restaurants in the place, not counting the bar. She thought they could even eat by the pool. Didn't that sound like fun?

By the third day Angie and Sam were bored. They'd walked on the beach, swum in the pool—the hotel had several clothing boutiques and they each bought a bathing suit, though Angie hated the straps on hers and didn't like wearing it. Even so, she attempted a few sluggish laps. She struck up a conversation with a good-looking young guy who turned out to be there with his boyfriend. They were both Brazilian. Lavinia suggested she invite them up to the suite and Angie told her not to be ridiculous. They called Bonaparte, who never picked up his phone. They took the hotel's shuttle service across the bridge and wandered around until the heat drove them back to South Beach and the mercy of the hotel. Lavinia spent her time by the pool reading one paperback after another procured from the gift shop in the lobby. They ordered room service three times a day or ate in the hotel bar. If Lavinia were at loose ends, she didn't let on. She seemed to be having a great time. Their plan was to stay a week, but Lavinia thought two might be better.

"I never thought I'd say this, but I'm sick of the sun and heat," Angie said when Lavinia couldn't hear.

"Yeah."

"And frankly, I need to go home and get used to being alone again." There was no sadness when she said this. She added that Matt was supposed to be all moved out and she was worried he might have taken something that wasn't his, like her television set, though that would be easily replaced, if so.

Sam nodded without really hearing her. She was at the dining room table, working. The poem she'd begun in Bonaparte's van took shape.

> The wafered trunk is a miracle of strength
> Against the quickening wind
> Graceful, resolute
> Withstanding any cruelty, any blow, any offense, any slight
> You once could too
> But no more

The day she broke the window and threatened her grandmother with the frying pan ended the slaps she took, but not the cold words and eyerolls, the high-pitched mimicking voices of her grandparents. Sometimes her mother joined in, and that was horrible. Sam had hated her mother for years. That was why she ran away to LA. The grandparents were dead by then and Flora was left alone. Sam sent her a postcard to say she got a job at a local Ramada Inn cleaning rooms. She didn't say where she was living or give her a number where she could be reached. Flora called every Ramada Inn in greater Los Angeles looking for an employee named Samantha Clarkson until she found one that said they had a Sam Clark. The name change was done at the courthouse before Sam left Dunston. Her mother's persistence in finding her both surprised and annoyed her. She assumed she couldn't handle being on her own, but during their one long-distance phone call Flora just asked if she were all right and never begged her to come home.

She didn't even suggest it. Sam made that decision on her own not long after.

Then a grandfather Sam didn't know died. He lived in Dunston and apparently was well-off. His son was her mother's rapist, so the story always went. Flora told Sam to look up the son—her father—and get her share of whatever inheritance had been left to him on the grounds that he never did right by her. Only, he'd tried to. Over and over and Flora refused. It was all part of the elaborate ruse to keep her parents at bay, but it didn't work. Flora must have known Sam would learn the truth when she met her father, and whatever explanation Sam would demand from her later didn't outweigh the money she hoped Sam would share, assuming there would be any. There was quite a lot, not from the grandfather because her existence had never been made known to him, but from her father who had invested a tidy sum to be handed over when she might come looking for him. The day she did, he said he thought often of contacting her, but felt it better for her to make the first move. Sam didn't give Flora a cent.

Now Flora lived only a few miles from where Sam was then. Sam hadn't told her she was in town. It was almost as if she were afraid to.

She went into her bedroom and picked up her phone. Her mother answered right away.

"Hi! I wondered whether you'd call again. How are you?" Flora asked.

"I'm in Miami."

"Really? Why?"

Sam explained about Lavinia offering her and Angie the trip. Flora asked where she was staying, and Sam told her.

"Wow. Pricey," Flora said.

They paused. When it was clear Flora wasn't going to invite her over, Sam suggested it.

"I won't stay long," she said.

"Okay. Chuck's out. I could use some company."

Flora gave her the address. She asked Sam if she had a car and Sam said she'd call a cab or use the hotel's service.

"What service?" Flora asked.

"They have a shuttle service. I don't know if it goes as far as your place though."

It turned out not to, so Sam asked the valet to summon a cab. There were several waiting and the first one in line swung into the half circle that separated the hotel from the street. The driver jumped out and opened the back door. He looked like a teenager.

Sam told him where she wanted to go, and he punched the address into his phone. He said it would take about an hour, but that it was a straight shot along the freeway.

"Really? How many miles is it?"

"Says eighteen."

"Traffic must be bad."

"Welcome to Miami."

Sam hesitated.

"I have to warn you, I'm not too chatty with cabbies," she said.

"No problem. I'll leave you be."

Except he didn't.

He said his name was Esteban and he was studying for a real estate license. The way he figured it, with rising sea levels, and hurricane season getting worse every year, sooner or later the whole place would be a ghost town. He was going to make his bundle and get out of there before that happened.

"And go where?" Sam asked.

"Somewhere cooler, where there aren't any hurricanes. Or tornadoes. Or earthquakes. Earthquakes are the worst."

Sam asked how he felt about snow.

"I could get into it. Learn how to ski. You know?" Esteban braked hard for a sudden clot of traffic. The sun bore through the tinted glass of the car's windows. Sam put on the sunglasses she'd bought at the airport in Newark while waiting for Lavinia. They pinched her nose.

Sam asked Esteban if he had grown up in Miami. He said he had. His parents and grandparents came from Cuba. He thought Cuba was a place he'd like to visit but it was hard to go. The paperwork was a pain. American credit cards didn't work down there, so you had to bring cash, but not dollars. They said Euros were best.

"Doable, if you really want to visit," Sam said. She removed her sunglasses.

"Yeah."

He said nothing more and Sam was alone with her thoughts. She was nervous about seeing Flora. It had been almost three years, though they talked on the phone often after she and Chuck first moved south. Flora was always the one to call, and it was always to ask if she could have some of Sam's money. She stopped calling over a year ago, and they'd had no contact until Sam reached out to her the other day from Martin's apartment.

They passed dingy office parks and fast-food restaurants, then Esteban's map function instructed him to take the next right and informed him his destination would be on the left. A large sign bearing the name The Seabright welcomed them, and just beyond it were rows of mobile homes.

Esteban confirmed the address, then asked Sam if she wanted him to wait. She said she didn't know how long she was going to be. He gave her his card and told her to call the number on it when she was ready to go back. If she called the main number for the cab company, it would take a while for someone to get here. She asked about paying for the ride out, and he said he could charge it to the hotel, if she could could tell him the name the reservation was under. She did.

Sam thanked him, got out, and went up the walk, wishing her hands weren't empty. Lavinia urged her to buy Flora something in one of the gift shops, a small piece of jewelry or a scarf, and Sam browsed one store for a few minutes with an open mind but every time she imagined Flora looking at what Sam gave her, she hesitated. Then she gave up.

Two concrete stairs led to a wooden door with peeling green paint. A bright pink geranium sat in a pot to one side of the top stair. It had recently been watered. The concrete was wet around its base and drops of water on its petals held tiny points of sunshine. Sam stared at them, enchanted. It wasn't the heat that drew people down here, she thought, but the light. Boston was so dark now, and Dunston was too.

She knocked on the door and stood, waiting. She knocked again and heard someone moving around inside. The door opened and there was Flora in a blue tracksuit. Her hair had gone gray. That is, she'd stopped coloring it. She put a hand on Sam's shoulder in greeting, then asked her to come inside.

The home was bigger than it looked from the outside. Two recliners sat in front of a large television that stood on a table against the wall. Sam imagined Flora and Chuck sitting there every evening watching whatever they watched and talking. The kitchen had a round table and four upholstered chairs. It seemed like a cozy place to sit and drink coffee or play cards. Potted plants were arranged on the windowsill. On the counter was a tile with the imprint of a tiny hand—Sam's, as a child. She'd made it in school. It had broken and been glued back together.

"You lost weight," Flora said.

"Yeah, a while ago."

"And, what's all this?" Flora looked at Sam's hair.

"It was time for a change."

"Well, you look good."

"Thanks."

They paused, awkward now that the initial greeting was behind them.

"I like your place," Sam said.

"Thanks. We're happy with it."

Flora asked how long she'd be in Miami. Sam said she wasn't sure.

Flora ran her eyes over Sam's outfit, a silk blouse, and a pair of linen slacks she'd bought from one of the hotel's boutiques. None of her other clothes felt right for a visit like this. On her way out, Angie remarked that Lavinia's sartorial sense must be catching. Now, under her mother's gaze, Sam felt she'd chosen badly, then was defiant in a way that made no sense.

Flora offered her iced tea. Sam accepted. Flora gestured to the table in the kitchen and Sam took a chair. She put her backpack on the empty seat next to her and Flora said she still remembered her carrying it everywhere. She was surprised she hadn't gotten a new one after all this time.

"We're old friends," Sam said.

Flora put a tall glass of iced tea with a wedge of lemon in it down in front of her. There were children playing outside, calling to each other and laughing. Sam asked when Chuck would be back.

"Why?" Flora asked.

"I wanted to say hello, that's all."

"I'm afraid you'll probably miss him. He's getting a part for his truck. After that, he's seeing a friend in Fort Lauderdale."

"I thought you guys didn't know anyone down here." Then Sam remembered the sound of people in the background the day she called.

"This is someone Chuck used to know in Dunston. He and his wife moved down right around when we did," Flora said.

Sam's phone dinged. It was a text from Steven.

Tell me where you are. I mean it. I'm not playing games.

Flora looked curious. Sam explained that her ex was driving her nuts. She'd moved out and he kept wanting to know when she was coming back.

"The new guy, you mean?" Flora asked.

"Yes."

They went on sitting, listening to the children's voices. One turned angry, and there was shouting. An adult yelled for them to stop what they were doing, and, after a moment, there was quiet.

Flora watched her. Sam wondered if she regretted her being there.

"I need to ask you something," Sam said.

"Okay."

"Do you ever get flashbacks?"

"About what?"

"You know about what."

Flora looked out the window over the sink. A car started. The driver revved the engine, then drove away.

"You always did get right to the point. Okay, yes, I do. I had it worse than you did, though you probably don't think so," Flora said.

"You had to put up with them longer, that's all."

"Well, that's a lot, isn't it?"

Flora removed the slice of lemon from her glass and dropped it on the table.

Sam said she understood why Flora lied about her father, why she felt it would protect her from her parents. But after they died, and it was just the two of them, why did she tell her the truth then?

"I'm sorry," Flora said.

"That's not an answer."

"It's the only one I've got."

They fell silent again. A woman across the street called out, "Filbert, stop that at once!"

Flora explained that Filbert was a dog. In case Sam was wondering. Sam said she hadn't wondered at all.

Flora sipped her tea. Sam didn't touch hers.

"I think you have more to say," Flora said.

"It's hard."

"Why don't you pick up where you left off? When you called, I mean. You said you felt like you were about to fall apart, that Steven got in trouble with a student, and I don't remember what else."

Sam brought her up to date on the situation with Gail and said there was also a colleague who was gunning for him. That's not why she left. She left because he wouldn't let her talk about herself. Everything had to be about him.

"Men are like that," Flora said.

"Is Chuck?"

"Not as bad as some. I talk at him a lot. I'm not sure he always hears me, but he pretends he does."

"What do you talk to him about?"

"Just daily stuff. We had to get the swamp cooler fixed last week. He was slow getting on that, and I nagged him a little."

Sam said she was sorry she didn't give her any of her father's money. She didn't think it would be right. She hoped Flora understood that.

"It wasn't easy to accept, but it's your money, not mine, and I could have taken what he offered, if I hadn't been such a scaredy-cat."

"Why didn't you go away with him? Leave those jerks behind?"

"Don't speak ill of the dead."

"Answer the question."

"Because as stupid as it sounds, they needed me. And I thought you would need them. And I wanted their help raising you."

"Didn't you love him?"

Flora paused. Her eyes had a queer light then.

"Yes. But I couldn't inflict my parents on him. He didn't deserve that."

"And I did?"

Flora raised her hands in a gesture of surrender. She said she was so young at the time, and damaged in ways it took her years to fully appreciate. Sam asked her to specify. Flora said she had no confidence in herself, didn't think she was worth anything, was afraid of everyone and everything. She understood why Sam left to go to California before. In her shoes, she would have done the same thing.

"And then I met Chuck. He convinced me I wasn't a loser," Flora said.

Sam took a sip of her tea. It was delicious, earthy, and floral at the same time.

"And I understand why you changed your name. You had to shed them, and me, and just be yourself," Flora said.

Sam said the problem was she didn't know who that person was. She thought she did. But she had disappeared from view. Flora asked her why.

"Well, I think it was a two-step process. First, I threw myself into making Timothy happy, protecting him from himself, guiding him toward smart choices, though it never worked. Then I met Steven, and he seemed to know what he was doing and what he wanted, so I felt like I could rest, ride his coattails, as it were. I let him call the shots on everything. It seemed like he needed to, like it was so important to him to take me under his wing."

"But you don't feel dependent on him."

"Not at all."

"Did you feel dependent on Timothy?"

Sam said yes, in the beginning, when she was starting on poetry and thinking of applying to school. She told Flora she dropped out.

"I'm sorry. You were so gung-ho," Flora said.

"I was. But the politics of higher education suck. I'm glad I saw that, but that's another identity that's gone."

"You're a poet though. Isn't that your identity?"

"I think so."

Sam had more of her tea. Outside, the children laughed and called to each other.

Flora said she didn't know when they'd have another chance to sit like this, just the two of them, so she wanted to take a moment and tell her a little bit about her grandparents, the people they were before she was born, when Flora was young, before Linda found religion and Herbert lost his job at the furniture shop and went crazy.

"I didn't know about that," Sam said. It was startling to hear Flora use their first names.

"He got laid off. He wouldn't get out of bed. He decided he was of no use to anyone anymore, and that he might as well go out back and shoot himself in the head."

Flora said his past was troubled already. His mother was unstable, his father drank, his sister ran away with a traveling salesman. He had to hold his parents together. Learning how to build furniture saved him, in a way. Linda's childhood wasn't much better. Poverty never makes for a happy family. Her father was disabled, and her mother cleaned houses—the same thing Linda did later on. There were four brothers, all of whom took flight as soon as they could, which left Linda unwillingly at the helm. That's what they had in common, really, and what drew them together. They met at church. Religion provided solace and purpose, though they took it too far, in the end.

"That's an understatement," Sam said.

"I know they were awful to you but try to see that they were trying to keep you safe."

"By telling me how bad I was?"

"By telling you always to be better."

"Then they should have followed that advice themselves."

"Agreed."

Flora said the day Sam broke the kitchen window changed everything. Not the event itself, but what Sam said right afterward. Her parents pulled further into themselves, down to a point where even their faith brought no comfort. Then came illness, which Sam surely remembered. Herbert's emphysema got the better of him, and he went downhill fast. Linda's heart had never been strong.

"They died only a few months apart," Sam said.

"Yes."

"You were so sad. I didn't understand why. All I could think was that I was free, and you were too."

"I was sad because they were my parents. You'll be sad when I die, even if you don't think so now."

Sam said nothing.

"My point is they weren't always terrible. They were also loving," Flora said.

Sam pushed away her glass of tea. She asked her to please come to the point.

"They're a part of you, whether you like it or not," Flora said.

"I don't like it. I've spent my whole life dealing with what they did to me. And to make up for it, I enabled the bad behavior of other people, because that's what I did when I was a kid."

Flora said she was young enough to change. The future was all up to her.

The children were quiet outside.

Flora asked her if she were certain things with Steven were over. Sam said she honestly didn't know.

"Are you thinking of getting back together with Timothy?" Flora asked.

"Sometimes."

"Has he cleaned up his act?"

"According to him."

"Well, then."

Sam said that, for now, she was going to enjoy the rest of her time in Florida, work on her poems, and look ahead to Dunston. She needed to find a new place to live.

Then she stood. She was ready to go.

Flora didn't ask her to stay longer. She stood up too and gave her a quick hug.

"Thank you for seeing me," Sam said.

"Please stay in touch."

Sam saw a tear in Flora's eye. She went outside and was met with a wave of heat and humidity. She pulled out Esteban's card and called. He didn't pick up. She called again and he answered. He'd be there soon, he said. He wasn't far away.

Sam sat on Flora's steps in a small but blessed patch of shade and waited. Inside, there was no sound.

She didn't know how much time passed until Esteban's cab pulled up. Her mind was quiet, and she let it stay that way. In the car, she closed eyes and must have dropped off because time passed more quickly than it should have.

When they reached the hotel, Esteban confirmed that it was okay to put the charge on her hotel room. She said it was.

"Call me anytime and take care," he said.

Up in the suite, Angie was watching TV. Lavinia appeared in a new ankle-length dress patterned with palm trees and said they had dinner reservations at a great Cuban restaurant in about an hour and she hoped Sam would join them.

"Of course. That sounds lovely."

Lavinia looked at her closely.

Sam went into her room, closed the door, drew the blinds, and lay on the bed. In seconds, she was asleep.

Chapter Fourteen

As quickly as she decided Florida was a must, Lavinia said it was time to go home and bought their tickets. There was no discussion. Angie and Sam had gradually grown used to their lazy, lavish routine. Angie accepted the faults of her swimsuit and spent hours by the pool every day reading, with Lavinia at her side. Sam wrote there, or in the suite, or on the deck outside their living room.

Lavinia said Sam could stay with her when they got back to Dunston. Sam was happy to accept. Soon, she'd look for a house to buy. No more renting. Her investment portfolio would allow the purchase of a modest home if it were in good shape structurally. Cosmetic fixes she could handle and even enjoy.

Angie was glum at the idea of leaving. She hadn't heard from Matt, and the gravity of their separation seemed to be hitting her again. Steven stopped texting, and Sam was relieved. From Flora there was nothing, and though Sam had expected that, she found herself hoping for a quick line saying how good it had been to see her. The chill in their relationship had thawed a little more because of their visit, but there were years of difficulty still firmly in place. Any ease or openness was something they'd both have to work on, and now, Sam found the prospect exhausting.

Martin contacted her again. His message said he was sorry to hear about her and Steven, and hoped she was doing well. He still didn't have the keys. Steven wasn't returning his calls, he said. He wasn't sure what to make of that. Sam sent him a text message saying that if Steven hung onto them, Martin should change the locks.

Steven was being an idiot, ignoring Martin. He might need more papers for his research, or some other information that only Martin could provide. But Steven's plight was no longer her concern.

By the time they were changing planes in Newark, Angie's mood was darker than it had been since she came to Boston. Sam was tired of her, and tired of Lavinia too. Lavinia was a sympathetic person, but she was all business for most of the trip and wasn't much fun to be around. As they waited at the gate, Angie sullen and Lavinia lost in a magazine, Sam took herself a little distance away and called Steven.

"Hello?" he said.

"Hi. Why aren't you giving the keys back to Martin?"

"Where are you?"

"Newark airport. I'm going back to Dunston."

Steven said he'd returned Martin's keys that morning and all the relevant papers were now at the townhome where he was going through them. He said the work was slow but picking up speed. Sam asked if the document transfer included Edith's diaries. Steven said he didn't know.

"I should ask him to mail them to me before the place is sold. They might get lost in the shuffle," Sam said.

"I don't think he's selling it after all."

"He changed his mind?"

Steven said Martin hinted at this but gave no details. Then he asked if Sam were ever going to come back to Boston and talk things through.

"So, now you want me to talk," Sam said.

Steven sighed. He said he didn't have time for this.

Sam hung up.

By the next afternoon she was all settled in Lavinia's oversized guest room. Angie was back at her place and said she'd be in touch later with a full report on everything. Sam didn't want to talk about Matt anymore and hoped Angie would reach out to Lavinia instead. Sam didn't want to talk to anyone, so later that same day when she wandered into the kitchen to make herself a cup of green tea, she was taken aback to find Mark sitting on one of the counter stools playing on his Gameboy. He looked up and smiled brightly at her, and she instantly regretted wishing he weren't there.

"What are you doing here?" she asked.

"I come over after school now so Lavinia can spy on me."

"I see."

"My mom doesn't trust me since, well, since that thing."

"It's a long bus ride over here, isn't it?"

"Yeah."

Sam filled the kettle and asked why he hit that other kid. Mark said he was harassing some girl, and no one did anything about it.

"Didn't you tell them that? The people at school, I mean," Sam said.

"Yeah. They didn't care. Defending someone doesn't matter as much as punching someone."

Sam said to look at it from the school's point of view. He said he had, but he'd do it again, if he had to.

Mark opened a small bag of potato chips he pulled out of his backpack. He looked at Sam and asked what she was doing there. Wasn't she living in Boston now?

"Things didn't work out so well up there," she said.

"Bummer."

Lavinia entered the kitchen and asked Mark how his day had been. Mark said he got a good grade on an English paper and a lousy grade on a math test. Lavinia barely registered his reply. She looked at Sam and asked how she was feeling about things.

"Fine," Sam said.

It felt like the house was getting smaller by the minute. She took her steeping cup of tea and fled upstairs where she'd set up a workstation at the desk by the window of her room.

"Her Face Curls" finished itself while the tea grew cold.

Take from the chest the dress you wore
When she pushed you
Into the river
Down the stairs
Under the bus

Her face curls

Slip into that dreadful rayon
Snagged at the cuffs
From the fight to stay alive

You bested her

It's okay not to be wanted
As long as she keeps her hands
To herself

But she won't

Her face curls

Planning her next attack

Make for the door while her back is turned
Wake sweat-soaked from another nightmare
Remind yourself as your heart now slows

She's gone

Sam put her pencil down and reviewed her work. Nightmares into poetry, she thought. And the Medieval alchemists thought they were onto something!

She took her journal to the window and read the poem aloud. The stanza breaks worked. Last summer, at Middlebury College, she read to a small audience of professors and students. At the time she was proud of being introduced as a promising young poet working toward her degree. It let people understand her place in the scheme of things, a place she had since abandoned.

Professor Morris's email remained unanswered, and as Sam typed out a cheery greeting, saying she was certain her decision to withdraw from school was the right one, she recalled the professor's involvement with Dunston University's literary journal. It tended to publish professors from other schools, or students in various MFA programs around the country, so to take something from a former student who had yet to publish a book-length collection would be a risk. Yet she asked if the professor would read the poem and pass it up the line if she found it worthy. Steven would laud her effort, then caution her about certain disappointment.

His email address was at hand in her recent correspondence, and she attached the poem with a note saying this is what she'd been trying to tell him that night, and that she didn't expect reading it would change anything between them, but she wanted to share it with him, anyway.

As she watched a light snow fall, she fell into a distinctly somber mood. She called her father and left a message saying she'd like to see him today, if he had time. Then she gathered up her dirty clothes and carried them downstairs to the laundry room tucked behind the kitchen. Mark was still at the counter reading. Lavinia was stirring something in a pot on the stove.

Sam started the wash, then returned and asked what Lavinia was cooking.

"I don't really know. I thought I should get something started, but I suppose we could all go out."

Then Lavinia asked if Mark would be joining them for dinner, and he said maybe. His mom had a meeting after work and said she'd be by to get him around seven. Lavinia said Potter would be home from the bar soon and wouldn't want to eat whatever she was making, not that she'd settled on anything yet. She asked Sam what she felt like having. Sam said anything was fine. She added that she was hoping to see her father sometime that day, and she wasn't sure yet when that would be.

"Oh, let's just go out," Lavinia said, turned off the pot, and wandered out of the kitchen.

Mark watched her go and shook his head.

"She's weird," he said.

"A little, I guess."

Mark hopped off his stool and got himself a cookie from the bag on the counter.

"Did you know her before you met my dad?" he asked.

"I met her once with your Aunt Angie."

"She's another weird one."

"Am I weird?"

Mark studied her as he chewed his cookie. His resemblance to Timothy was unnerving. He even stood with his arms crossed, just the way Timothy did when he was thinking something through.

"Well, you write poems, so I guess you're sort of weird. Unless that makes me a jerk for saying so."

"No, I am on the weird side. And you're not a jerk."

Sam's phone rang and she went into the hall to answer it. Her father said she could swing by his office then if she wanted. His last patient canceled. Sam said that sounded great, and to give her about half an hour.

Mark wasn't in the kitchen when Sam returned, and she heard the sound of a television drifting up from the basement.

Her father's practice was in a single-story, red-brick building near campus surrounded by trees that provided rich shade in summer and early fall, and now stood bare and lacy against the chrome-colored sky. She'd been there only once, three years before, when she came to meet him for the first time. Her plan had been to tell him who she was, but he already knew. She was the spitting image of his late mother, he said, and produced a black-and-white framed photograph to prove it.

The waiting area had a sofa, a coffee table on which magazines were neatly arranged, and several potted plants. The leaves of the rubber tree were shiny, and Sam had an odd pang thinking of her father dusting them with care. She knocked on one of the double doors that led to her father's office, and he asked her to come in.

She hadn't seen him since the summer before and that thought caused momentary wretchedness. He came around from his side of the desk, embraced her warmly, then took her coat. He was in his early fifties, without a trace of gray hair. His wool slacks had a sharp crease, and his button-down shirt was well-pressed, yet he gave off an air of casual goodwill intended to put people at ease, Sam thought. He offered her tea and she said she didn't care for any just then. He gestured to a pair of modern blue leather chairs in front of the window. She sat in one and discovered that it swiveled. His did too. He explained that this allowed patients to sit facing him, or not, depending on their comfort level. She sat facing him.

"Thank you for seeing me," she said.

"Don't thank me. You're my daughter. I'm always happy to see you if my schedule allows it."

The silk scarf around her neck felt uncomfortable so she removed it, folded it into a tight square, and put it in the pocket of her jeans.

When after a moment she said nothing more, he said, "Flora says you saw her in Miami."

"She called you. What did she say?"

"That you looked well."

"Do you think I look well?"

"I do, yes."

"Well, I don't think I am."

He said nothing, just continued to gently study her.

"Why don't you tell me what you wanted to see me about," he said.

She explained about breaking up with Steven. She said he didn't want her to talk about herself, that he was focused on himself only and it felt like she was suffocating.

"And now you can breathe," he said.

"It doesn't feel like it."

Again, the gentle gaze.

"You see, I don't think I'm cut out for relationships. I always get them wrong," she said.

"What if you're not the one getting things wrong?"

She said she knew she made excuses for people, put up with bad behavior, and always thought she could change someone. That kind of thinking was foolish, as she found out with Timothy.

"Is he still drinking?" her father asked.

"Not nearly as much."

"So, you're in touch with him. Or, have news of him."

She said he came to Boston with Angie.

"And how was that for you?" he asked.

"Strange.

"I can imagine."

"I thought he'd ask me to get back together with him, but he didn't."

"Sounds like he's moved on."

She nodded.

"Have you?" he asked.

She said she didn't know. That was the problem. She didn't seem to know anything anymore.

He asked how her writing was going, and she said it was going surprisingly well. She just finished a really good poem and sent it to a former professor asking if she might send it up the chain at the university's literary magazine. She said she also sent the same poem to Steven to show him what she would have said, had he granted her permission to speak.

"Did you need his permission?" her father asked.

"No. But I gave up trying to make him listen. The past is important. Even my own mother understands that."

Sam then shared what Flora said about her parents, how she painted them as sympathetic people, worthy of compassion. Her father asked if Sam felt compassion for them.

"No," Sam said.

"It's healthy to be able to admit that."

She said the thing that never made sense to her was why Flora didn't protect her. Her father suggested that she might not have known how.

"There's nothing to know. Someone hurts your child, you make them stop," Sam said.

"Flora couldn't stand up to them. And she knew you could, or you would eventually."

"Are you saying she knew I'd be okay?"

"Aren't you okay?"

"I don't think so. I can't be. I keep ruining things."

Her father said it was clear to him that Sam liked to help people, give them what they needed, but she didn't know how to help herself. Was he right about that?

"Yes," she said.

"I say, look at the evidence. The situation with Timothy became untenable, so you got out of it. People who don't know how to help themselves don't do that. Ditto with Steven."

"But didn't I just give up on them?"

"Didn't they give up on you first?"

Sam leaned back in her chair, exhausted. Her father said he'd make her that cup of tea now and went into a tiny galley kitchen at the back of the office. Through the window, a thin patch of blue sky was visible before being covered by clouds moving up the valley.

A few minutes later, her father returned bearing a tray with two cups of tea. He set it down on the window seat next to their chairs.

"What do you really want, Samantha?" he asked, then apologized. He said he should use her chosen name.

"It's okay." She poured some milk into her tea. It swirled lusciously and made her think of happiness, the kind she'd felt living at Steven's.

"I want to work on my poems," she said.

"You said you were writing just this morning."

"Yes."

"Well, then."

The tea needed sugar, but she didn't ask for it.

He asked her where she was staying. She said with Lavinia, but she wanted to cut that short. Lavinia could be kind, but they'd seen a lot of each other recently and Sam needed a break. The same was true for Angie.

"You think of them as your extended family, don't you?" he asked.

"I suppose I do."

"Well, remember, we're here too and would love to see more of you."

She said she was sorry she didn't come by more often. She asked after her stepsiblings. He said Janet just got a promotion at the lab where she worked, Derrick wanted to move to Vermont and take pictures, though his mother was discouraging him in this, and Lisa was narrowing down the list of colleges she'd apply to next year.

"And Maureen? How's she?" Sam asked.

"She's well."

Maureen was her father's wife. Sam wondered how she felt about him being in touch with Flora. Of course, he'd be open about why it was necessary, but even so, past entanglements tended to cling. Edith could speak to that and did, in her diary.

They chatted for a while longer and then it was time to go. She thanked him for seeing her.

"I remember the first time you came here. You were much less sure of yourself then," her father said.

"Good to know I'm going in the right direction."

She promised to call him soon.

She'd turned off her phone during the visit and when she brought it to life, she saw a voice message from Martin. She put it on speaker and listened to it as she drove.

He had something to talk over with her and would appreciate a call. It had to do with the apartment.

Sam thought she hadn't been thorough in her final inspection of the place. Steven could handle whatever it was, but then he wouldn't, would he? She saw him in the townhome, pecking away at his laptop, looking up and remembering she wasn't there anymore to wait on him.

But he'd done his fair share of waiting on her, too.

There was no one home at Lavinia's and Sam figured they'd all headed out to dinner.

Her phone rang. It was Martin. He said he was sorry to bother her again and hoped she didn't mind. She asked what was wrong with the apartment and he said nothing, he'd expressed himself badly before when he left his message. He wanted to broaden the scope of The Hedgerow Press with the money currently held in trust. The apartment might become a base of operations, an office, if you will, where applications could be reviewed, and interviews held.

"For what?" Sam asked.

"People applying for grants and scholarships. I'm starting a foundation to foster the growth of literary arts, especially poetry. I'm even naming it after my mother, though I suppose that sounds silly. But 'The Edith Alistair Foundation' does have a certain ring, don't you think?"

Sam asked what any of this had to do with her.

"I want you to run it with me," Martin said.

"What? Are you kidding?"

"I've had a change of heart, Sam. Pro-bono law work is fine, and it's useful, but I can do more. I did a lot of thinking in the Bahamas about myself and who I am, and what's best for me now. Time away is often good for that."

He asked if she'd at least think about it. He knew it would be awkward for her to be back in Boston with Steven there too, but it was a big town, and they didn't have to cross paths. She asked if she could work remotely. He paused.

"Yes, of course. But I'd love to have you around. Please forgive me if this sounds odd, but the truth is, I find you inspiring."

"I can't imagine anyone finding me that."

Martin said he admired her dedication to poetry, and Sam said she didn't see how he could tell.

"I'm a good judge of character, at least, I like to think so," he said. Then he paused again and said if she were interested, they could start working out details. Organizing everything was going to take a while.

"What will my role be?" Sam asked.

He said she could read the applications, see who had heart and who didn't. He thought they should avoid academics and encourage lay people, people without a formal education, in other words. Sam said that sounded good to her, but she needed to think about what her short-term goals were. She said she would let him know soon.

Lavinia and Potter returned, minus Mark. Lavinia explained they dropped him off at home. Her mood was bad, and Potter was tight-lipped. Lavinia said she was going to take an aspirin and get off her feet. When she left, Sam asked Potter what was going on.

He got himself a glass of water. His sports shirt was damp under the arms, and his thick gray hair was ruffled, as if he'd stood out in the wind. He said dinner hadn't gone too well. They invited Timothy to meet them at the restaurant. He'd been drinking beforehand and spoiling for a fight with his son. Mark didn't know what to do, and Lavinia told Timothy to lay off. That led to some raised voices, and Potter was afraid they'd be asked to leave, but Timothy put a lid on it long enough for them to all finish eating. Potter was sure Mark was going to tell his mother what happened, and Timothy would be asked to steer clear for a while.

"He's a damn fool. He wants to get in good with his son, and what does he do? Shows up loaded and picks on the poor kid," Potter said.

"Timothy was so much better," Sam said.

"Yeah, when?"

"Up in Boston."

"That was all for your benefit."

Potter apologized for sounding cynical, but he'd been down that road himself, and the plain truth was that Timothy just hadn't decided to be sober. Oh, he could do it, all right. He knew how. He just didn't want to, and Potter was fed up.

He said he was going to see how Lavinia was doing. He also said he was glad Sam was staying with them for a while. She was always such a steadying influence, but she didn't need to worry, no one was going to ask her to deal with Timothy again. She'd served her sentence on that one.

An hour later, her plane ticket to Boston had been bought. Her flight was early the next morning and as she pulled out the suitcase she had so recently put away, she prayed the weather would hold and snow wouldn't fall.

Chapter Fifteen

Sam told Martin she felt like a yo-yo, the way she'd been bouncing from place to place. Then she apologized for using that metaphor. A ping-pong ball was more apt. They were dining in an elegant Back Bay restaurant to celebrate her joining the foundation. Her lamb was underdone, and Martin reminded her that she'd ordered it medium-rare. He asked if she'd like to send the plate back and she said no, of course not, it was still delicious. Around them people spoke softly, so they did too. Sam leaned forward and said the atmosphere bordered on holy.

Martin asked if she attended church and said she'd been dragged every Sunday as a kid but once she was old enough to effectively resist, she never went again.

"You?" she asked him.

"My parents were atheists."

Martin signaled the waiter to pour out more wine.

Sam steered him back to the foundation. She wanted to favor women applicants, and wanted to offer some, or all, a publishing contract with The Hedgerow Press. They could call it their New Poet series. The name wasn't original, and they could work on a better one, but then again, it was accurate. Martin was keen to publish underrepresented voices, and for him, this meant gays and lesbians, along with people of color. Sam said she wasn't sure how she felt about asking a person's sexual orientation on an application form, or their racial background, for that matter. She suggested they read blind and simply choose the best people based on their writing sample.

"Oh, dear. What if they all turn out to be white men?" Martin asked. Their plates had been cleared and the waiter gave them dessert menus and left.

"Then that's how it will be. I don't believe in denying talent because of the body it comes in."

"I don't think that's what I was suggesting."

"No, you wanted to skew toward a particular subset of the population. That's different."

The waiter came right back to ask if they wanted dessert and Sam said no. Martin said he'd had his eye on a slice of chocolate mousse cake. Sam said he should have it then. Martin asked the waiter to bring it.

"I'm sorry. I didn't mean to sound harsh," Sam said.

"You didn't."

"I just think we should try it my way and see what we think."

Martin said he wasn't sure he was the best person to review the writing samples and suggested they could get Lisa Tettle involved to help Sam with the workload.

"You read a lot of poetry, don't you?" Sam asked. The dessert arrived, and Sam eyed Martin's plate lustily.

"I do."

"Well, you know what you like. That should be enough of a qualification."

"Perhaps."

Sam said they could both read and have Lisa Tettle review the biographical information on the applicants. After a manuscript was chosen, or at least put in the "likely" pile, they could see who the author was.

"My mother used to say you could tell a poet's gender just from the way they wrote," Martin said.

"I don't know if that's true."

But Steven had said the same thing, once. Sam thought men were just as confessional as women, but they wrote about sex and hard luck and women wrote about the state of their souls. That was too simple, though, wasn't it?

She said she didn't know if she would be up to the task. She might not have any idea what the hell she was doing.

"Don't back out on me now," Martin said.

"I wouldn't dream of it."

She'd expected to find it odd, living at the apartment, and didn't. She took the room Timothy had used during his stay. It was large and Martin had updated it with modern furniture and heavy curtains that kept the drafty windows from admitting cold air. And it was quiet, even though the street below was often busy. Sometimes when she woke up, she didn't remember at first where she was, and rather than finding this alarming, she let her mind drift until it settled calmly on her new reality.

Martin was in and out a lot those first few days. He was busy getting settled in the condominium he'd recently bought. Along with that, his ex had finally been discharged from the hospital, and Martin was making arrangements for follow-on home care. Sam suspected that the ex's health was generally poor. Martin said Aaron had mobility problems, respiratory problems, and suffered from loss of appetite. When he wasn't at Aaron's, he applied himself to the new foundation. Sam felt they needed to begin with the granting process and then move on to the publishing project. Where grants were concerned, Sam wanted to support working poets who had a collection in progress. The decision would be based on the work itself, how the poet described their perceived mission, and what else the poet did with their time. Did they have a family? Children? What did they give back to their community? Martin wasn't sure that information would be relevant. Sam said it was relevant, completely relevant. What could be more important than the personal challenges a poet created against and within? Look at her, for instance. She came to poetry after finding a slim volume left behind by a guest in a motel room it was her job to clean. The awe she felt from the poems she read stayed with her to the next job at the Lindell retirement home, where the rooms were never vacant but occupied by people decades older than she. The air was thick with their memories, even if they said little. The past was all around, like faint perfume. Seeing this, feeling it, expanded the world, made her see that there was so much beyond her own small, painful life. To write was to meet that world. To write poetry, specifically, was to rejoice in it.

Martin put down the tumbler of whiskey he'd been enjoying and looked at her over the top of his bi-focal glasses.

"I can see why I thought you would be good for this position," he said.

They were in Edith's former office, which Martin had also spruced up with two new desks, computers, and hardwood flooring. The fussy wallpaper remained. Martin explained that removing it was a big project, one he didn't want to undertake just then. The papers Steven didn't use were now stored in a handsome credenza on which sat an abstract marble statue. The two desks were pushed together so Sam and Martin faced each other but only when they weren't staring at their computer screens. At first, Sam didn't like the idea and Martin begged her to give it a try. After the first day she was used to it and told him it was good to be reminded of how flexible she was.

Another issue was to decide how much money each grant should contain, if the recipients should get the same amount, or if there should be a sliding scale where people with lower incomes would get more, and better off people would get less. Martin was in favor of a sliding scale and Sam overruled him. Next, they needed to get a handle on how to make people aware they could apply for grants in the first place. Since they wanted to stay out of the academy Sam thought they could write to small presses, bookstores, and place an ad in writer's magazines. Martin considered her remarks and said he remembered his mother talking about soliciting submissions for her new press, way back when.

"She put a notice in the window of her bookstore and every poet who would walk, crawl, or roll came in with a manuscript to drop off. There were over fifty hopefuls. Isn't that something?"

Sam didn't look forward to being inundated with requests but understood each would need her attention. Her concerns, when expressed, prompted Martin to offer her a salary which she declined. She was happy to volunteer. Working for goodwill, rather than for money, would make her efforts genuine.

Lisa Tettle, with whom Martin had spoken, said they should focus on writer's magazines and web pages to advertise the grants. Small presses were overwhelmed with work and bookstores tended to focus on author readings when it came to publicizing events. If they found one that published their own newsletter in print or online, that might be something to pursue.

As the days passed, Sam applied herself to drafting the grant announcement:

Unpublished poets lacking an academic degree are encouraged to apply to the newly established Edith Alistair Foundation. Winning applicants will have a demonstrated ability to write startling, evocative, important poems and hope to publish a book-length collection. Grant funds will be used for the sole purpose of making time for the poet to accomplish this task. Please submit a writing sample of no more than thirty pages and a letter of intent to the following address.

Martin asked what she meant by letter of intent.

"I want to see how they view what they're doing, what their goals are, why they think their work is valuable," she said.

"To bare all, in other words."

"After writing poems, that should be a no-brainer."

Martin's mood had improved, which meant Aaron must also have improved. He talked about buying new furniture and new window treatments for the entire apartment. Sam said she hoped he understood when she said she wasn't particularly interested in decorating.

"My mother would have said that made you unusual, for a woman," he said.

"Unusual in the 1960s, but not now, surely."

Steven sent a text message saying he'd found a shirt and three pairs of socks she left behind when she fled. He was happy to mail them if she sent him an address. She texted that she was back at the apartment, and could collect them in person, if he were okay with that.

They agreed on the following Tuesday afternoon. The train was slow, and her mood suffered, but the walk from the stop was improved by a burst of mid-February sunshine. As a child she saw winter as a time when everything lay in wait, asleep, but that wasn't true. The ground was always busy, tree roots alive and working, though surely less robustly than in warmer weather. Timothy loved winter. Sam loved all seasons except winter. Winter was both a price and penance, though that was unnecessarily grim, wasn't it?

Dave's car was in its usual place and Sam recalled how nice he'd been to her the night the pipe broke. She thought for a moment of stopping in, but that didn't feel right.

Steven didn't come to the door until after Sam knocked a second time. He looked well, and she was relieved to see that he was taking good care of himself. The townhome was in good order too. It was as if she'd never been there, though of course, her tenure hadn't been long, not even a month.

They hugged and Steven kissed her on the cheek. He thanked her for coming. He took her coat. A light lunch was laid out on the dining room table consisting of pasta salad and fresh fruit. Sam helped herself to a chunk of cantaloupe and asked where he'd managed to find a ripe one that time of year. He said it definitely took some looking.

He had a pot of green tea staged and ready to serve. As he went to bring it in from the kitchen, she saw the wall had been repaired.

He asked how she liked Miami.

"Oh, it was so-so. It was great to be where it was sunny and warm, but then it became too much of a good thing," she said. He poured out the tea and told her to help herself to the pasta salad. She did.

"How's Angie bearing up with everything?" he asked.

"Okay, I guess. I haven't talked to her for a while."

"You're busy with the foundation."

"You know about that?"

"Martin mentioned it when I finally got around to returning the keys."

She asked him what he thought of the whole idea.

"I think it's wonderful, naturally. A lot to take on, too. Will you have enough time for your work?" he asked.

"So far, so good."

"I enjoyed the poem you sent me, by the way."

"Thanks."

She wanted to know how things were going with his research, and if he'd found a particular angle on The Hedgerow Press.

"I've concluded that Edith Alistair's commitment to it reflected what was going on in her own life at various points," he said.

"I'm not sure what you mean."

"She didn't keep much psychic separation." The salad contained small pieces of chopped celery, and his chewing was loud and crunchy.

"What are you basing that on?"

"Her diaries."

"You read them?"

"Not all, but enough to get a real sense of the woman. She was quite a character. It's fascinating all the things she doesn't talk about that are somehow there, lurking on the page."

"You told me I was obsessed with them, then you read them and find them worthwhile."

He wasn't put off by her tone. He regarded her as he might a whining student lobbying for an easier assignment.

"I shouldn't have used that word. You weren't obsessed, merely . . ."

"Curious."

"Exactly."

"In a way you found silly and sought to ridicule."

"I wasn't nice."

"You weren't."

"And hard to be around."

"Not in the beginning. After a while, yes. Particularly when you were worried about the grant."

"Fair enough."

Sam ate her salad and drank her tea. Speaking honestly always made her hungry, as if truth required greater fuel than tact.

There might be a poem in that.

"Look, I made mistakes too," she said.

He dabbed his mouth with his napkin. A quiet settled in him as he waited.

"I was on the rebound. There's no question about that. I assumed all kinds of things about you because it made dealing with leaving Timothy easier," she said.

"I know."

"I don't want you to think I don't care for you, because I do. A lot, in fact."

"I'm glad to hear it."

"But you wouldn't let me talk about my past, and that hurt."

"So, tell me now if you like. Unless you're in a hurry."

"Are you sure?"

"Of course."

She supposed there was nothing to do but begin at the beginning, and as she described her earliest memories, then progressed through elementary school, she saw how her grandparents changed, just the way Flora said they had. After she stood up for herself, she and her mother became isolated. They ate their meals alone at one time, then her grandparents ate theirs. No more sitting together, no more forced conversations. After they died, peace was slow to occupy that sad, leaning house, but it came, though only for Sam until her father's arrival in her life shifted things once more and the lie Flora told grew enormous. So, she left for LA right after changing her name.

"I used to be Samantha Clarkson," she said.

"I had no idea."

She searched his face to see how her tale had affected him, but he looked just the same.

"I'm surprised someone from school didn't report them to the authorities," Steven said.

"I never talked about what went on at home."

"Bruises?"

"They were careful about that. They tended to hit me on the back because marks didn't show."

"Calculated abusers."

"Let's just say they had an instinct for self-preservation."

Steven said the one he didn't understand was Flora, standing by day in and day out.

"She was waiting for me to grow up and act for us both," Sam said.

"That's a remarkable insight."

"Stop it."

"I'm being serious!"

Sam held up her hands. She apologized for being overly sensitive.

Steven cleared the plates and returned. The sun filtered through the blinds and showed a layer of dust on the top of the bookcase.

He asked if she were relocating to Boston permanently. She said she didn't think so, she missed Dunston too much. The city was a lot to manage when you weren't used to it. Her plan was to get the first round of applicants approved, find a new place in

Dunston, and continue her involvement with Martin remotely. The apartment was lovely, of course, and she was getting spoiled with having so much space, but she'd adapt. One thing she'd learned about herself over the years was that she was excellent at adapting.

"Let's try again. You and me. With some new ground rules," Steven said.

"Are you serious?"

"I miss you, Sam. You make sense of things for me."

"Does that mean that without me you're senseless?"

Steven threw his head back and laughed. Then she did too. When they'd stopped, she thought about what he said.

"You make sense of things for me too, but I'm not sure it's a good idea. At least, not now," she said.

His disappointment was clear, even as he tried to conceal it.

"Well, keep me in mind while you're here. And drop by once in a while. It's lonely being on my own so much. I hadn't expected that, though Jordan has been wonderful. We see a lot of each other, and he's promised to introduce me to some of his circle," he said.

Now his tone was sad, and she felt a dire heaviness in her chest.

He said if there were anything he could to help with the foundation to let him know, though between Martin's financial generosity and Sam's poetic acumen, it sounded like they had everything covered.

"I don't know about that. I think I've bitten off more than I can chew," she said.

"You'll do great."

She asked if he were going to follow through and mount a defense against Professor Baker. He said he'd been in touch and suggested that they clear the air.

"You know what he said? That he never feels he can be honest with me. I assured him that he can," Steven said.

Sam held her tongue.

"That's wonderful. I bet things will work out just fine between you," Sam said.

"We used to be friends. Well, we were friendly from time to time. That's not quite the same thing, is it?"

She said she should be on her way. She thanked him so much for the lovely lunch, and for returning the things she left. She promised to call him soon, maybe tomorrow. If he weren't too busy, and the weather stayed decent, he could show her around Harvard.

"Sure, that'd be great!" he said.

Waiting for the train, with her socks and shirt stuffed into a used brown paper bag, the sky thickened, and the sunlight faded. The visit had been hard, but she was glad she'd gone. Then her thoughts turned again to the work she'd taken on, the sheer scope of it, and she felt something she'd only ever felt writing poetry—powerful.

The train came and she was lucky to find an empty seat. She pulled out her journal and searched for the piece she'd begun a little while ago about the candle and the lantern. She found it. It didn't read right.

With her pencil she crossed out that first attempt and started over.

You're a candle in a glass lantern
And when I light you, you burn
Beautifully, a dance of energy
Releasing, finding your way to me

Yet we know, deep down,
Love cools when you
Realize you made a bad bet

Affection fades, the heart hungers,
We hollow from the inside out

And so I wonder, gazing at the blackened wick,
If you disappeared because I
Didn't love you enough

But then I see—know—you're
Still out there, burning as brightly as ever,
Perhaps for someone else, or just by
Yourself, alone

Not bad for the spur of the moment. Except that this moment had been there for a long time now, waiting to be given voice.

She put away the journal and pencil and sat with her backpack in her lap. The city glided quietly past the window. This was not a place she belonged, but being here now was imbued with purpose. Like Edith, decades before, the idea of shaping something, guiding it, and watching it grow, took hold.

Happiness was a shock.

THE END

ABOUT THE AUTHOR

Anne Leigh Parrish is the author of sixteen books spanning short stories, novels, and poetry. Known for her dedication to environmental causes and women's rights, Parrish has recently ventured into photography, further enhancing her creative exploration of the world. She resides in the South Sound region of Washington State. To learn more, visit her at anneleighparrish.com and laviniastudios.com.

ABOUT THE PRESS

Unsolicited Press is based out of Portland, Oregon and focuses on the works of the unsung and underrepresented. As a womxn-owned, all-volunteer small publisher that doesn't worry about profits as much as championing exceptional literature, we have the privilege of partnering with authors skirting the fringes of the lit world. We've worked with emerging and award-winning authors such as Amy Shimshon-Santo, Elisa Carlsen, Sommer Schafer, and Laura Gaddis.

Learn more at Unsolicitedpress.com. Find us on Twitter and Instagram @UnsolicitedP.

www.ingramcontent.com/pod-product-compliance
Lightning Source LLC
Chambersburg PA
CBHW061122310726
48974CB00002B/646